I0760603

the cottage

N.D. HAUPT

The Cottage

ISBN 978-1-956611-08-3

Cover design and content layout by Houseal Creative
Edited by Rivers Houseal

Nogginnose Press
PO Box 96
Smithville, AR 72466 USA
nogginnose.com

To Charlton, always,
and to Justice, Courage, & Favour.

Life is a story.

What a gift from God Almighty
that I get to live it with you.

1

PROLOGUE

CIRCA A.D. 1830

The Pearls got into his blood by accident.

He was twenty when he found them in a forgotten cave. It was supposed to be a simple hike up one of many nearby mountains, a way to clear his mind and relieve the stress of his university studies.

The storm caught him by surprise. There was no sign of impending weather when he started, but as he reached the top, clouds boiled, and an eerie wind sent him hurrying back the way he had come. Gales of sleet raked the air before he was halfway down the trail.

He ran for the first shelter he could see, an outcropping of rock slabs that loomed near the base of a massive pine. With all the deftness of a man on adrenaline, he scrambled into their shadows. With any luck, he could get out of the worst of the sleet before he was soaked to the skin.

To his surprise, the shadows gave way to a cave mouth large enough to step inside with little more than a head tilt.

The prospect of a dark cave was daunting. Staying out in the freezing deluge seemed worse.

He stooped inside, wary and out of breath. When his heart rate slowed and his breathing evened, he glanced around. He knew full well that he might not be the only creature looking for shelter. The air had the musty smell of dirt and old animal droppings.

Something skittered in the darkness. He flinched and almost bolted for the mouth of the cave, but his rational mind held out and listened. The sound had disappeared further into the cavern. Whatever it was, it had run away, not toward him. Still, his skin crawled. He didn't like not knowing his surroundings.

His clothes clung to him, damp and uncomfortable. Shivering, he sat down and pulled his knees toward his chest.

Frigid wind howled through the cave mouth just beyond his feet. Cold overcame apprehension, and he turned to move farther into shelter.

That was when he saw them. There were three, small but unmistakable, glowing with a faint, warm light a few yards away.

He froze. *Eyes?*

But no, these did not blink or move. The light was soft. Inviting.

He crawled closer. All thoughts of wild animals fled. He saw only the light, beautiful and alive, drawing him as water does a parched man.

He pulled himself up and picked his way over the treacherous floor. It was uneven and jagged in many places, pockmarked with cracked stone and ragged tree roots.

He reached the lights, and his heart nearly burst.

They were infinitely, utterly, magnificently beautiful.

Colors—for they must have been colors, though he had never seen their like—whispered through curved surfaces smooth as pale glass. Their iridescence was soft, but piercing. A cool fire held in the confines of liquid stone.

Each was gripped by the tree, partially enclosed by roots that had long ago traversed the cave's ceiling and continued their downward journey through the stony floor.

Trembling, he reached and attempted to pry them from the grasp of the tree roots. The roots held firm. They were gnarled and timeworn. Bark flaked under his hand, but the wood did not budge.

He pulled a penknife from his pocket and went to work on the top root. If he could get that one out of the way, he thought he could dislodge the stones.

It was a grueling task, sawing enough of the root away to strip it back. He was glad he had always kept the little knife sharp. Finally, he clicked the knife closed and dropped it back in his pocket. With his feet braced and his hands clutched like iron, he gave a mighty pull. The root groaned and snapped.

The sudden release landed him in a heap on the cave floor, but he hardly noticed. He jumped to his feet and scrambled forward. All other thoughts melted away. There were only the stones, silent and riveting. As if in a dream, he reached a hand and dislodged them, one by one, from their ancient nest.

They sat on his open palm, three soft lights in a world of dark.

The stones weren't large, perhaps each the size of a quarter dollar coin, but perfectly round.

They were neither heavy nor light. A hint of warmth emanated from under their surface like spring sunlight, and he could swear their swirls of light moved like tiny rivers, though he couldn't see the precise moments of change.

Pearls. That was the closest description he could come to. They must be pearls. Pearls that were not pearls. Soft stones of vivid, aching beauty.

He stared at them for uncounted minutes while the thunder boomed and the wind howled outside the cave.

Silence pulled him from his reverie. The storm must have stopped. It was time to go. He closed his hand around the Pearls, turned, and stepped toward the cave mouth.

Perhaps his legs were stiff from waiting. Perhaps his mind was distracted by beauty. Perhaps the tree sabotaged him, lifting a root to prevent its long-hidden treasure from being taken. Perhaps he simply missed his footing.

He tripped, and the Pearls fell, making only the softest clatter as they tumbled—one, two, three—onto the stones of the cave. He dove for them, but not fast enough. They rolled into a crevice and stuck there under a sharp bridge of rock with an opening only large enough for his fingertips.

He would get them. He had to get them.

It took hours. He chipped bits of rock away with his penknife until the blade broke, then strained, scraped, and smashed, desperate to clear enough space to reach through to where the Pearls rested, shimmering, a perfect contrast to the cold, dark stones of the cave.

He was running out of time. The light at the cave's mouth was fading into evening. Shivers racked through weary muscles. His wet clothes felt icy cold, and his feet were numb. He had to get off the mountain.

Finally, he thrust his hand through the opening, which was only slightly larger for all his efforts. Jagged stone tore at his bones and skin, but he forced it through anyway.

He screamed.

Reaching as far as he was able, while the rocks bit at bones and nerves, and blood began to bead and run in trickles, he managed to grip one Pearl with the sides of his fingers. He pulled it close to the opening and grabbed it with his free hand. Repeating the process, he retrieved the other two, then yanked his mangled hand out of the crevice.

He sat, shaking. Blood spilled into the sleeve of his coat. His entire arm burned with vicious pain. He had won. There were the Pearls, safe again in his possession.

He reached for one and let it rest in his injured palm. As the Pearl pressed against torn flesh, heat seeped from the stone, straight into his blood. He felt it move through his wrist and arm, a powerful light.

He snatched the Pearl away from the wound. It scared him. But the act was done.

What it meant, how it changed everything, he did not yet know.

2

GEORGE

CIRCA 2023

George parked behind the red sedan. There was no other vehicle in sight on the dirt road besides his own, and the shiny red one still had a temporary license stuck to the back window.

"Kathleen must be doing pretty well for herself," he mumbled, picturing the contrast of his own decrepit station wagon.

He had found her number on a real estate flyer at the dentist office. He hoped she wasn't one of those overbearing, I'll-do-anything-for-a-sale types. The less conversation, the better. She had seemed eager on the phone, but at least the flyer saved him the trouble of sorting through internet listings or asking around. He only needed her here to see the place so she could tell him what it would take to sell it.

George had not even known his Uncle Barry owned a second property, much less expected it to show up in his inheritance. The house was old, though, and too far out from town. He didn't intend to keep it.

George glanced in the rearview mirror. He was a plain man. Thirty years old already, though it still surprised him to think it. Average height, nondescript build, pecan-colored eyes that stared back at him without enthusiasm. There had been a time when those eyes were full of light and laughter.

That seemed long ago.

George smoothed a hand over faded brown hair, sighed, and opened his door. He swung his bad leg out first. It had been twisted since babyhood and surgically corrected as a child, but it never could bend well at the knee. It splayed out a bit and, on bad days, caused a painful limp. George pulled out his right leg, the good one, next. He stood, and shut the car door behind him.

"Mr. Morgan?" the woman asked, beaming a smile. She glanced at the gimpy leg.

"That's me."

"Kathleen Stanwell, Better City Realty. Thrilled to meet you." She shifted a stack of papers, keys, and cell phone to one arm and reached the other hand toward his.

George shook it quickly. She met the firmness of his grip, though her hand felt clammy on his own dry palm. He stuffed his hand back into his pocket.

"So this is the place, huh?" Kathleen said, still smiling. She gestured toward the house. "Looks like something out of a storybook."

George turned to face the house. It was small and plain.

"I certainly understand why you might sell it," Kathleen said, stepping forward to stand next to him. She stepped too fast and dropped half the papers.

"It's awfully small," she went on, jumping to retrieve the scattered pages. "Someone could always get rid of the house and rebuild on the lot, though." Kathleen stood and forced a flustered glint behind another enthusiastic smile. "Best I can find, this property has never been listed before. The house has got to be at least a hundred years old. Did your uncle leave any other information about it?"

"Nah," George said. He edged away from Kathleen and looked over the stone front, the simple porch, and sloping roof line. It was a mix of greys and browns. Rough-hewn stones held both colors, and the wood siding was weather-warped and faded from its original tones.

There was no garage attached. The driveway, just a worn track through the grass, cleaved before it reached the house and led further back to a small, wooden barn with a split rail fence around it. The barn, if empty, might prove to be big enough to work as a carport, with the doors left open and the fence out of the way.

George returned to the front of the house. It was well-situated. The front yard was more ground cover than grass. Patches of clover grew among a smattering of short green leaves and tiny stalks. A reel mower would make quick work of that maintenance.

One massive maple tree, the biggest he had ever seen, towered near the house's east face. The other trees were all out back.

The house sat comfortably away from the dirt road, a dead end lane with no other homes in sight. *A cottage,* George thought. *That's the appropriate word for it.*

Kathleen glanced up and down the lane, shifted the keys in her hand, and cleared her throat. "May I see inside?"

George remembered that was why she had come, and nodded. He led the way to the front door and turned a key in the lock.

"Thank you," Kathleen said. "I'll just pop in for a minute, then wait out here. Take all the time you need to look around; there's no hurry." She aimed another cheerful smile in his direction and started through the house.

George stepped inside a moment behind her, glad for the solitude. He limped through the cramped entryway into a pleasant living room with wood floors and a stone fireplace. The fireplace was empty, but a blackened grate and chimney showed evidence of much use.

The walls were vertical wood planks covered with a thin coat of whitewash. He could see the wood grain through the wash. It gave the room a cabin feel without overdoing the wood's natural color. George had always thought that too much of the same wood made a room feel claustrophobic.

He wondered how long, exactly, the house had sat empty. It did not look at all run-down. Aged, perhaps, but in a comfortable way, as if the former occupant had spent most of a lifetime there and only left recently. He had expected more dust.

Why had Uncle Barry never mentioned this place? It seemed he had held onto it, but never done a thing with it. The will had listed it as Morgan Family Property, along with the parcel number and address. There was a note that the previous owner was Abel Morgan, whom George knew to be Uncle Barry's father and his own grandfather. He could only conclude that the property had been passed as an inheritance to his uncle, who had kept it and passed it to George.

George had been raised by Uncle Barry and Aunt Pam, once his parents died when he was seven. His aunt and uncle had no other children, so it did not surprise him that he was the sole inheritor.

Why his uncle had never told him about the house remained a mystery. That question itched the back of George's mind, but he didn't bother thinking too far into it. There was no answer to be had at the moment. Here was the property, and he was the unexpected owner.

George realized, much to his surprise, that he liked the feel of the space. He had not predicted that. True, he was more than ready to get out of his apartment back in town, with the yappy dog next door and the upstairs neighbor rattling the ceiling all hours of the evening. Town, with all its bustle and noise.

Now that he thought about it, he wouldn't need to be going to town very often—not with his two-weeks' notice already filed at the accounting office. A bit of a commute for groceries wasn't that big of a deal, was it?

George stood still and listened. Nothing. He furrowed his brow and continued perusing the cottage.

He didn't need much space. It was only him, after all. A fresh breeze filtered through the open front door. It smelled of sunbaked grass and summer pine. George breathed it in. It was so quiet here. He could work better in the quiet.

Off the left side of the living room, George found a kitchen with space for a small table. These walls, too, were whitewashed, as were the few cabinets that hung in a neat row.

One window in the far wall let in sunlight, dappled by the maple leaves dangling near its outer face. Below the window was a stone sink set into a smooth, wooden countertop. George eyed the faucet. There were no knobs, only a single pump handle. Gingerly at first, he tried the handle. It rose smoothly, only squeaking as he pressed it back down. After a few pumps, water gushed through, brown and stale-looking at first, but then clear and clean.

Good enough.

George wiped his hand on his jeans and tried the drawers on either side of the sink. Both slid smoothly. That was nice. The kitchen drawers back at his apartment had cheap runners that jammed far too often. They irritated him.

He turned and scanned the remaining space, pausing to stare at the old-fashioned iron-top stove with its claw-foot legs and multiple oven doors.

"Good grief, do people still use those things?" George muttered to no one in particular.

He grasped one of the front handles and turned it. Metal grated on metal. George shuddered at the sound but brought the handle to its full twist. He pulled. The door swung open with surprising ease.

Peering inside, George examined the empty, cast iron expanse that, as far as he could tell, required an actual fire for cooking. Bits of ash still clung to the corners.

He shook his head, latched the door, and stepped back. *Unnecessary anyway.* He rarely cooked with anything but a microwave.

There was no fridge or any other appliances, but off the left side of the kitchen he found a pantry with shelves and a cellar door. The cellar proved larger than expected, but empty, save for a straw broom in the corner and an unsavory number of cobwebs.

George left the kitchen and crossed through the living room to the other side of the house. There he found a large bedroom where windows gathered sunlight into bright rectangles on the floor. A narrow staircase spiraled upward in one corner of the bedroom. George navigated the spiral, only putting his bad leg down to steady himself while his good one did all the work.

He opened the door into an attic room, complete with sloped ceiling and a solitary window facing whatever lay behind the cottage. The attic walls were bare wood, but a welcome honey color that seemed appropriate for an attic. The whole room felt warm and inviting, full of possibility.

George walked to the window and looked out. There was not a soul in sight. Only the acre or so of backyard with scraggly patches of grass and a few trees basking in the late summer heat. The backyard disappeared into a forest of smooth, grey trunks and leafy branches.

According to the description of the property in his uncle's will, the forest behind was uninhabited. That meant guaranteed quiet. George saw what looked like a footpath in the edge of the woods. A walking path perhaps? He needed walks, both for writer's block and for limbering up his leg.

He listened.

Silence.

Maybe town was overrated.

From the front door, Kathleen cleared her throat. "Mr. Morgan?" she called, her cheerful tone relentless. "Still need a few minutes? Or are you ready to talk about pricing?"

George needed more than a few minutes. He needed days. Weeks. Months of quiet to think, and work, and create.

He thought of the neighborhoods back in town. They were Midwest American cookie cutter neighborhoods. Houses all alike, pocket-sized yards that stared into the neighbors' back windows, privacy fences that offered little privacy. Neighborhoods were crowded. All concrete and door-to-door salesmen.

He would only be able to afford a basic subdivision house there. The inheritance from Uncle Barry was large, sure, but he would have to be careful. He figured between the inheritance and his own savings, he could live comfortably for four years. After that, he would have to get creative.

He hadn't expected such a large sum. He had not, for that matter, expected Uncle Barry to die so soon. Maybe it was wishful thinking, assuming his uncle would still be around for awhile. Mid-seventies seemed too young to die.

The doctor said heart attacks were very normal for men that age, even men of decent health, like Uncle Barry. But George still found it hard to believe he was gone. Then again, every other person he had really loved was gone, so it shouldn't have surprised him. Heck, twenty-three was too young to die too, and that hadn't stopped...

George shook his head. There was no use going down that road. The point was that Uncle Barry had been the last to go.

He had left everything to George. Over two hundred thousand dollars, his remaining personal possessions, and this rural property that George hadn't even known about. George had not known, either, how much money Uncle Barry actually saved. He was not stingy, by any means, but he and Aunt Pam never seemed to have much. They had lived simply and seemed content to keep it that way.

About the time George graduated college, they sold the house they had lived in for thirty years and moved to a ground-level, rented townhome with no yard to upkeep.

They hadn't bothered buying another car once their sedan kicked the bucket. Aunt Pam said she would just as well walk as drive anyway, since they were within walking distance of anything important, and Uncle Barry said he would rather walk with her than drive on his own. So that was that.

They would go to the movies once in awhile and order take-out when no one felt like cooking. Then Aunt Pam died. It was a short, brutal fight with lung cancer. Uncle Barry didn't do much after that. He ate microwave meals and ambled around town with George on the weekends.

All that money just sat in the bank. He gave it all to George when he passed away.

George wondered how much his aunt and uncle had scrimped to leave him such a large gift. It would be like them to think that way, to purposely save more for his benefit. The inheritance was his ticket away from the corporate world. He was grateful.

Still, though, they had not been wealthy. It would hold him over while he got his writing career off the ground, but not much more. If his writing didn't take off, well...

George would not let himself think that way. It *had* to work. And for it to work, he needed a place to write.

He looked around the attic room once more, then out the window at the emptiness of grass and forest.

This would do.

"Mr. Morgan?" Kathleen was at the bottom of the stairs.

George cleared his throat. He could hear the surprise in his own voice when he said, "I'm going to keep it."

George moved in two Saturdays later. Getting the cottage ready did not take long. He had hired Kathleen's suggested inspector, in awkward apology for not listing the cottage with her after all. Her cheerfulness remained unshakable.

The inspector, armed with lengthy checklists, was thorough. George was satisfied to hear that the cottage was in sound condition, considering its age.

"Tight as a drum," the inspector had said in apparent surprise.

"You'll have to run some electricity," he had added, making some notes on his clipboard and shooting another curious look around the little house. "Doesn't look like it's been updated a smidge, but it's still solid. Kind of eerie, ain't it? Just turning onto the road gave me the heebie-jeebies. It's too..." The inspector scrunched his forehead and thought for a second. "Bygone, I guess."

"It doesn't bother me," George answered.

He had thanked the inspector, hired an electrician to run enough line for a fridge and a few outlets, then called a moving company for a truck and some extra hands.

The move only took a couple hours. He never kept much in the apartment anyway. George straightened his couch and the little coffee table, put sheets and his old blue afghan on the bed, and arranged some books on the nightstand. A worn paperback of Herbert's *Dune* topped the current stack. He cycled through it every couple of years.

The rest of his books fit on one bookshelf, a white particle board structure he had bought several years before. He unpacked the remaining volumes onto its shelves and organized his collection of Star Wars figures across the top.

Liese had always teased him about those figures. But she knew he liked them. And he knew that she liked that he liked them. So they stayed.

The figures had been in the basement when the fire happened. Only basement items had been salvageable. Other than the action figures and a few books and blankets, everything else he had now was stuff he had picked up second-hand.

George didn't spend much time cooking, so unpacking the kitchen was hardly a chore. He set the coffee pot in the corner and arranged a small jumble of mismatched dishes and silverware into the drawers.

The only difficult part had been getting his desk into the attic. Between Max and Jerry, the hired movers, they had heaved, pushed, pulled, and finally squeezed the heavy desk over the last bit of spiral stair railing and through the doorway.

George had directed them to the wall with the window, where they set the desk against the window sill with a final grunt.

"Couldn't leave the beast downstairs with the rest of them, eh?" Jerry had said, wiping sweat from his forehead with one hand and massaging his back with the other. He shook his head and chuckled. "Those stairs are something else."

"Nah," George replied.

He hadn't bothered explaining. That desk was his pride and joy, if he had one. It, too, was from Uncle Barry, though gifted several years ago, just before Aunt Pam died.

It did not look like anything spectacular to the average eye. Just an oaken desk with drawers down both sides and a work surface marked by tea stains and coffee cup rings. To George, though, it was a haven.

George waited until very last to unpack his writing things. It was almost eight o'clock by the time he straightened the rest of the house and microwaved a mini lasagna for dinner. He washed his fork and placed it back in the drawer, wiped the small counter clean, and mounted the stairs.

The single bulb lamp on his desk cast a cozy glow through the attic. He could see nothing through the dusk out the window. But tomorrow there would be trees and sunlight, perhaps an occasional bird through the quiet. Maybe he would take a walk on the forest path tomorrow afternoon when he hit his usual lull.

He thought of the lonely path disappearing into the trees.

Maybe he would wait on that.

George cleared his throat. It sounded loud in the solitary attic. He stacked notebooks on one side of the desk. A spider skittered across its web on the window corner and began work on a lodged housefly. George did not mind a spider if it stayed where he could see it.

He set an array of pens near the notebooks and parked his thesaurus in easy reach. In the middle of the desk he placed his laptop, ran the charging cord to the newly installed outlet, then stepped back and surveyed the scene.

Yes. This would do very nicely.

Last of all he pulled out the picture of the beautiful, brown-haired woman. The woman's eyes laughed. They looked right at his. Her mouth was frozen in a half smirk, the edge lifted in some secret mirth, as if he alone shared the joke.

Man, he missed her.

George stared at the picture for a long moment. He traced the edge of the woman's face with one finger. A belly-deep sigh escaped him. The sigh of a man whose world has long been grey.

George wiped the glass clean with the edge of his shirt and placed the frame gently on the desk. He edged it back until it sat next to the lamp, bathed in the light of the single bulb.

Finished.

George clicked the lamp off and clumped down the stairs to bed. Beneath the familiar ache, a thrill of tense excitement set his heart pounding. He had done it. He was in his own house, away from the apartment he had never liked, past the long-awaited exit from nine-to-five office life. He had contemplated a change like this for years.

True, the rural cottage was unexpected, but George thought it was an improvement from his original plan. He wondered briefly what his ex-colleagues at the accounting office would think if they knew how nervous he was.

As if on cue, his last day at the office forced its way forward in his memory. They had thrown a farewell party for him. Not because anyone there cared much about him leaving. They threw a party for everyone who quit or retired.

It was always the same routine—a tray of stale cookies in the break room, the Farewell banner hung up on the wall with its corner still torn from when someone had pulled it down years ago without loosening the tape first. A few handshakes and "Good luck" comments before people glanced at watches and moseyed back to desks.

Kirk Johnson had come over while George took a regrettable bite of cookie. "Well, George."

George had winced. Kirk was a loud talker by nature. Standing next to him was like being blasted with a megaphone. George shook Kirk's hand and forced a polite smile around the wad of cookie.

"Off into the world, huh?" Kirk boomed. He grinned, showing almost all of his shining white teeth.

"Not really. Just changing careers."

"Whatcha' planning to do now? Doesn't get much better than bookkeeping and taxes." Kirk had chuckled at his own sarcasm and glanced around the room to see if anyone else appreciated it. No one was paying attention. A few colleagues chatted in the corner. Others were sipping coffee on their way back to cubicles.

George cleared his throat. "Still working out the details, but, uh, I'm mostly going to be writing."

He instantly regretted this statement. *Keep it to yourself,* he had chided, as Kirk's eyes shifted from bored to incredulous.

"Write? Like, books?"

"Something like that." George had glanced at the other faces now watching him. He took another bite of cookie and wondered how much longer until he could make his exit.

Kirk did a grunt laugh, the kind that means, *That's ridiculous, but I'm not going to say it out loud.* "Well, good luck with that. If you ever need a job back, I'm sure there'll still be space for you here." Kirk had guffawed loudly and checked for reactions before meandering to the coffee pot.

In the dark bedroom of his cottage, George stood still for a moment, then pushed the memory away. This would work. It had to. He would never slink back to an accounting job asking for a paycheck.

George climbed in bed. His leg ached from all the extra stooping, lifting, and carrying. He kneaded his thumb along the length of his hip and grimaced.

Through the window, he heard the soft sound of trees blowing in the night breeze. His breathing slowed, matching the trees in their gentle exhales of night and nature.

He couldn't hear that sound without dislodging a particular memory. It was a simple one. Funny that such a little thing would stick with him. Liese stood next to him on a chilly night in their backyard. They were looking at the moon. She was wearing that old yellow sweater she liked so much, but it wasn't quite warm enough. She had hugged her arms around herself and leaned into him.

"Do you ever think the trees talk to each other?" Liese had asked, out of the blue.

"What?" George had glanced down at her, amused. His brain was numbers, logic, and space stories. Hers was watercolors and Narnia.

"The trees," she had said, giving him a playful slap on the arm. "In the wind. Do you ever think they're having a conversation?"

George had listened to the leaves rustling. The breeze was cold. "Nope."

She'd smacked him again and laughed. "Of course not." Then she pressed against him once more, resting her head on the sleeve of his jacket.

George sensed her contemplative mood. He could picture the exact look in her eyes without needing to see it. These were the times she would expound on art, literature, and life's meaning.

But not this time. She only said, "I do." Then she had stood quietly, leaning into his warmth and listening to the wind.

George lay still as a rock in his empty bed. The breeze blew, sometimes soft as a whisper, sometimes hard enough to rattle a branch against the window. *Just nature.* But he relaxed. Excitement for his new home and writing possibilities once again took hold in the center of his sternum and held on.

Tomorrow. Tomorrow he could begin his work in earnest.

As George drifted toward sleep, he thought, for just a second, that he heard music. Faint strains, almost inaudible. Something stirred in his soul. He snapped his eyes open and listened.

Nothing. Just the wind.

Perhaps it was only the beginning of a dream. George turned over and fell asleep.

3

GEORGE

CIRCA 2023

Fire. Fire, and madness, and night. George was running. Running like his heart would twist out of his body, shred to pieces and burn. It already had.

It was too late. He knew it was.

He saw the last of the roof collapse in an explosion of smoke and sparks, saw the siding peeling back from the walls, blackened and burning.

Not this. Please, God. Not this. Not her.

Hoses stretched like enormous snakes from their firetruck coils. They gushed water from metal mouths, spewed foam and spray into the furious heat. Firemen bustled, yelled.

George saw the neighbors huddled in knots up the street. Away from the road where the truck lights whirled. Away from the house that was burning to the ground.

He lunged forward. His bad leg reeled, but he forced it ahead. He would have kept right on running. Would have hurtled right into the flames. Maybe there was a chance. Maybe she wasn't gone yet.

Strong arms grabbed him. They held him back.

"It's too hot," a man's voice yelled. "It went too fast, I'm sorry. No one's been able to get in. Was there anyone inside?"

George's legs buckled. He was falling. Falling.

George woke. Sweat drenched his forehead. His heart pounded, frantically at first, then slower, regulating back to the methodical rhythm of the present.

He was alone in his cottage. The bird clock ticked on the wall, one of his thrift store finds. He felt around for a flashlight and held it up. The minute hand clicked into place. Four o'clock. But no bird song piped through the room. That part was broken, thankfully. George would not have bought the clock otherwise.

He sat up and dragged his legs over the side of the bed. Five years. Five years since the fire, and still the memory plagued his sleep. Not as much, now. Not nearly as much, but it did come.

George stood and shuffled to the kitchen for a glass. He pumped the tap and watched the glass fill with water. He drank, sighed, dragged a hand over his face.

Maybe it was the memory of Liese in the moonlight that had brought back nightmares of the fire. Or maybe it was Uncle Barry's funeral a few weeks ago. Too many funerals. First his parents when he was just a kid, then his wife when the house burned down. Aunt Pam passed away a few years back, and now Uncle Barry.

Good grief. He was only thirty.

Only. Ha! Time marches on, stubborn as a mule, and not nearly as pleasant.

George clicked a light on. He may as well get up. It was still dark out, but not for long. He would get some extra work done on his novel. He never could fall back asleep after that nightmare anyway. George groaned, stretched, and flipped on the coffee pot.

Within a week of moving to the cottage, George had his new routine down. He woke to his alarm each morning as the sun rose. He pulled on his usual Levis and plaid button-down, then hummed the old Bonanza theme song while he brewed half a pot of coffee. He would pour himself a mug, navigate the spiral stairs, and get to work at his desk.

He was a writer. He knew he was, though his old coworkers at the accounting office did not agree.

He had worked at that office for eight years. Eight years tracking receipts and expenses, reconciling accounts, and sorting tax forms. Other than the paycheck, the only thing he liked from that job was his trashcan basketball record. Thirty-two paper wads in a row, tossed from his cubicle into a wastebasket on the empty desk next door. No one else knew about the record. He saved trashcan basketball for midday while his coworkers were out for lunch or chatting in the break room. *Paper wads and wastebaskets*. There was probably a good metaphor in there somewhere.

With increasing frequency over the last decade, George spent his evening hours typing away on his laptop, building descriptions and stories word by word, sentence by sentence, compiling thoughts that seemed much easier to express when written.

He had not shown his stories to anyone until about six months ago. After many misgivings and much wrestling of the mind, George submitted a short story to a writer's magazine, telling himself he was foolish for doing so. He wasn't ready yet. He still had too much to learn.

To his shock, a number of weeks later George found himself staring at an acceptance letter and a check.

It was possible, after all.

So, on the last day of August, George sat at his oak desk in the attic of the little cottage, sipping lukewarm coffee between long, thoughtful stares at the page on his screen and fervent bursts of typing. He made a sandwich at lunchtime and took a short walk down the road.

Upon his return, George heated water in the microwave and plopped in a tea bag. The tea was a personal conundrum. He preferred coffee, but by the time he crossed out of his twenties, afternoon cups of coffee left him tossing and turning long into the night.

George picked up the tea. Weak, and less satisfying, but he was getting used to it. He worked better with something hot to sip.

George headed back upstairs and tried to work. He stared at the last paragraph from the morning. Typed. Erased. Stared some more. His brain moved like cold molasses. He sighed and shifted in his chair.

A fly buzzed by the window. George gave his local spider a disapproving look and swatted the fly with one of his notebooks. He drained the last of his tea and paced, trying to stretch the kinks out of his bad leg.

The air felt stuffy. He should buy a fan to put in here. George walked to the window and looked out.

Perhaps he would try the forest path today. He hadn't yet. Something about it made him wary.

Maybe it was the way it disappeared so quickly into the trees. George didn't like not knowing what was around a corner. It might be an ideal walking path, though, and he would never know if he didn't find out.

George snapped the laptop closed and thumped downstairs. On Tuesday he had trimmed overgrown patches of lawn with a reel mower, and yesterday he had gone to the grocery store for cans of soup and microwave dinners, so there was no excuse today that would use up the afternoon lull.

George pulled on his tennis shoes and stepped outside. The afternoon was warm, almost hot. He looked forward to the onset of fall. He could feel its beginnings in the recent night air, that crispness that whispered of cool days and fire-building. For at least a couple more hours today, summer would prevail.

He pushed his hands deep into jean pockets and started down the forest path. It was only a dirt track, wide enough to walk comfortably if he kept an eye out for stray branches, and there were plenty of those to contend with.

George nudged broken tree limbs to the side with his good foot as he walked, and even stooped to remove a larger one. If he was going to use this path, he reasoned, he might as well clear it sooner than later.

After a quarter mile or so, the trail ended at a much wider one. This new path led both left and right and was considerably larger and less cluttered. It was more a narrow lane than a footpath. The dirt was packed hard as stone. A few sticks lay strewn near the edges, but no larger branches. This lane looked, for all George could see, well-kept.

He stopped to rest. Leaves rustled lazily in the breeze. Grasshoppers skipped over the dirt and disappeared. He looked at his watch. Half past three. George glanced up and down the lane. Both directions looked equally solitary. He hesitated, wishing he knew what lay around each bend, then turned left.

After a bit more walking, George felt his tension ease. It was beautiful in the forest, all greys, greens, browns, and cheerful nature noises. George grinned at a bird eying him from a branch up ahead.

"Where's your song, huh? Nothing to worry about from me. I'm one of you out here."

He hummed Bonanza again and limped along, watching for more birds. He had been walking five minutes or so when a rattling reached his ears from further up the lane.

George broke off humming. He stopped. An animal? Unlikely. The sound was too steady. A person? George squinted, but the lane curved not far ahead. Whoever it was would be this side of the curve by the time he saw them.

George turned and quickened his steps back toward the home path, swinging his lame leg along like the wooden limb of a pirate. The rattling grew steadily louder.

Maybe forest management, he thought. *Maybe they're going to do some tree clearing.* Surely that was it. *Who else would be back here?* It was only wooded wilderness, according to the paperwork his uncle left.

He was still a few paces from his trail when he heard, "Hullo!" The rattling ceased. "Hullo," the same voice called again.

George stopped and turned. On the near side of the curve, still too far to see the driver clearly, stood a pony hitched to a wooden wagon. The driver quickened the pony and drove toward George.

George stiffened. He hated interactions like this. So obligatory and awkward.

The pony halted a few yards from him. On the wagon seat sat a young man. He was clean-shaven but ruddy, and looked to be near eighteen. His clothes could have popped straight out of an old western. Denim overalls and a white, collared shirt stained with dirt. He had the sleeves rolled up over strong, sinewed forearms.

The kid pushed a wide-brimmed hat off his forehead, revealing sweaty blond hair. He held the reins in one hand and leaned forward, staring at George with a strange, unreadable expression. "Who're you?"

George rubbed sweat off the back of his neck and glanced behind him at his own worn footpath. He cleared his throat.

"George Morgan," he said. He waved, turned onto the footpath, and hurried toward home.

"Wait!" the young man called. "Wait, how'd you get here?" He was clambering off the wagon.

George's neck prickled. What was the deal? He hadn't seen any trespassing signs. He turned around and put both hands up.

"My mistake," he said. "I thought it was public land back here."

The kid stopped at the entrance to George's footpath. He stood in a half-stride, arms tense and eyes wide.

"How'd you get here?" he asked again. His voice sounded strained, as if it had stuck partway up his throat.

George dropped his hands. He filled his cheeks with air and let it out like a leaky balloon. How should he answer that question? It seemed obvious. The kid must be pretty touchy about anyone coming on his property.

"Walked," he said finally. "Sorry about the intrusion." He turned toward home.

"Mister, wait!" the young man called again.

George heard twigs crack in quick succession. Was the kid chasing him? He turned quickly. "That's far enough." George shot him a stern look. "This is my land here, and I'd prefer you leave me be."

"But—"

"That's far enough."

George eyed him coolly. The young man looked stricken, half-terrified. *What on earth?* Was he mad, or scared?

George turned homeward again and hurried away. Maybe if he escaped fast enough, the kid would leave well enough alone. With his mind thus occupied, George didn't pay close attention to the path. His bad foot caught on a branch he hadn't pushed far enough away the first time through. He sprawled headlong and landed hard.

He swore and pulled himself back to his feet. His knees and arms throbbed, and his head spun. He glanced toward the lane, but the young man was nowhere in sight. George heard a shout, then the clatter of pony hooves and wagon wheels tearing into the distance.

He shook his head. *Good grief. That kid was a piece of work.*

George brushed dirt and leaves off his shirt and straightened.

How long had it been since he had fallen like that? Twelve years, probably. Not since his freshman year of college, when he had made a fool of himself tripping over a curb and wrecking into a girl on the way to class.

George couldn't help glancing behind him a few more times as he walked home. It was just a teenage kid and a pony. But the kid's expression...it made him uneasy.

"Of all the luck," George grumbled, closing the cottage's back door behind him and kicking his shoes off. "What's the use of a lonely walk if it isn't lonely?"

He would stick to the first little forest path from now on, he decided. That one was on his property and clearly no one used it. It was a pretty walk, though not very long. He could tidy it up and pace it more than once, for more exercise or longer spurts of writer's block.

"A pony wagon?" George said aloud to no one in particular.

He shook his head, looked for a moment at the empty coffee pot, then sighed and made a fresh cup of tea. He would try again to make some progress on his novel before the day ended.

After two more hours and only a few brittle paragraphs, George gave up. He hauled the little wastebasket to the opposite side of the attic and threw paper wads until dinnertime. Thirteen. He would have to work on that.

George closed his laptop, and went downstairs to make dinner. He had just pulled a pasty-looking chicken Alfredo out of the microwave when a face peeped in the kitchen window. George jumped and sloshed Alfredo sauce on his hand. He swore under his breath and dropped the container on the counter.

The face was gone. It had been a girl's face, maybe fourteen or so. Big, astonished eyes and a smattering of freckles. George shook the sauce off over the sink and rinsed cool water over his smarting skin.

"Blasted neighbor kids," he muttered.

He checked the window, but there was no one in sight. He stepped to the living room and looked out toward the woods. Two figures were running out of his yard. By the time he opened the back door, they had disappeared into the trees.

He almost shouted after them. Inside he seethed, but yelling at neighbors seemed a little much. He settled for chucking a weed in their general direction.

Only the birds and cicadas answered.

George glanced around, feeling foolish. He cleared his throat, yanked the door closed, and turned the deadbolt.

First thing next morning, while the coffee pot sputtered in the kitchen, someone knocked on the front door.

4

INTERLUDE

LETTER #1

D.F.,

Though it's quite against my original inclination, I've decided to compose a history of the Magister, the Order of the Gifted, and all those strange events that occurred. I will attempt to do so here.

I won't tell it all in one go. I do not have the energy at this point for a lengthy narrative all at once. Do what you will with these letters. I trust your judgment on with whom to share them, and when. Many have been affected.

The story of the Magister finding the Arbor Pearls in the roots of that once great tree has been recorded elsewhere, and you have heard it before. I will not waste time and ink on what is already known. Rather, I hope to tell what happened after—the powers he cultivated and passed to others, the forming of the Order of the Gifted, and what became of all. Some details have been lost, as is the nature of man and his pursuits, but much has been retained through my own careful research and many firsthand accounts. May you see and understand.

Sincerely,

G.

In A.D. *1830, the Magister first discovered the Pearls. Shortly after, he found that these strange stones, by mixing with his blood, had endowed him with new abilities.*

It was quite an accident, this knowledge. Much like the finding of the Pearls.

He learned movement first.

A glass tipped off the edge of the table, knocked by the careless toss of a book. He lunged by instinct. Not because he thought he could stop it shattering, of course, but simply because that is what one usually does when something fragile falls.

But it did stop.

As he flung his hand forward, the glass stopped midair. Hardly believing what he saw, he kept the glass suspended as the last of its contents splattered on the floor below. His hand remained outstretched, his body rigid with shock and concentration. The hand ached. It was still covered with deep scabs and bruises, reminders of his efforts to retrieve those beautiful Pearls.

Slowly, ever so slowly, he eased his hand downward, willing the glass to follow. It did. The glass settled unbroken on the wood-plank floor amid a puddle of water.

He felt irrationally tired. He lowered himself to the floor and stared from the glass to his hands until the shadows deepened to dusk.

He practiced. Days, weeks, months—willing objects to move short distances, then longer. Slower, then faster.

He lived alone, so it was not difficult to keep a secret. He had a modest, rented house near the university at which he studied. Friends came at times, but never without warning. He knew their class and work schedules as well as his own and could predict their visits like a train schedule.

He was quick with his work and did well in his classes. His professors praised his abilities. Several had already recommended him to become a professor after graduating.

Now there were the Pearls. Why he, of all people, should find them on that mountain, he did not know.

He would use them, though. They frightened him, but he would conquer that as he conquered anything else that frightened him: through control. As long as he stayed in control, there was no reason to be afraid.

They were given to him, after all. He was not one of those people who attributed life's mysteries to chance. Power came from somewhere, or someone. He didn't bother to think much into who or what.

The Pearls were given to him, and he would use them. He would receive their gifts and make the most of them.

He got better. He gained precision and clarity in each object's movement. He built endurance too, though any use of the power still taxed his strength.

Within six months he could lift a full bottle of wine without touching it, send it hurtling from one end of the house to the other, and have it land unharmed on the windowsill. The effort fatigued him, but not like it used to. He was getting stronger.

The more his capability grew, the more he wondered what else was possible.

Every night before going to sleep, he lifted the Pearls from their hiding place and set them on a square of black velvet in the middle of the kitchen table.

He would stare at them, freshly astonished by their beauty, hungry for their secrets. He studied the lines of light and color. They were forever shifting. Not that he ever saw them change, but no matter how many times he looked, they were always different. Infinite.

He held them, gingerly at first, then with more confidence. He brushed his fingers over their smooth exterior. They were always cool to the touch, but only at the surface, as if a heat glowed within, a deeper power just beyond reach.

One night, after many months, he took a hammer and a sharp nail and drove the point with all his might toward the center of a Pearl. The Pearl careened across the table and smashed a wine bottle, sending green glass shattering to the floor.

The nail stuck, embedded to its head in the table.

He recovered the Pearl and stared at its untainted surface. Then, as if by sudden decision, he picked up a piece of glass and drew it across his arm until the blood ran.

He pressed the Pearl to his marred flesh. Its peculiar warmth seeped into his veins. He held it there as long as he dared, swallowing back fear that rose and jerked at his thoughts, screaming that this was too much, too beautiful, too big for his human frame.

But no. He pulled his arm free and waited, panting. His heart pulsed and tingled. His mind calmed. He was in control. He would take it slowly, learn carefully.

As long as he was the one in charge, he had no reason to be afraid. The power was locked in the Pearls. The Pearls were his. He could receive their gifts over time, like drinking sips of water from a magic well.

He bandaged his arm and returned the Pearls to their hiding place. He was more capable now than he had been. He could feel it.

5

GEORGE

CIRCA 2023

George flinched and turned toward the door. He waited. The knock sounded again.

He sighed and set his empty coffee mug back on the counter. If this was some kind of prank, he was going to have a thing or two to say about it.

He stepped to the door and pulled it open. There stood the young man from the wagon, and with him the girl George had seen in the window yesterday evening.

From the looks of them, George assumed she was the boy's younger sister. They both wore wide-brimmed hats and clothes of old-fashioned fabric. The boy had the same shirt and overalls from the day before, and the girl wore a simple, calf-length dress with dirt smudges on the hem. Her hair hung in one long, blond braid over her shoulder.

They jumped when George opened the door. Both teenagers gaped at him. He looked from one to the other.

Why did they seem so surprised? They had knocked on his door, after all. He saw no sign of the pony wagon. Had they cut through the forest?

"Can I help you?" George asked when it became clear they were not going to be the first to speak.

They only stared at him, eyes wide. Finally, the young man cleared his throat.

"Well, we ain't certain," he said, hesitating just a fraction of a second. "I'm Harlan Stone. This here's my sister Hanna."

The girl cocked her head. Her eyebrows cinched, drawing her freckles close together. "How'd you get here, sir?"

They spoke with a tight, slightly drawled accent, more intensified than the Midwestern speech George was used to hearing.

"Excuse me?" The words came out stiffer than he intended.

The girl's eyes narrowed and hardened. "Harlan said he saw you on the road."

"Hanna." Her brother elbowed her in the arm. "Give 'im a minute."

Hanna jerked her arm away. "I just want to know what he was doin' on the road." She turned back to George. "We don't see new folks here. You'd be the first in a right long time."

"Oh, uh..." George shifted his feet. They must not want him back there any more than he wanted them on his front porch. "Sorry about the road. Is that your land back there?"

"Our place is a mite further up," Harlan said, interrupting his sister when she started to speak again. "That's Jasper's land other edge of the lane from the old path back of here."

"I see." George rubbed an eyebrow, glanced around, wedged his hand in his pocket. "I uh...I was just out for a walk. Didn't realize anyone lived back there."

Harlan and Hanna looked at each other.

"You..." Harlan began. He crammed his hat back on his head, then took it off again. "You been here long? In this house, I mean?"

"About a week."

Again a look passed between brother and sister. George scratched the back of his head. "How about you?" he asked finally. "Have you lived around here awhile?"

Hanna snorted. "You could say so."

She surveyed George's attire and turned to consider the battered station wagon in the open barn. "Where'd you move from?"

"If—" Harlan cut in, "you ain't bothered by us askin'."

George *was* bothered, but he figured he should try to behave better than he had done yesterday.

He would much rather they left him alone. *But best not to burn bridges,* as Uncle Barry would have reminded him, even if this particular bridge seemed to be a couple of odd-brained teenagers.

"Just from Hillsboro, about fifteen minutes north. Wanted something quieter."

Hanna coughed.

"Do they...do folks have those in...Hillsboro?" Harlan gestured to George's station wagon.

Hanna looked at it too, her head cocked to one side and eyelids scrunched. "What is it?"

"It's a pile of junk," George chuckled, hoping to lighten the mood. He noted the seriousness of their expressions and coughed. "But cars, yeah. Everyone drives cars there. Or takes the bus."

Harlan and Hanna stared openmouthed.

"Cars. To drive in." George looked from one to the other. What was their deal? And why had he tried to crack a joke? Things were weird enough without him attempting to bring in a sense of humor. These people were obviously cracked in some way or another. He hesitated, trying to think how to wind up the conversation without being rude.

"What in tarnation is a bus?" Hanna asked finally, but Harlan elbowed her again.

George coughed into his shirt sleeve. "Does Jasper drive a pony wagon too?"

Harlan glanced again at the car, then back at George. "Jasper's got a horse. Some of the others have ponies though. And a few have donkeys."

George searched Harlan's expression. Not a smidge of humor. This was getting weirder by the second. George cleared his throat.

"How many live back there? In the forest…area?"

"All of 'em," Hanna mumbled.

"All of them?"

Harlan put a hand on Hanna's shoulder. "Look, Mister, uh…Morgan. You coming here is…unexpected. Not in a bad way," Harlan hastened to add. "Just odd for our…our usual way of things."

George shifted his feet. "Look, I don't want to cause any trouble. I'll stay off your road back there and keep to my own property if you'd like."

"No, no," Harlan said, his eyes widening. "That ain't what we mean at all. What we mean is…" He looked to Hanna.

"Would you come by this evenin'?" Hanna asked. "Close on to six?" She grinned, and George saw a hint of amiability. "We're havin' roast and beans. It's awful good."

George opened and closed his mouth so many times, he felt like a gasping fish. *Dinner?* He had hardly met these people. And they were absolute weirdos. He didn't want to talk to them, let alone have dinner.

"I…I don't…that is…"

"Please, Mr. Morgan," Harlan said. "We sure would appreciate it." He glanced over George's shoulder into the cottage, then back to the old station wagon. His brows were knit tighter than fishing knots in a hurricane.

Hanna grabbed her brother's arm and dragged him down the porch steps. "Six o'clock. Just turn right onto the road from your trail there. Same way you saw Harlan a goin' yesterday. We're only another quarter mile up."

Harlan nodded. He glanced at George's lame leg, paused for a second, then tipped his hat to George before placing it back on his head. The two of them turned and strode away, not toward the road out front, but sharply left toward the side of his yard. George stared after them.

"Six o'clock," he mumbled.

But by that time the two teenagers, overalls, hats, and all, had disappeared around the corner of the cottage.

George stepped inside and closed the door. He stood with his hand still on the knob, then hurried to the back window and looked out. Sure enough, they had headed for his little path and, he assumed, the forest lane.

"Roast and beans?" He shook his head and turned away from the window.

George glanced at his watch. Just after seven. He was usually in the attic by now with his manuscript open and his coffee half-gone.

"Neighbors," he mumbled, returning to the kitchen. *Cracked neighbors, at that.* This had not been part of his plan. Why couldn't they just leave him alone?

George poured his coffee and tromped upstairs. He settled into his chair and leaned back, letting the coffee mug's heat seep into both hands. Had that really just happened? Had he really just agreed to have dinner with some backwoods neighbor family who couldn't seem to decide if they thought he was the devil or their new best friend?

Apparently so.

George groaned and set his mug aside. He could call the police. Alert them of two teenage harassers trespassing on his property, possibly a whole community of nutcases hiding in the woods. But what would he tell them?

"Hello, officer? Yes. There are neighbor kids violating my rights. How so? Well, they snuck around my yard. One of them looked in my window. Then they knocked on the front door and looked at me really weird. Yes, yes, and they said there are more where they came from. They were wearing weird clothes too. No, no gang symbols, just out-of-date stuff, overalls and all that. What else? Uh, then they invited me over for dinner."

Right. A lot of good that would do. *He* would probably end up being the one on the county watchlist.

He could buy a dog. Nothing crazy, like a pit bull or a doberman, just something smart enough to be intimidating if needed. Something to ward off people like Harlan and Hanna Stone.

George pictured a Saint Bernard drooling on his couch and quickly nixed that idea. He only liked dogs on a case-by-case basis. Besides, he was allergic. He had found that out the hard way when he was ten years old, and Uncle Barry brought home a beagle from the animal rescue.

"Barry Morgan, what on earth?" Aunt Pam had exclaimed. "What about Kit?"

Kit was Aunt Pam's long-haired cat who lurked around the house and snarled at everyone but her.

"Kit can deal with it, Pam. A boy's gotta have a dog."

He had handed the beagle to a wide-eyed, grinning George. George held the squirming beagle against his chest and rubbed his cheek on the brown head. He was smitten. Absolutely delighted.

Aunt Pam had smacked Uncle Barry on the shoulder, then leaned over and kissed him on the cheek.

George knew that beagle was his. The beagle had whined and wriggled. It licked George's cheek, his chin, his nose. George laughed. He had plopped to the floor like a sack of potatoes and hugged that squirming dog against his chest, burying his face in its fur.

A dog. His dog. His very own dog.

Then his eyes had started stinging and watering, and his nose felt like someone had stuffed it full of cotton. He tried to ignore it. But he had sneezed, and sneezed again, and felt his chest start to tighten until he clutched his sternum and let the beagle drop to the floor.

Uncle Barry had taken one look at his face and ran for the nearest drugstore. Aunt Pam stripped his shirt off and shoved him into the shower with the water on full blast.

The beagle peed on the kitchen floor and ate Kit's bowl of kibble.

That was the end of having a dog around. By the time George's face quit hurting and he could breathe freely again, Uncle Barry had returned the beagle to the rescue.

"Welp, George-o," Uncle Barry had said when he came back. "Sometimes we've gotta take life's lemons and do our best with them." He slapped George on the back and handed him a goldfish glubbing silently in a plastic bag.

"Best we can do for now," Uncle Barry said. He had glanced at Aunt Pam across the room, then leaned close and winked. "At least this one won't eat the cat food."

George chuckled at the memory. The goldfish swam in circles in a bowl for two weeks before Kit got ahold of it. They didn't bother with any other pets after that.

He stretched and took a drink of coffee. No police. No dogs. He might as well show up for dinner and see what happened. If it got too crazy, he could always move.

George rolled his eyes at that thought. That was what he had just done, wasn't it? Moved to escape crowds and neighbors?

He sighed, opened his laptop, and pushed the power button. He had come here to get away from town and have a quiet place to work. Surely a couple of neighbors wouldn't throw too big a wrench in that plan. It was just dinner.

Just get in, be polite, get out. It was as simple as that.

6

LUX

CIRCA 1873

Lux Crane did not consider himself to be a very complicated person. Particular, maybe, but only about some things. He liked to learn. Being in charge didn't appeal to him much, but maybe that was because the opportunities for authority had been so rare.

Lux had grown up as an only child with no father, a boy in his mother's shadow. It still felt that way, much of the time.

His mother insisted on control. She had been like that his whole life, and he had done little to challenge her. Not for twenty years, anyway. It was starting to chafe at him.

"Again," his mother demanded from her seat by the window.

Lux stood and readied his hands. She knew more than he did. It was that simple. He was still learning, and she was the only one around to teach him.

"It is fire, Lux. Remember that. Fire has—"

"A life of its own, yes. I remember."

How could he forget? He had the burn scars on his ankles, and the unpleasant memory of failure. The fire, only a stick blaze at the time, had been too much for him. He had tried to hold it together, but it had slipped out of his grasp, slipped and burst and devoured the bottom of his trouser legs before he had time to do anything. His mother had yanked it free and thrown it back into the hearth.

She had pulled the burning out of his legs, too. Drawn it from his skin before it had time to melt deep into his flesh. It hurt still, and scarred, but not as badly as it might have.

That was months ago. Lux was stronger now.

He concentrated. His breathing steadied, slowed. *In…out.* He braced his hands and focused on the flames licking the bricks of the fireplace across the room.

One. Lux felt the heat of his Gifts coursing through his veins. This was a gentle heat, like the feel of sun on skin, but within his blood. It surged, speaking without words to the fire on which all his focus rested. Every fiber of his hands tightened. The fire obeyed. He willed the flames into a single ball that pulsed and writhed over the grate.

Two. Lux lifted his hands, still braced in open air. Across the room, the fiery orb rose. He pulled it toward himself. It left the confines of brick and floated in the middle of the room, a mass of light roiling like a nest of snakes, tame but deadly.

Three. Lux twisted his hands toward each other. The ball of fire condensed. Blue heat surged in its center. Lux's breathing came faster. Perspiration beaded on his forehead. He felt control slipping through his fingers like melting water. A tongue of fire lashed toward the floor, another toward the wall.

Focus. He forced his breathing to slow and deepen. Carefully, he gathered the wayward flames back to their center. He loved the feel of it. Fire was not still or silent like glass and furniture. Those things had energy too, but much less. Fire was movement and power.

Four. Lux stretched his hands apart. His fingers and tendons held steady, tense as piano strings. The fireball lengthened into an ellipse. He set it spinning, slowly at first, then faster. The flames crackled like static in a lightning storm.

Five. With a final thrust, Lux sent the flames hurtling back to the fireplace. There was a loud pop as it hit the grate. Sparks exploded into the room. Then quiet. Only the simple sputtering of a tame fire in the hearth and the huff of Lux's breathing.

He dropped his hands to his sides.

"That was almost a disaster," his mother said. Her voice held its usual softness, its well-bred, lilting tones, almost regal. But her eyes were stern. She looked sideways at him, one eyebrow raised.

Lux was used to her harsh critiques. She had been that way as long as he could remember. Even when he was a little boy, she expected perfection. Or at least as near to it as he could come. His capabilities were nowhere near her own.

"I brought it back in bounds." Lux used a shirt sleeve to wipe sweat off his forehead.

"It should never have left the bounds at all." His mother stood and paced the floor, her long velvet skirts swishing at each turn. "Fire is a rabid dog, Lux, not a puppy. Apart from living things, it is the strongest force you will master. Let it any looser, and it would explode. The whole room would be burning before you had your wits back together."

Lux gritted his teeth, but nodded. "Yes, Mother."

He poured a glass of water from a nearby pitcher and drank. It was cool and clear, and spread, silent and calm, through his insides. *Water. The conqueror of fire.*

His mother turned toward the window. "That's all for today. I'm tired."

She stood tall, shoulders straight and proud. One slender hand hung by her side. The other rested on the windowsill. She looked at the hand on the windowsill, turning it palm up, then down, then up again. She sighed and clenched it into a fist.

"What about water?" Lux asked.

She tensed and turned to face him. "What about it?"

"When will you teach me to harness water? We've done wind, and still objects, and fire as small as a candle flame and large as that one." He gestured to the fireplace.

"You aren't ready for that."

"Not ready? You said yourself that fire is the strongest non-living force."

"That's different. Water is too dangerous."

"How?"

"Because of what it can do, Lux. If it were to reveal us..." She clamped her mouth shut and turned back to the window.

"Reveal us how?"

She whirled toward the door. "Not now, Lux. I'm tired."

She was afraid. Lux could hear it in her voice. *Afraid of what? Water?* That did not make sense. He knew she could manipulate water. He had seen her do it. Just little things—pulling a spilled puddle off the floor and sending it to a potted plant; that sort of thing. What was dangerous about that?

"Does it have to do with the Code?"

His mother paused at the door. She looked at him. Lux saw the tension of her mouth, the mask of stern authority over that deep-seated unease. For a moment, her eyes softened. She lifted a hand, reached toward him.

Her hand dropped. The mask returned.

"It has to do with many things, Lux. Trust me."

With that, she left the room.

Lux felt his chest tighten. Always the unspoken, always the fear. His mother's look, her tone, they crawled through him like a mole in the dark. He swallowed. Something was wrong. Something was always wrong.

Lux had spent almost the entirety of his twenty years here in Green Meadows. He was not quite six when he and his mother came here, she as strong as life itself, and he just a scrawny child.

He was small for his age, then. The other boys in Green Meadows were sturdy, rugged lads. They had been hauling hay and farming crops with their fathers from the time they could walk. Lux, on the other hand, was thin and pale. When he was not training in the Gifts with his mother, he spent his time reading books or lying on a tree branch, talking to the birds.

With little interaction among other children, Lux did his best to be friends with the forest creatures. His mother had taught him to observe and talk with the animals, using the Gifts to listen to their chatter and contribute some of his own. It was a far cry from having children as friends, but better than nothing. He took pleasure in knowing that the animals were not afraid of him. They would come near and let him see their way of life.

Deer lived by poetry, squirrels by scolding. Foxes let him trail along to dens of frisking young. Birds hopped aside to show him nests of eggs perched among the highest tree branches.

So Lux was not really alone, though he longed for the companionship of other boys.

He wasn't scared of the Green Meadows boys. He just didn't belong with them. Once, when he was seven, he had been waiting outside the hotel while his mother paid for their meal. It was the only hotel in town, a simple boarding house that offered lunch or dinner to any paying customer. Lux and his mother used to stop there sometimes to eat. While he waited, a few boys about his age swaggered over and began to poke fun at him.

"Bastard," they had called him. "You don't even know who yer daddy is, do ya?"

Lux had not bothered answering. He hauled back and punched one of them in the nose. They left him alone after that.

They were right. He did not know who his father was.

He had asked his mother. It wasn't the first time he asked her. She gave him a long look, and, as before, changed the subject.

"They aren't mean boys," she said, referring back to the incident. "Not really. Otherwise they wouldn't have let it go that easily. They just want to have power over someone. You didn't give them any."

Lux never had managed to get on very well with them. He didn't know how to interact with a bunch of ordinary children. He was not ordinary; his mother often told him so. He was Gifted. He would learn powers they knew nothing about.

"Treat them with kindness," she had said. "You are Gifted to contribute to the good of others. But we are not the others. They won't understand you. They can't. Better to keep some separation."

Lux obliged, though at times he lingered behind his mother in town, staring longingly at groups of laughing children playing tag in the schoolyard. It was a small school. Green Meadows was only home to a couple hundred people, mostly farmers and a few storeowners. They lived in cottages of wood and stone.

Lux and his mother lived in a mansion. She had paid a huge sum, unheard of in those parts, to have her mansion built in record time by as many men as could be spared from their farms. She gave them high wages and earned their respect—though not their understanding.

The cottagers looked at his mother with fearful awe, as if she were some kind of queen. She rewarded them with benevolence and financial help and effectively sealed herself and Lux as reigning nobles in a land of paupers.

Lux, to his relief, grew in height and bulk as he got older. Puberty helped, and clearing trees in the sun. His mother made him do it without the Gifts, though sometimes he used them anyway to gather stray sticks. It was faster to stand in one place and beckon the sticks to a pile than it was to walk around picking them up one by one.

"It's good to put your hand to things," she had told him. "Besides, you need some muscle on your bones."

That much was true. So, he chopped and sweated while he turned into a man. He ran, too. Their land stretched for thirty acres, over the grassy meadow and through scads of trees. As a teenager, Lux would run for hours.

He had started with a trampled path around their property. It climbed the low, tree-covered hills and leapt a creek in the valley. Sometimes he would pause to strip his clothes off and lay in the shallow water, letting it burble over his skin and wash the sweat away.

Then he would be off, dashing over hill and vale, sending a hurried greeting to rabbits and deer that startled in his wake.

Eventually he left the confines of his mother's property and took to running through the town itself and the neighboring roads.

Green Meadows, named so for the three humongous grassy fields situated amidst the forest, had been only prospective farmland when the first settlers came.

Hillsboro, the nearest settlement at the time, had grown to a thriving village. When the railroad crews laid tracks through Hillsboro, more and more people congregated into its acreage. Crowded farmers pushed out for miles in search of uninterrupted space.

Green Meadows had just four families, to start. Others came, and soon they formed a village of their own along the central meadow. It never grew large—not without a railroad. The people seemed to like it that way.

Those without meadowland on their property cleared trees for planting. They grew and harvested. Some abandoned farming altogether and built stores by the central road, bringing supplies from Hillsboro or from the city far away.

This was the Green Meadows that Lux knew, but he never felt fully part of it. He liked to run its paths, though. He learned to converse with the cottagers and wave to them as he ran by. Most would tip their hats and smile politely. Some of the adults would offer him a dipper of water, or call to him to pause for a bite to eat. Sometimes he did. He was ravenously hungry in those growing years.

He would thank them and continue on until weariness cramped his muscles and sent him staggering back to his mansion on the edge of the farthest meadow.

There was one running path he liked best. After he had left the mansion and passed through town, the road narrowed slightly and entered the forest. He would go by the lanes to several farms. These cottagers he rarely saw, since the trees stood between the road and their cropland, but sometimes they would be hauling a wagon load to town and pass him on the road. One of these was Mr. Rainwater, who never failed to greet him if he passed.

Toward the end of the Rainwater land, another lane branched on the opposite side of the road. It was overgrown with weeds when Lux first found it. Since then, he had been over it enough times to pound the weeds flat.

The footpath led to an abandoned cottage at Green Meadows' southern border.

The cottage was in good shape, sturdy but ownerless. It stood on a small plot of land beside a massive maple at the edge of the forest. In appearance it was much like the other cottages Lux had seen: a simple structure of wood and stone with a peaked roof and small porch.

He liked the feel of it. Maybe it was just the way it sat alone, part of Green Meadows, yet separate. Maybe it was the feel of the house itself.

The door was not locked. Lux had gone inside numerous times. It felt like his own hideaway, a secret place that only he knew. A peaceful place.

Of course others knew about it too, but no one went there. He had asked Mr. Rainwater about it once on his way back from a run. Lux had seen him coming from town and stopped to ask what he knew of the cottage. He figured it wouldn't hurt anything, and Mr. Rainwater had always been nice. Lux didn't tell him he had been inside the cottage, just that he had seen it and wondered whose it was.

"Ah, that's old Wallace Humphrey's place. Or was, anyway," Mr. Rainwater had said in his booming baritone drawl. "He didn't stick it out long. Tucked tail and moved back east after a year or two."

"So nobody owns it now?" Lux had asked, swiping hair off his sweaty forehead and glancing back toward the footpath.

"Not that I've heard of. I think Wallace let the deed go. He had no care in keepin' the daggone thing."

Mr. Rainwater had leaned down over the wagon side, bracing himself on one beefy arm. "He thought the place was jinxed or somethin', even though he built it himself," he said, green eyes twinkling as if he were sharing a secret. "For my part, I think he was just lonely and discontent, and didn't have enough land to do much of anything with."

Mr. Rainwater had sat up straight and gathered the reins. His horse, a powerfully built bay, shook his mane and snorted. "I was in that house at least a dozen times a'fore he left. It seemed alright to me." He chuckled. "Man should've found himself a wife."

He had waved to Lux and clucked to the horse. Lux, satisfied, asked no one else about the empty cottage. It was his. His hideaway. Not even his mother would think to look for him there.

Not that he did anything extraordinary at the cottage. But the knowledge itself was enough. He had a domain of his own. Away from his mother's expectations, away from the cottagers he would never belong with. It was a refuge in the borderland between the two.

He would walk through its few rooms, climb the attic steps, lie in the patch of sunlight by the window and watch the inevitable spider skitter across the ceiling.

Sometimes he would invite the spider closer. He would reach for it, draw its attention with his Gifts. It would drop a web and descend from the ceiling. When it came to rest on the back of Lux's hand, he would study the creature, noting the way its legs moved as it stepped across his palm.

Lux marveled at the patience of spiders. They were meticulous, careful, always willing to wait. On intricate webs that would rival the greatest artists, spiders watched and waited. Prey must come to them. There was no hurry.

Lux was not so patient. His adolescent blood thrummed with restless questions. But there were not, as yet, answers. So he ran mile after mile and savored the interludes in the empty cottage.

In summer the heat grew stifling. Lux would open the window and summon a breeze, reaching his hands, beckoning with the Gifts in his blood, until wind blew the hair off his forehead and stirred the room with respite.

Winter was a bigger problem. He didn't know how to summon heat with the Gifts and was afraid to light a fire for fear of neighboring farmers coming to investigate.

He would rather keep it secret.

He didn't stay long on those cold days, but let the peace of the place settle into his mind before closing the door firmly behind him and returning to the woods.

Thus it remained for a few years, until Lux tired of it. It was the same routine over and over. By the time he reached the age of seventeen, he was antsy for something else.

Now, at age twenty, Lux's commitment to learning all he could from his mother was beginning to wane. He had not been to the abandoned cottage in years. It meant little to him now, other than being a pleasant memory from younger days.

He had been to the city twice in the last three years. Quick, careful trips to get supplies when Green Meadows came on hard times. His mother sent him with egregious hesitancy and warnings to keep his head down and be careful.

Lux relished those trips, though the warnings scared him more than he liked to admit.

He had been tempted to stay in the city. But that would betray his mother. He loved her, despite his frustrations. It would kill her if he left without warning. Besides, he still had more to learn.

He worked hard to hone his Gifts. His mother taught him diligently, but she also held much back. He knew she did.

He needed to get out. He needed reprieve. He needed something to change.

7

GEORGE

CIRCA 2023

That evening, at a quarter to six, George started down the forest path. He paused when he reached the wider lane, tucked in the edge of his wrinkled button-down, and ran a hand over his hair.

Should've combed it, he thought, then instantly corrected himself. He had nothing to prove to these people. *Just be friendly and get out of there as quickly as possible.*

It had crossed his mind that he might be visiting one of those old-style holdout communities who insist on antiquated ways of life. Or maybe he was accidentally joining a cult. Was "roast and beans" some kind of secret code phrase? Or, worse, were Harlan and Hanna and their parents just the kind of friendly neighbors who expected to treat him like long-lost family? Maybe that was why they had been snooping around his house. Maybe it was a "mi casa es su casa" type thing, and dinner was just a formality to etch it into the unspoken neighborly contract.

George took a deep breath, nudged a stick out of his way, and turned right, the opposite direction from where he had walked yesterday.

The woods held the busy stirrings of nature preparing for evening. Toads belched in the shadows. Birds flew among branches, red and grey flits amidst a mirage of green. Up ahead, a fox darted across the road. The air still felt sticky from a long day of sunlight.

George waved a fly away and traversed the unfamiliar lane. At first he saw only forest. The road proceeded around a curve and up a gentle rise. At the top of this rise, George saw a worn dirt track turn into the trees. He smelled woodsmoke long before he saw it wisping through the branches.

Hoping he was at the right place, George turned up the track and soon came to a cottage much like his own—though this one was larger and far more lively.

Flowers lined the front edge. He recognized gaillardia and a few bunches of lavender. The rest were beyond his knowledge. Liese would have known what they were. She loved flowers and had taught him many classifications, but he had forgotten most of them now.

He heard the lowing of a cow from somewhere beyond the house and the prattle of hens much closer by. George paused and watched the hens waddle about the yard, their quick heads bobbing and pecking for whatever it is that hens take so seriously.

A collie rounded the corner of the house and eyed George warily, her black ears perked at attention.

"Just visiting," George mumbled. He ascended the porch steps and knocked. Harlan answered the door.

"Mr. Morgan," Harlan said, shaking George's hand.

"Just call me George."

"Oh. Er, George." Harlan pulled the door wide. "Come in."

George ducked into the house. He stopped in the entryway to pull off his shoes. They looked odd—a pair of thrift-store Nikes next to old-fashioned clogs and leather boots caked with mud. George eyed the boots, then nudged his shoes into neat formation and stepped into the living room.

This living room looked much like his own, the same windows and stone fireplace. It was larger, though, and more simply furnished. There were a few wooden chairs and a low table near the fireplace, a colorful quilted tapestry hanging on one wall, and an oil lamp burning on the mantle.

Not into using electricity, apparently, George thought. Maybe the holdout community thing was actually true.

Hanna peered around the doorway from what George assumed was the kitchen. She grinned and went back to her work. The way she grinned bothered George.

She looked...he thought for a second. *Conniving? Nah, too negative. Mischievous? Unpredictable?* That was it. Unpredictable. George was wary of things, or people, who were unpredictable.

That had been the one beauty of a job in accounting. It was all numbers and spreadsheets with clean, predictable outcomes.

He tried being unpredictable once. "Part of the healing process," his counselor had said. "Give yourself permission to live a little." Some coworkers had invited him to Friday night drinks one evening, so, on a whim, he agreed. He finished the night with a sour pit in his stomach and a lot of stories he had never cared to know about his colleagues.

After that, he had accepted that spontaneity was a thing of the past. Predictability was much simpler. No more surprises. No more loss.

"Sure glad you came, George," Harlan said, as Hanna disappeared again into the kitchen. Harlan led him to the fireplace. Rich scents of meat and gravy filled the air, far more savory and enticing than the pasty odor of his usual microwave meals.

"Smells good," George said, sitting on the edge of a scuffed wooden chair and stretching his bad leg out to rest.

"Hanna's real good at cookin'." Harlan handed George a cup of water and sat in another chair a few feet away. He cleared his throat, fiddled with his hands, then tipped a finger toward George's leg. "What happened to it?"

George looked down at his rigid knee and the shin that ended in a crooked ankle. "Not sure. Just always been that way."

Harlan nodded but didn't ask further. "Jasper will be by after supper," he said after a moment. "He would a' come sooner, but he had some things to tend to at home."

Another neighbor to meet? That's just great. George said nothing. He sipped the water Harlan gave him. The two men sat opposite each other in silence. George glanced around the room to avoid eye contact. *Why'd you put yourself in this situation?* He chided. *You hate this sort of thing.*

He had to admit his own curiosity, though. What were these people doing out here as if they had missed the turn of the century? No cult vibes so far. Were they hermits? Minimalists? Homesteaders holing up in case of disaster? And why the strange interest in him? He knew nothing of this area.

There was not much to look at that would give excuse for avoiding Harlan. He studied the tapestry hanging on the opposite wall, but that, too, ran out of interest. It was a simple quilt block pattern of green squares and blue stripes. The green had little flowers on it, like something he would expect to see on a grandmother's easy chair. Not that he knew much about grandmothers.

He shifted his gaze back to the fireplace and fidgeted with his water glass. Harlan crossed an ankle over one knee, tapped his fingers on his kneecap, switched legs. Neither spoke.

They both looked relieved when Hanna called for suppertime.

Even at the table, there was, at first, only the sound of forks, knives, and chewing. Harlan kept his eyes fixed on his plate. Hanna, on the other hand, stared fixedly at

George between bites. George tried to ignore the blatant inquisitiveness.

Despite the awkward atmosphere, he was savoring every bite of that meal. Tender meat, fresh peas steamed to perfection, baked beans dripping with sauce, thick hunks of homemade bread slathered with butter.

George couldn't remember when he had eaten anything so good. Aunt Pam had been a decent cook, but more along the lines of grilled hamburgers and adding a dash of this or that to boxed mac n' cheese. Liese, on the other hand, couldn't cook worth a dime, other than spaghetti noodles and jar sauce. They had eaten out a lot.

George scraped the last bit of gravy from his plate and leaned back with a contented sigh.

"You eat much venison?" Harlan asked.

George sat up, his ears buzzing from the sudden question after so much quiet. Venison. George looked at his plate in surprise. "That was venison? As in, deer meat?"

Hanna butted in. "Course. We only eat hunted meat. Deer, mostly, or rabbits. A few wood turkeys now and again."

"You don't raise your own meat?" George thought of the cow and chickens he had noticed outside.

"Cain't," Hanna said with a bit of scorn. "If we did, there'd be none left."

Harlan glared at his sister.

"So, Mr. Morgan," Hanna said, after a glance at her brother. She set her fork down and clasped her hands on the tabletop. "You know much about music?"

"Hanna Stone," Harlan exclaimed, eyes widening.

"Well I ain't gonna just set here pretendin' like all's apple pie and roses," Hanna shot back.

Harlan pushed his chair away from the table. "No need to be haulin' ahead though. We've just met him. Don't be scarin' him off before we even know how he got here." He stood. "Apple pie sounds good, though. Didn't I see one?"

Hanna sniffed. "It's by the stove."

While Harlan found the pie, Hanna watched George, her brow furrowed and lips pursed.

George shot Hanna a thin smile. He cleared his throat and took a sip of water to fill the silence. Finally he met Hanna's eyes.

"I uh, don't know much about music," George said.

Hanna sighed.

"Nothin' wrong with that," Harlan said, returning to the table. He set the pie down and began slicing it with a long knife. "I don't neither. Jasper does. Hasn't played much, though, since..."

George waited while Harlan piled pie onto plates and passed one to him. "Since what?"

"Oh, well, the Lady..." Harlan sat down and shoved a hand through his hair. "Look, George, I'm sorry for all the secrecy, but we've got to be careful, you know?" He edged his chair back. "What all do you know about Green Meadows?"

"Green Meadows?"

"We're on the outskirts here. The main part of town is a mile or so that a'way." Harlan pointed the direction that would lead past George's little forest path and further up the lane.

"Are there meadows here?" George asked around a mouthful of apple filling. "In the forest?"

Hanna leaned toward her brother. "I don't think he knows a thing about 'em, Har. Look at him. Looks as confused as a bat in the daylight."

George choked on his pie.

"I don't mean daft," Hanna said, shooting an apologetic look at George. "I just mean, he's clearly not from around here. That seems plain enough."

"Well, it's better to make for certain," Harlan said. He pulled at his shirt collar and glanced toward the door. "I wish Jasper would come," he sighed. "Look, George. You sure you don't know much about music? It's just... you bein' here and everything."

Harlan took a deep breath, and tried again. "We'd sure appreciate it if you told us a little about yourself. Where you come from. How you came to be in that house."

George's last bite of pie felt thick and sandy. Irritation rose in him like water in a clogged sink. They had come to his house, asked him to dinner, for crying out loud, and now they were acting like he had butted in on some secret society. They should have left well enough alone. He was all for getting along with neighbors, but this was too much.

He set down his napkin. "That's my business. And your business is yours."

Harlan opened his mouth to speak, but George interrupted him.

"Look," he said, pushing his chair back to stand. "I appreciate dinner. I really do. You two are asking a lot of questions, though, that aren't yours to ask." George looked from one face to the other. "I could ask a few of my own. Like where your parents are, for starters."

Harlan looked at the ground. Hanna's face flushed from white to red and back again. Her eyes flashed. George could practically see her jaw muscles tightening like bolt screws on a stubborn hinge. Maybe he should have left his questions out of it.

George cleared his throat. "I don't mean any trouble. And I'm sure you don't either." *I think,* he clarified to himself. He had not entirely ruled out the cult possibility. "I'll stick to my own property, alright?"

"It ain't about you bein' on the road," Hanna snapped.

George looked at her in surprise. She had a lot of fire in her, for a hermit teenager.

"Well then what *is* it about?"

"How you're here at all. No one gets in here." She slumped and looked away. "Or out." She mumbled the last bit. George couldn't be quite sure he had heard it right.

"George, please." Harlan stood tall and looked George in the eye. "I'm sorry about all the questions. I should've..." He took a deep breath and blew it out. "Wait for Jasper to get here. Please. He'll be able to explain better'n we can."

George looked at the young man. He was strong and capable. There was a depth to his expression that George could not quite pinpoint. He looked at Hanna. She was watching him. The fire was gone. She looked tired.

George thought of a fawn he once tried to rescue. He had been twelve years old at the time. The fawn was caught in a fence. George was walking home from the bus stop when he saw her. It had been a rotten day at school—he remembered that. He was fuming about the general cruelty of middle schoolers, especially boys who mimicked his limp, or who taunted him about his parents being dead, as if the accident were his fault.

He had kicked a rock off the side of the road and seen something flinch. When he looked up, there was the little fawn—the front half of her through the wire fence square, and the back half still out toward the road. George had stopped still. She had watched him, her spotted sides heaving fast, scared breaths, but her eyes as dark and infinite as two deep pools. She hadn't moved a muscle as George stepped carefully toward her, edging as quietly as he could so as not to scare her any worse. He couldn't see where she was caught. Maybe she just needed a little lift to get her back legs through?

When he was right up next to her, he reached his hands, inch by inch, toward her tawny flank. All in a second she had leapt forward, cleared the fence wire, and bolted into the tall grass. He stayed for several minutes, scanning the grass swaths for another glimpse of her, but she was gone.

His heart, he remembered, had felt lighter. Buoyed up by the sheer beauty of that fragile creature.

"Alright. I'll wait for Jasper." George heard the words come out of his mouth before he realized he was going to say them. He glanced at the Stone siblings. "But no more nonsense."

They agreed.

That was unexpected.

8

LUX

CIRCA 1873

Lux sat on the front porch of their mansion that night. Hours of practice taming the fire had worn him out. His limbs felt rubbery. He hated being so easily weakened. Strength built at such an irritatingly slow rate.

Lux stretched and leaned back in the wicker chair. It creaked, temporarily startling a nearby cricket into silence.

He often sat here before retiring to bed. The covered porch ran the full length of the house's front face. It was his favorite part of the mansion. Deep enough to keep the rain off, open enough to let the night breeze have its full effect.

Lux watched the trees swaying beyond the porch. They danced in silhouette against the moonlit sky. The cricket rejoined the chirping chorus of its fellows, a symphony of tiny croaks without a conductor. He inhaled deeply and let his tension ease.

He was going to the city. His mother had told him at dinner—a modest fare of beef, gravy, and potatoes, much simpler than their usual variety.

"The drought has progressed too far," she had said. "That farmer, Tom, came today, and told me that the cottagers' crops are dying in the fields. He didn't even have the greens Reuben ordered for us."

She had waved a hand at her plate as if that summed up the problem. "We will need to order a load from the city to keep everyone upright through planting time."

She hummed cheerfully and scooped a bite of potatoes. Lux had paused, watching her. Scared of Gifts with water, excited about getting food for the townspeople. He did not understand.

His mother was the most powerful person he knew. Granted, that was not saying much, if it was only a matter of how many people he knew. The two of them were an elite economic class amongst a smattering of cottagers in the middle of nowhere. Other than some vague memories from boyhood and the couple of careful trips to the city in recent years, he knew little of the rest of the world.

"There are people here that we can help," his mother had said countless times in his growing up years. "That is the whole purpose of the Gifted. To help people. The cottagers need our Gifts as much as anyone in the city. Let's make the most of it. We'll never let them know, of course; that would be breaking the Code. But we will help them."

The Code. That invisible, terrifying set of rules that governed the Gifted. And the Magister, the strict ruler of them all. *Never break the Code. Never anger the Magister.* Lux's mother had ingrained him with those two truths for his entire life.

They had helped the cottagers. But so little, as far as Lux could tell, with anything that required the Gifts. Sure, his mother had kept a wagon from tipping once in awhile, and she cleared the street when heavy snow came. But mostly she helped by using her wealth.

She financed loans to keep the cottagers afloat in hard times, ordered food when a drought got bad; that sort of thing.

Lux did not understand. Why not go to the city where there were more people and countless opportunities? But his mother was terrified of the city. That much she had made clear, though she would not tell him why—other than not wanting any run-ins with the Magister.

"We're safer here," she would say. "We can do plenty of good here."

She never would explain any explicit grounds why she, with all her power, wanted to stay here, in such a small town as Green Meadows.

His mother was powerfully Gifted. She had abilities of which he had not even scratched the surface, and it irked him that she did not teach him more. She talked about the Gifts, the Code, and the Order of the Gifted as a matter of urgent knowledge. She herself seemed hungry for more Gifts, more power.

"I could have done incredible things," she had said more than once, staring listlessly out the window. "If he had just..." Then she would stop, as if remembering Lux was there, and say nothing more.

But concerning her son's abilities, she had no such fervor.

"Quit pining ahead," she would say. "I will give you what you need as you are ready for it. Learn well with what you have. Trust me for the rest."

He tried, but that trust was getting harder and harder to come by.

Lux watched the moon sink behind the trees. The conversation about his upcoming trip to the city had been brief.

"You will need to send an order to the wholesale," his mother had continued from across the table. "Use the same place as last time. It seemed safe."

She sipped water from a crystal glass. "Do you think you can have it settled by end of next week? Travel out there the week after?"

Lux had agreed, glad to have a reason to leave, even if only for a few days. His home in Green Meadows felt tame, now. Too tame. He wanted to find his place in the wider world. He wanted to contribute to the many, not just the few.

His resolve to return here after his errand was weakening.

But he still had more to learn. It irked him. He had little choice in the matter, though; he could not learn without her.

Lux sat silent on the porch as the trees rocked their nighttime lullabies, and the stars hung like bits of diamonds in the inky sky.

What did his mother know that he did not? He wanted to find out.

He just didn't know how.

9

INTERLUDE

LETTER #2

Time is relative to its context. One week is long for the child waiting on a birthday. Fifty years is a blink of an eye to the aged woman at her husband's funeral.

By 1840, the Magister found that time's relativity was more poignant for him. It was, in fact, mostly irrelevant, except for the way it affected those around him.

He was unaffected by time.

It was because of the Pearls, of course. Their endless mysteries both terrified and soothed him. The time factor became apparent after a decade of learning. Ten years of letting the Pearls' nectar seep into his blood while he shook with fear.

He did it rarely, always carefully. He was too scared to do otherwise. The Pearls, he reasoned, could kill him. They could fill his human frame to bursting and shatter his veins with light.

They had the opposite effect instead.

He saw people around him aging, but he remained the same. His hair was still thick and brown, with not a speck of grey, though nearly all the men he knew had begun a salt and pepper look by the time they reached their early thirties.

The skin of his face was smooth, apart from a few lines of early adulthood. When was the last time he had been sick? Five years ago, he remembered—and even then it had been a mild cold, while those around him contracted vicious coughs and fevers.

The Pearls...so painfully beautiful. So mesmerizing. So dangerous. They gifted him now with the first hints of immortality.

He had learned much else from them already. Controlling the movement of objects was only the beginning. He could uproot full-grown trees if he wanted. The effort barely fatigued him.

It was much harder to manipulate the life of something. He had started with seeds, willing them to sprout and watching the seeds tremble and split. After months of work, he was able to coax green tendrils to break through their husks and reach slender tips toward his fingers.

He owned a vineyard now. He had built it from the ground up and done quite well. His house was spacious and comfortable—elegant, refined to his tastes.

Though numerous universities had reached out about higher education programs and possible teaching contracts, he had decided to go on his own instead. He wanted space, time, and money. The vineyard gave him options.

The vineyard workers never came to the house. He liked it that way. The housekeeper came every afternoon to tidy up and cook dinner, but she always left by six o' clock.

His workers were diligent and quick to heed his demands. The grapes grew in luscious abundance, and the wine received high praise from his buyers. He had practiced using his new abilities for more minute changes in crops and fruit trees, first in his own vineyards and then in larger farms. Farmers on the outskirts of the city never knew why they had seen such strange patterns of sudden blight in their wheat fields and peach trees, followed by a seeming reversal, though nothing had changed in sun, rain, or soil.

In fact, for years now they had enjoyed fields and orchards virtually free of disease. Their crops grew even in drought. Moisture seeped into the roots while all the ground around them cracked under dry heat. They never saw the man in their fields late at night, willing water from underground reservoirs to fill the thirsty roots.

Some attributed the phenomenon to a late thaw the previous spring. Others shook their heads in wonder and whispered prayers of thanks.

He, the holder of the Pearls, observed, and learned, and practiced.

He learned the ways of animals too. They were more difficult than plants, of course, but not complicated once he found them out. He simply reasoned that if the Pearls gave him power over green things, perhaps they would apply to other living things.

He was right.

Insects came first. Something small and more easily manipulated. The Magister gathered ants from the garden and let them loose in an empty bathtub. They swarmed the copper floor, chaotic in a mad rush of interrupted pursuits.

The Magister studied them. He reached toward one ant in particular, steadied his hands, focused the Gifts coursing through his veins. He could feel the power surging toward the ant. It was like light, invisible to the eye, but with its own warmth and strength.

Nothing happened.

Something was not right. Perhaps he had to work with things as they were, not try to manipulate them outside of their nature. He tried again, this time including the ants as a group. Maybe they did not act as individuals.

The Magister braced his hands, focused. The ants halted. Thirty black dots on the bathtub floor. Gently, carefully, he bid them to move, easing his hands in the air to encompass the little army.

The ants marched toward each other. Paused. Lined up in straight, even rows of ten.

On cue of the Magister, they filed up the inside of the tub, over the rim, and down to the floor. The Magister led them through the house and back to the garden. Once there, he released the tension in his hands and let the power cease. The ants scattered their various ways, merging with the rest of their company working tirelessly in the dirt.

He watched them for a moment before returning to the house. Living things. Not just plants. What else would be possible?

Animals proved more complicated than insects, but with time and practice, he was able to understand and hold simple communication with them. The effects were subtle at first, and varied depending on the animal. Animals had personalities. Animals had brains and decisions, even if they were instinctual.

Birds, for instance, varied as much by classification as a turtle might compare to a lion. The chickadees were friendly little things with bright personalities and simple ways. He spent weeks learning to comprehend their chatter and direct his Giftings to communicate with them.

The speaking was not audible. Not on his end, anyway. A chickadee might flit to a branch, cheep a little, and peck at a pinecone. The Magister, if he stood very still and lifted a hand toward the bird, could focus his power on the little creature and speak to it with his mind. He might ask it to come nearer, to tell him whether it was frightened or what it had seen that morning. The chickadee would generally comply without much hesitation.

An eagle, on the other hand, was a regal bird with high opinion of its own position in nature and little regard for the affairs of men. When the Magister sought to speak with one, it declined with mild disdain.

So it went with mammals and fish, amphibians and reptiles. Each species had its unique mind and would respond in different ways. The Magister took care to learn as much as he could. He must work with the animal, not against it. They were not his puppets...though he could influence some with tremendous effect.

He turned then, of course, to people. The Magister learned to read much in the eyes of a person. People were not to be tampered with. Not like an animal. People had souls and minds, hearts that resonated with wildly wonderful and difficult experiences and feelings, all while pumping blood through warm, frail bodies.

For they did seem frail, now that he really looked.

His gaze was sharper and more cunning than it had been before the Pearls. He watched city dwellers rushing about their business, farmers toiling over their fields, children shrieking in play.

Only the children looked truly happy, truly whole. The rest seemed more like half-living shells, so tired and worried, so frantic over little mishaps and changes, so quick to succumb to sickness and death.

He found he could, at times, relieve sickness. It took years of practice. Some of his trials ended in death, but some revived. He did better with external troubles. He could more easily isolate and draw out an infection in a wound than he could a virus in the blood.

With enough practice, though, he believed he would be able to manipulate even what was in the blood. He practiced on animals first, then in the emergency ward of the hospital, sneaking in at shift changes and posing as a nurse.

He could also cause terrible pain. He found that, too, by accident. It shook his nerves so badly that he left off his work for weeks.

Pain was cruel.

Pain was a weapon.

Pain could also be a tool.

He would not use it, he promised himself, unless in dire circumstances. Unless its purpose was for a more ultimate good. He breathed easily again and went back to his work.

The world around him seemed more and more at his fingertips. He chose to look at it as opportunity, not power. He was honing a set of Gifts that could shape the course of the world for the better.

Objects, plants, animals, people—they were always breaking, always on the brink of disaster. He could help keep it together. It seemed he alone, of all people, could see clearly. It was thrilling. And lonely.

Unless, he realized, he could bring someone along. He could teach someone else to work with him, infuse someone with the Pearls, just a little, and teach some of the Gifts.

One person came to mind immediately. It was an obvious choice.

He had one friend. One real friend, anyway.

There were the old university acquaintances and the business men who talked about money and bought his wine. His parents were long dead, and he had no siblings.

He did have Cyrus, though. He had met Cyrus in his university days, a student a few years younger than himself. The two had connected from the start. He had taken Cyrus under his wing, taught him the ins and outs of the ancient campus, brought him into his social circle, and, later, introduced him to influential business leaders.

Cyrus was intelligent and active, moved easily around people, and was not tempted by their petty games.

He never was quite sure what deeper element he had seen in Cyrus that made him care for him as a brother. It just happened. Cyrus was the Jonathan to his David, he liked to think, though "soul-knitting" seemed a bit over-descriptive.

Cyrus was like a brother, though. A smart, cunning younger brother.

He would tell Cyrus about the Pearls. He would be careful, of course, but he knew already that his long-time friend would want to take part.

He could trust Cyrus. Cyrus would handle power well. He, the holder of the Pearls, would give the Pearl nectar in small doses. He would oversee Cyrus' acquisition of power. He would give it slowly, teach him how to use it.

Together, they would do great things.

I have found something that you must see.

That was all the note said. It was enough. Cyrus was used to his simple, direct messages. With other people, he used more words to keep up appearances—or maybe because more words were necessary with people who did not know him well. But Cyrus would not need any more convincing.

Even so, when his friend arrived the next day, ambling up the walkway with long, relaxed strides, he took his time telling him about the Pearls.

He wanted to be careful…so careful…to do it right. Too much power too quickly was dangerous for anyone. Of all people, he did not want Cyrus to get hurt.

He told him first about finding the stones, about the strange way they seemed to seep into his blood, about the terror that accompanied each dose, and about his accidental discovery that he had gained extraordinary abilities.

Cyrus demanded a demonstration and stared, dumbfounded, as he slung a half-full wine glass across the room and brought it back unspilled, with a few simple movements of his hand.

More demonstrations followed. They talked through possibilities, the endless possibilities, of such power. The risks, the uses, the fun, all the ins and outs of a Gift like this.

Then he told Cyrus about the seeds and the crops, the truth of the farmers' fields, and the reason his own vineyard thrived so well.

His friend was flabbergasted. Again the demonstrations—simple ones, with sprouting seeds. The others would have to be shown over weeks and months. Again the conversations and mounting tension of excitement and somber reality.

By the time he explained what he was learning to do with animals and people, Cyrus had no more words. He told Cyrus how his aging ceased.

Then he showed him the Pearls.

Silence prevailed. Only the rain swashed gently outside the curtained windows, and the mahogany clock ticked on the mantle.

When Cyrus could speak again, they talked long into the night.

Amidst the words, and wonder, and questions, a plan began to form. A good plan. A great plan.

Cyrus learned quickly, though not as quickly as he himself. He administered the Pearls in sparing, rare doses. As much as he loved his friend, he knew, like an anchor in his gut, that he must always stay a few steps ahead. He must never let Cyrus' abilities reach his own.

The very possibility seemed preposterous. He was a decade ahead of Cyrus already, and he had far more of the stones' power running through his blood.

But still, he held to the anchor. He must always be the one in highest power. He must stay in control. It was the only way to be sure of safety for himself, for Cyrus, and for all they would affect.

They sometimes discussed where the Pearls came from. He called them, in more formal terms, the Arbor Pearls, hearkening to the roots of the ancient tree where they had lain for unknown ages.

But where were they before the cave? Before the tree? Had the great Power who made all things hidden them on that mountain until the opportune time? Were they wrought from stars beyond all reckoning of human knowledge? Did they emerge from the very life core of the earth?

He did not care to consider very deeply on such things, but Cyrus was one to ponder layer under layer.

He cared only that he had found them. They were given to him. He would keep them and use them.

As Cyrus grew in the Gifts of the Pearls, their talk turned to more practical possibilities. They could do more, achieve more, affect more, if there were more of them—more people with the Pearls' power. Not with the same capabilities as themselves, of course. That would be too dangerous.

But what about simple things? What if there were a group of Gifted people dedicated to benefitting society at large? People who could shift things in subtle ways, always in secret.

It would never do to have the general public making a rush for power. They would choose carefully, and have strict rules and governance. These would be privileged individuals, like-minded types who would use the Gifts well, keep them secret, and always stay loyal to him.

Cyrus would be his mouthpiece, his right-hand man.

He would be the overseer. The originator. The bestower of knowledge beyond their wildest dreams. He would be the Magister.

Yes, he could stay elite and mostly unknown. They would make sure he was feared. They could not risk anyone trying to break the rules.

They began work on the rules—the Code of the Gifted, as they came to call it. When it was finished, they searched out their first members.

The Magister sold his vineyard and bought a mansion in the city. Cyrus found it, an emblem of past wealth for some forgotten family. The house had been empty for years. They turned it into a place suited for their needs.

The Magister would live there in an extravagant apartment hidden behind secret doors, a space utterly unknown to all but Cyrus and the housekeeper.

Cyrus had advertised for a housekeeper and found an eccentric old woman named Gertie. She wanted the job, and swore allegiance to the Code, though they gave her none of the Pearls' power.

The main part of the house they fashioned into an opulent gathering place for receiving and training new members. Cyrus would live nearby, but in a smaller, separate house he had purchased with his own funds.

For all the lesser members knew, Cyrus was the shoulders, and the Magister was the head, an omniscient presence in the mansion, seeing all that went on without being seen himself.

They did not know how often he walked about as any normal passerby in the city. They didn't realize how much he slipped through secret doorways and watched their doings in the mansion, or how much he did his own work.

Five years after the writing of the Code and the mansion's completion, there were fifteen members of the Gifted.

They had found them in universities and various trades—each one a person who stood out for one reason or another, and whom, after various testings, the Magister and Cyrus believed to be both capable, loyal, and committed to keeping a secret of great importance.

Only after the testing—of which the individual knew nothing—did Cyrus approach him or her with the offer of joining the Gifted.

Cyrus always approached that conversation with utmost care. Smooth speech was a talent of his, and he had not yet failed to gain the enthusiastic desire and gravest promise of loyalty and silence from each person.

Only one member had later broken the Code. Braxton Smallguard, a promising young man, got it into his mind that the Magister should not be in charge. He demanded a rewriting of the Code and started trying to convince other members to join him.

He was reported, of course, and punished accordingly. None of the Gifted had ever seen him again. The Magister knew that a rogue member with Gifts could not be tolerated.

When a new member swore loyalty to the Magister and the Code, he was allowed one awed look at a Pearl while Cyrus held it to a small cut in his palm.

That was all. One good look; one dose. But no one forgot the beauty, however brief the glimpse.

Then the training began. Cyrus started them on small things: moving a pebble across the floor without touching it, then gathering many pebbles into a pile. As the months and years progressed, they worked on more difficult tasks. They learned to recognize the inherent energy of all objects and manipulate them according to need. Shifting wagons out of ruts, coaxing heat from what looked like dead coals, drawing water into the roots of thirsty plants.

Some select members were given a second blood dose of the Pearls and trained further. These practiced basic animal languages and the art of pulling a simple sickness from a body. But those were rare. Most members were kept to only one dose.

Such was the method of the Magister and his right-hand man. The appropriate members were few and far between, but they preferred it that way.

There should not be too many, too soon. That could be disastrous. They must always be careful.

It was in year six that they first saw her.

10

GEORGE

CIRCA 2023

No one spoke for awhile. Harlan pulled out a knife and whittled a stick of wood he had taken from his pocket. Hanna cleared the dishes. George sat and mused over this unexpected predicament he was in.

Do I know much about music? he repeated to himself, rubbing a knuckle along his bad hip.

Aunt Pam had taught him about music. Uncle Barry liked music too, but it was another level with Aunt Pam. They almost always had the radio on, both at home and in the car. Uncle Barry loved classic rock. Aunt Pam liked just about anything.

When George was thirteen, Aunt Pam had paused the radio dial on a station playing opera, and George had asked to change it.

"You listen good, George-o. This song is life-giving to people somewhere." She had leaned her plump, parlor-tanned arms across the counter and looked him right in the eye. Her voice was deep and raspy, damaged by years of cigarettes. "Music is part of being human. It's the human experience. There are all different types of people in the world, all different cultures."

She had tapped a *Reader's Digest* lying on the countertop. "Did you know, George-o, that there are places in this world where the people don't have any written language? Can't read or write the words they speak? And some places people know a dozen languages, and other places the folks think cows are more important than the humans. There are people that spend their lives studying books, and people who just look for enough food to survive each day. But all of them..."

Aunt Pam lifted her chin, still looking at George. "All of them have music. It's a universal language. Tells you where people come from."

She had grinned and tossed a dish towel at him. "These particular people come from the Italian opera. Enjoy it for what it is."

Then she had turned up the volume until even Uncle Barry called for mercy from the garage. But George had listened.

He still paused at random stations on the radio sometimes, just to appreciate them.

The fire sputtered, bringing George back to the present. Harlan was putting a fresh log on the embers. Hanna clattered dishes in the kitchen.

George sighed and leaned back to stretch. Near the fireplace was a large metal basin half full of logs. He noticed a tin bucket of kindling within reach of his chair and picked up a piece. It wasn't paper, but it would do. He tossed it toward the log basin. *One.*

Harlan looked at the logs. He glanced at George. George rubbed his shoulder and pretended not to notice. When Harlan turned back to the fire, George picked up another wood chip. He tossed it. *Two for two.*

Harlan looked up again. George studied the tapestry on the wall.

"Everythin' alright?" Harlan asked.

George glanced at him. "Sure. Sure. No problem."

He drummed his fingers on the chair arms and lazily skimmed the room. Harlan turned back to the fire. Another chip. This was fun. Like outwitting the enemy in a game of sharks and minnows. He tossed it. *Three.*

Harlan whirled toward him, his eyes a maze of perplexity, and his mouth open as if to speak.

But just then Hanna walked in with a steaming mug in each hand. "Tea?"

"Yes, please," George said, feeling quite cheerful.

Harlan cleared his throat and took the other mug.

George settled back into his chair. He was beginning to like the Stone siblings, despite himself. He could not explain his intrigue with them. But he was intrigued.

Perhaps it was just the uniqueness of their circumstances. Once he had started writing, he paid attention to unique things. Odd things. Out-of-the-way things.

He rarely met people who fit those descriptions, though, at least to his definition. Most people, in his mind, were quite normal. Until now.

The Stone siblings were different. Strange, and a bit uncomfortable, but in a way that piqued his curiosity. Perhaps they would make good characters for a novel. Where, he wondered, were their parents? He wished he hadn't put his foot in his mouth with that one. And who was this Jasper fellow?

Hanna joined them in the living room with another mug. George studied his own. It was a simple, brown ceramic with a navy blue crisscross pattern painted into the gloss. He hesitated to take a sip of the actual brew. It smelled like wood chips and applesauce. George examined it, trying to be inconspicuous. He had just tried a taste and decided that the floating objects were in fact bits of wood and shriveled apple when a knock sounded at the door.

Harlan jumped up and glanced at George. "That's him."

George stood as Harlan strode to the door and pulled it open.

Jasper stooped through the doorway. He was a man of hulking size—at least six and a half feet tall, thickly muscled, and wider than two of George put together. He had curly hair, dark enough to be almost black, and a bushy mustache above a grim mouth. He stared at George with piercing green eyes and held out a beefy hand.

"Jasper Rainwater," his voice boomed.

George's hand felt small in Jasper's meaty grip, but he squeezed as firmly as he could and looked Jasper in the eye.

"George Morgan," he answered, a little louder than he meant to.

Jasper was dressed in the same homespun look as his hosts. He looked at George for a long moment, then settled into a chair that seemed too fragile for him and accepted a cup of tea from Hanna.

"So you're a newcomer, eh?" Jasper asked, watching George over the rim of his cup. He spoke in a relaxed drawl, though his eyes gleamed with sharp intensity. He did not look angry, though, or mean. *Just...intimidating,* George decided. That was the word for it.

"Of sorts, yes," George answered, trying to keep his tone level. "I mean, new to this particular area. But I grew up in Hillsboro, just a few miles up the highway." He took another sip from his mug and wished his voice sounded less meek next to Jasper's rumbling tone.

"Highway?"

George nodded.

"And how'd you come by the house you live in now? Someone give it to you?"

"My uncle. He owned it, but he died recently."

"What's your uncle's name?"

"Uh, Barry Morgan," George said, feeling more and more uncomfortable.

Jasper stared at him for a minute without saying anything. He set his tea mug on a three-legged side table and leaned back in the chair. It creaked in protest.

"We haven't seen hide nor hair of a newcomer here in a long time," Jasper said.

"Not for leastways a—" Hanna began.

Jasper shot her a look. Hanna gave an awkward cough and closed her mouth.

"A long time," he repeated.

George looked from one person to the other. Clearly there was something they did not want to explain.

"No newcomers at all," Jasper went on, leaning forward. He rested an elbow on one massive knee and stared at George with such intensity that George half expected lasers to shoot out and burn him to bits.

"Not seen a soul near that house since...well, since it's been empty," Jasper continued. "Not seen a soul in Green Meadows at all apart from the couple hundred folks that live here." He cleared his throat and sat back. "So you'll understand that it strikes us a mite strange to suddenly find someone livin' in that house—someone with strange clothes and a big machine in his barn who says he's from Hillsboro, a place we also haven't seen in a mighty lot o' years."

George did *not* understand, but he wasn't sure what was most confusing: their bewilderment concerning him, or the odd details they included. *Big machine?* he thought. *Do they mean my car?* He remembered the pony wagon and Harlan pointing out the station wagon from George's front porch.

George cleared his throat. "Do none of you ever leave the forest? Or, um, Green Meadows?"

Hanna snorted. George fought back a surge of annoyance.

"Used to," Jasper said. He ran a hand through his dark mop of hair.

George was getting fed up with the riddle manner of their talking. He wished he was back in his own cottage, alone and unencumbered. *Get to the point!* he wanted to snap.

But he did not. He drank the gritty tea. He cleared his throat. "Why not now?"

Jasper looked up. "Why not now, what?" The intensity had faded. He looked weary, like a tree so weatherbeaten that it can't quite hoist its branches up.

"Why do you not leave now? Leave Green Meadows?"

Jasper released a belly-deep sigh. He opened his mouth, then closed it again. Finally, he met George's eyes.

"Do you know the Lady?"

"The *whom?*" George remembered Harlan mentioning the same title earlier. His patience waned. "No. No, I don't know the Lady. I don't know the Lady, or Green Meadows, or any of the rest of it." He looked at Harlan and could not hide a tinge of exasperation. "I thought you said the point here was to fill me in."

Harlan's eyes widened. "It...it is," he sputtered. "Us too, I hope. It just...I don't know if...well, leastways..." He glanced at Jasper.

"Oh, for goodness sake," Hanna blurted from her seat near the fireplace. "He doesn't know nothin', that's plain to see. Just get out with it, will ya'?"

"It's stuck."

All fell silent at Jasper's statement.

"I'm sorry, what?" George asked.

"All of it is stuck."

George squinted. "All of *what* is stuck?"

"All of life. All of everything."

George stared at Jasper. He felt like a little boy listening to bits of conversation behind a closed door and trying to make sense of it.

"What do you mean *stuck?*"

"I mean I haven't aged a day in the last hundred and fifty years. Neither has my wife Lillian, nor Harlan and Hanna here, nor any livin' soul in Green Meadows."

George set his tea mug, slowly and carefully, on the side table. He tried to remember if this was somehow a dream. He had woken up this morning, correct? Yes, he had. He had followed his same routine as usual. He had walked the forest path to arrive here after a day of work in his cottage.

George looked at the three people facing him from their various chairs about the room. All stared at him with solemn expressions.

"A hundred and fifty years?" George asked, hearing the incredulous tone of his own question.

Jasper nodded. "Might not look it, but I assure you we feel it in here." He thumped his chest. "A hundred and fifty years of time repeatin' itself like hands on a damn clock." He glanced at Hanna. "Sorry," he said quickly.

Hanna shrugged and crossed her arms, watching George.

"Not repeatin', I suppose," Harlan added. "Just...not movin' forward."

Jasper stood and paced the small living room. "Seasons come, seasons go, planting, and harvest, and work. But all the people…"

Jasper stopped and gazed out the window where the light sank toward dusk. It was a long moment before he turned back toward the small group of listeners, and when he did, it was with a heaviness in his eyes that George could almost feel settle on his own shoulders.

"Stuck," Jasper finished.

No one spoke. George scrutinized the faces before him. Not a hint of jest or humor. George remembered driving through the eastern plains with Uncle Barry when he was fourteen. They had passed a feed lot packed with cows. The stink of manure came through the car's ventilation system. George had noticed the way those cows stood in their pens, meandering helplessly through the crowded dirt. *They look sad,* George had thought at the time, as if they understood the proverbial noose around their necks, the long-suffering they had been forced to accept.

The way Jasper and the Stone teenagers looked at George now…it reminded him of those cows.

George leaned back in his chair. He felt the polished wood slide against the fabric of his shirt. He didn't like the feeling; it was too slippery. George rubbed the back of his neck and leaned forward again.

"So time is only stuck for the people here? Not for anything else?"

"Us and what we own. All the livin', breathin' things," Jasper said. "People and animals. My cow keeps on, my chickens keep on."

"Ellie out there's been here with us the whole time," Harlan said, gesturing to the collie lying in a patch of fading sunlight in the front yard.

"And the material things we own, they seem not to wear out," Jasper continued. "But the trees keep growin'. The crops grow and harvest, and we plant again in the spring. The wild animals live and breed and die as usual. But us and our stock...nothin' changes. Some of us tried leavin', but..." He shrugged. "It just led us right back to town. Some folks tried other, more...permanent ways of leavin'." He glanced at Hanna. "Didn't work either. For all we knew, everything outside stopped too. We haven't seen or heard from anyone outside our own town in all these years. But then you showed up, and..." Jasper trailed off.

George considered this for a moment. He remembered Hanna's comment about only eating hunted meat. He wondered again if he was dreaming, but all his senses told him otherwise.

"Stuck," George said, staring at the frayed cuff of his jeans and the jaunty angle of his bad foot. "Huh."

He looked up at Jasper. "How did it get this way? How'd it get stuck, I mean."

Jasper blew his breath out as he sat back in the rickety chair. "No one knows for certain. There are lots of guesses, of course, and what not. Most everyone agrees it had something to do with the Lady, but she won't say a word about it. Stays shut up in her big house and garden and sends Reuben out to do her biddin'."

"Reuben?"

"Her groundskeeper. Bristly fellow."

"Brute, more like," Hanna muttered. "Blind as a post hole, but thinks he owns the lot of us."

"Well, he works for the Lady, and she almost does own the lot of us," Jasper said with an edginess in his voice. He sighed and scratched his powerful shoulder. "So Reuben acts as her lackey and runs the town. Tries to, anyway. Best to stay out of his way."

He cleared his throat. "All that rubbish ain't the point though," he said, eying George. "The point is that we've noticed changes these past days. Slight ones, I might add, but changes sure as daylight, and they seem to go along with your comin' to Green Meadows."

George straightened. "I have nothing to do with this."

"I'm not sayin' you caused it. I'm just sayin' you're here and livin' in that house," Jasper said. "Though it's been empty for a hundred and fifty years, ever since Lux disappeared."

"Lux?"

"There's a differ in the air," Jasper went on. "A freshness. Like the weight of time has lifted just a fraction of an inch. We knew somethin' had changed, we just didn't know what. But here you are."

Jasper lifted both hands. He shrugged at George. "Look," he continued, letting his hands drop. "We don't know how you came to be in Green Meadows, or what it all means, but it's the first time somethin's changed here in a long time, and I'm rarin' like hell to figure out what it is." He glanced at Hanna. "Sorry," he said again, then turned back to George. Jasper leaned forward and looked him in the eye.

"You know anything about music?"

"I, uh..." George floundered to get his thoughts straight. These questions seemed so random to his usually organized mind. Stuck in time, a lady with a jerk gardener, and now music? It reminded him of trying to make small talk at those stupid work parties he'd had to attend.

"I took piano lessons for a few years as a kid," George managed to explain. "But that's about it."

Jasper stood abruptly. "I have to show you somethin'." He strode to the front door.

George watched, bewildered.

"Come on, George." Jasper pulled the door open. "Time's a wastin'." He gave a sardonic chuckle and marched down the porch steps.

11

LUX

CIRCA 1873

Lux gathered his bag and disembarked the train. Other passengers milled across the platform through steam and a general haze in the air. It paired well with the clatter and noise of the city. Lux had always liked the city. Green Meadows was such a tiny civilization in a vast world. He did not understand his mother's fascination with it.

Lux hailed a carriage. "Barker's Hotel, please."

The driver nodded and clucked to the horses. Lux watched the buildings and people pass by his window. Men in business suits, women in dresses and fancy hats. Others were in less sophisticated wear—the ones hauling carts, sweeping the streets, or filling baskets with meat and produce to bring home to hungry mouths or an employer's kitchen.

Lux watched it all with quiet contemplation.

He wanted to do something for the world. Something of significance. His mother seemed content to be bank and overseer for a couple hundred cottagers in the forest. Lux was not. Here in this one city were thousands of people, most of them working themselves half to death in their vain efforts to survive.

Surely, with all his abilities, there would be a way for him to help the thousands, maybe the millions. He would be patient and bide his time. He must.

The carriage stopped. Lux climbed out and handed some coins to the driver. He dusted off his jacket as the carriage pulled away, then climbed the steps of Barker's Hotel, an elegant brick building with three stories of white-curtained windows.

"Ah, Mr. Crane!"

The desk attendant hurried around the edge of the polished counter and extended an eager hand toward Lux. He was an older man, and slight compared to Lux's sturdy frame and broad shoulders.

"Good afternoon, Mr. Hill." Lux removed his hat and shook the man's hand. "You received word of my coming, I presume?"

Mr. Hill bobbed his bald head with the enthusiasm of a woodpecker. "Of course, of course. Your room is prepared, as always. Spick and span, if I do say so myself, like a Christmas pudding. I have your key here waiting. Visiting on business, are you?"

As he talked, Mr. Hill resumed his place behind the counter and shuffled papers and a pair of spectacles away from a set of small drawers built into the desktop. He retrieved a key from the bottommost drawer and passed it to Lux.

"Business, yes." Lux took the key and nodded his thanks. "Shall I go straight up then?"

"Yes, yes, it's all cleaned and ready, tidy as a whistle. Enjoy your stay, Mr. Crane."

"As always. Thank you, Mr. Hill."

Lux climbed the spiral stairs to the top level and opened the door to room 15 at the end of the hallway. He locked the door behind him, tossed his bag onto a nearby armchair, and sighed with relief. It felt good to finish twelve hours on a train and find himself once again in comfortable quarters.

He looked at the large, fresh bed and the clean fireplace, pleasant with its white stones and empty grate. A glossy table stood across the room with a bowl of fruit in its center, and past it were the tallest windows in the hotel, curtains thrown open to let in the sunlight.

Lux always stayed in this room when he came to the city. It was just right. Not fancy enough to feel overdone or ostentatiously wealthy, but affluent compared to the more meager lodgings. He picked an apple from the bowl and took a bite as he stepped to the window. Lux looked out over the bustling streets.

So many people. So much possibility.

Fear crept into his thoughts, familiar as the shirt on his back. He swallowed and turned away from the window.

Lux dreamed that night, as he often did. Past events replaying themselves as vividly as if he were living them over again. He was a boy, this time. Four years old. It was dark, the dark of midnight when one has awoken very suddenly, heart pounding and mind scrambling to gather scattered bits of what is real.

Four-year-old Lux sat up. He had not yet learned to stay perfectly still, to control his breathing and force the scattered bits into immediate submission. He pulled his knees into a tight little mountain and listened. The silence rang in his ears. The dark pressed on his pupils. Lux stretched his eyes until they burned. Slowly the dark softened to familiar shapes. There was the edge of his bed, the small table, the window curtain with the ribbon coming loose at the corner. There was the door, and through it, a light. A dim light, reaching from somewhere that must be far beyond the hall.

Lux blinked once. Twice. From somewhere with the light, a sound trickled to him. The last of his mind fog cleared. His ears sharpened.

Someone was talking...but not his mother.

Lux climbed out of bed and padded to the door. The floor was cold. He had forgotten his slippers, but he didn't go back for them.

He stepped into the hallway, already knowing it was empty. The danger was not here. It was somewhere ahead. Somewhere toward the parlor. And it was danger; he could feel the warning creeping up his spine, prickling behind his ears.

Lux picked his way through the hall, past the sitting room with its clawfoot sofas that used to terrify him, and into the entryway. He slipped into his hiding place, the one he always used when he needed to spy on guests. It was an alcove in the wall, too small for any adult, but perfect for a four-year-old boy. His mother kept a fern there in a huge ceramic planter, and Lux had just enough space to squeeze behind it and settle into the crevice at its back. From there he could peek through the fern leaves directly into the parlor on the other side of the entryway.

There was a light on in the parlor. There was also a man. Lux could not see his face, only his shiny black shoes and the bottoms of his trouser legs. He must be sitting in the velvet chair, the purple one that Auntie always liked to use. She loved purple.

Lux shifted behind the fern and tried to see more of the man. He could not view past the trousered knees. This must be the man who was talking, though the legs remained still. They didn't bounce or act at all scared.

"And what do you think will happen then, Isabella?"

The voice was smooth. Too smooth. It sounded familiar, but little Lux didn't know why. He only knew he did not like it.

"You think the Magister will just ignore what you're doing?"

One of the trousered legs stretched forward a few inches. Lux saw a grey sock now exposed above the shoe.

The man's voice spoke again. "You know he doesn't take well to threats, perceived or otherwise."

His mother stepped into view from the opposite side of the parlor. Lux caught his breath. She paced past the lit doorway and back again, her skirts swishing as she turned. Lux wanted to run to her, to squeeze her tightly and hide his face against her familiar smell. But he did not. The prickling behind his ears kept him still, kept him watching and listening.

This time his mother spoke. "The Magister knows perfectly well that I am loyal to him." She passed the doorway again. "There is no threat, Cyrus. You know that."

"Ah, but does *he* know that? You've always had his attention. It remains to be seen which way the domino will fall." The grey sock disappeared as the leg shifted straight. "I can't protect you forever, Isabella."

"I do not need your protection."

Lux heard venom in his mother's voice. Cyrus must have heard it too. There was silence for a moment. The trousered legs did not move.

"You may yet." Cyrus' voice was as smooth as ever, though a bit harder, Lux thought. Silence again.

"I respect the Code." His mother did not pass the door this time. "I have no intention of breaking it. I only want to build my skills and to be as useful as possible. That is what the Magister wants." Her voice trembled the smallest bit. "I need him to trust me. The more skilled I can be, the more useful I can be."

Cyrus stood. Lux caught a fleeting glimpse of a tall figure with a suit jacket over his arm and dark hair slicked back from a pale forehead. The figure stepped away from the door and was lost to view.

"I believe you. But you'd better keep sure that the Magister believes you, too."

"I'll be careful."

Silence. Lux moved to leave his alcove, but Cyrus spoke again.

"What of the boy?"

Lux froze.

"What of him?" His mother's voice was calm, but Lux recognized the same wariness she used when she sometimes caught him eavesdropping.

"When will you register him?"

Silence. Then, "When he has learned enough. He's still young."

"Don't wait too long."

"I won't."

The arm of the suit jacket flicked into view. A pale hand pushed through the sleeve. Cyrus must be getting ready to leave.

Lux slipped out of the alcove and dashed silently back to his room.

Grown Lux, twenty-year-old Lux, Lux who knew so much more than that small boy did all those years ago and yet knew there were still things he did not understand, that Lux woke in his room in Barker's Hotel. It took him longer than usual to steady his breathing.

12

CYRUS

CIRCA 1851

Cyrus and the Magister saw her at the same time. They were coming back from the outskirts of the city when a woman crossed the riverwalk bridge.

Cyrus sensed his friend's sudden alertness. He, too, was struck by the woman's beauty. She moved with graceful purpose. Her head was high. Her eyes bright. Her hair a heap of striking auburn. Her figure tall and fashionable.

She paused at the top of the bridge and waited for another woman to catch up. A sister, apparently—smaller, sandy haired, with a more delicate build; similar features, though not of the same captivating quality.

The Magister had eyes only for the first woman. He watched her step off the bridge. She laughed at something the sister said. The sound rolled through the air like sturdy wind chimes tuned to utter delight.

The Magister's breath caught. He turned to Cyrus, grinned, and moved toward the women now perambulating further down the walkway.

Cyrus followed. He did not try to stop his friend. He had seen him interested in other women, but never very seriously. This, Cyrus felt immediately, was different.

It didn't take long to form an acquaintance. Cyrus knew the Magister also would not wait long to invite her into the Gifted. He had to admit, there was something very intelligent about them both—the auburn woman, Isabella Crane, and her older sister Ada.

Isabella was the only person, besides Cyrus, to start learning the Gifts directly from the Magister. Cyrus was there too. He did much of Ada's training, but the Magister insisted on teaching Isabella.

Cyrus was not surprised, but he did worry. He was concerned that his friend was letting affection for Isabella cloud his greater judgment. He brought it up to him once, but the Magister laughed.

"You miss the forest for the trees," the Magister said. "She will be one of our greatest assets. Wait and see."

Cyrus waited. He watched. Their work with the Gifted went on.

Sometimes his friend was jubilant, sometimes dark and brooding. Isabella came to the mansion daily. Ada came less often. When Ada was there, Cyrus often noticed her watching Isabella. He, in turn, watched Ada.

Isabella was headstrong, beautiful, talented. She was hungry for more. Ada was quiet and perceptive. She had a cheerful, quirky way about her and a studious twinkle to her personality.

Ada learned the Gifts well, too, but not as quickly as her sister. The Magister mostly ignored Ada. It was not out of spite, though Cyrus suspected that the respect his friend did show to Ada was largely for the sake of pleasing her sister. Ada, bright though she was, slipped easily to the background.

But not to Cyrus. He watched her, taught her, conversed with her, and felt himself more and more captivated.

Deep in his heart, embers, long dark, lit and burned.

He kept it hidden. Any knowledge of his feelings would do no good. Not right now. Cyrus' loyalty was to his friend, who had brought him alongside and given him great power.

The Magister needed him. The members of the Gifted were growing. Some were learning quite fast. There were rules to keep and training to manage, the city to study and Gifts to use. Cyrus was well occupied.

He would not risk endangering all that he and the Magister had built. Not for a woman. Not even for Ada. He could stand firm.

So he let nothing of his feelings be known. But he watched, and cared, and hoped—only to himself—that someday, somehow, he could win the heart of Ada Crane.

To anyone else, though, Isabella was the standout. Some of the Gifted took to half-jokingly calling her "Lady Crane," as if she were a noblewoman among the lesser members. Cyrus could not deny that she excelled more than any student they had yet had. He liked her. And he pitied her. She was nervous, though she covered it well. He could see her fear, buried deep beneath the beauty.

She was gaining power quickly. Too quickly, Cyrus thought. He had suspicions. He kept them to himself.

13

GEORGE

CIRCA 2023

George followed Jasper down the forest lane, past his own little path, and further on for a quarter mile or so. George gritted his teeth against the ache in his leg, but he was not about to ask Jasper to slow down. Actually, he appreciated that Jasper didn't offer.

When they reached a wagon track that branched away from the lane, they turned and arrived at another cottage. It looked to be about the same size as George's house, but with a tidy array of horses, chickens, and cow, much like the Stones' place. The scent of hay and manure mixed with the evening pine. It was an oddly comforting smell.

In the fading light, George could make out acres of fields beyond the barn in various stages of growth and harvest. He wondered if the meadow was natural or if they'd had to clear the trees for planting.

"Jasper," George said as he hurried to keep up with the larger man's strides. He dodged a pile of horse droppings.

"Yep?"

"Where are their parents? Harlan's and Hanna's?"

Jasper slowed. He stopped and turned as George caught up. Jasper studied George's expression for a moment before answering.

"They were out of town when time stopped workin'."

"But..." George's brow furrowed. He tried to make sense of the gravity in Jasper's tone.

"No one can get in or out. It's stuck. Those kids haven't seen 'em since the day they left." Jasper turned and walked on. By the time George could move again, Jasper was turning off the lane and motioning for him to hurry.

He led the way up the porch steps and into the cottage's entryway.

"Wait here," Jasper said in a hushed voice. "Lillian may be sleepin'." He disappeared into the front room. George heard a door open softly, then Jasper murmur something, and a woman's voice respond in kind.

A moment later, Jasper reappeared by the entry. "Come on in," he said, only slightly louder. "Lillian's resting in the bedroom, but we can talk in here."

He led him into the kitchen and lit a lamp on the table, adjusting the wick until it cast a pleasant light across the table's surface.

The table was beautifully made. It looked like redwood, or something similar. Deep rose-colored tones gave richness to the grain, all enhanced with a glossy finish.

Someone had worked intricate designs of forest life around the border. George could make out a stag standing on a hill, three eagles flying in a sweeping circle, a stand of pine trees with a fox hiding in their shade. He wanted to see more, but the lamplight only reached so far.

Did Jasper make this? George traced a finger over the stag's antlers. He supposed a hundred and fifty years would give a lot of time for perfecting an art form.

"Look a'here, George," Jasper said, pulling a set of papers from under his arm and laying them carefully in the lamp's glow. "Can you make any of this out?"

George stepped closer and peered at the pages. They were light brown parchment paper and a bit wrinkled, but the markings on them were clear. He looked up in surprise.

"Sheet music," he said.

"Yes, yes, but do you know how to read them? How to make out the notes? I learned some instrument work, but never the written stuff," Jasper said, his eyes glimmering with a hopeful urgency.

"A song?" George asked, his eyebrows raised. "This is what you wanted to show me?" He stared at Jasper. "Why? What does a song have to do with anything?"

"Well, we don't know just yet. But we know it's important. None of us knows how to read the notes though, so we can't learn it enough to find out."

"But...it's just a piece of music."

"Can you make out the notes?" Jasper's face was insistent. Pleading.

George turned back to the music sheets. This seemed ridiculous. *These people are claiming that I'm the first person they've seen in more than a century, and they want me to teach them a song?* He studied the topmost page.

"Every Good Boy Does Fine," he murmured, moving his finger along the staff lines. "F-A-C-E. This would be a D, F sharp, then G..."

He lapsed into silence, tracing his hand over some notes, the time signature, and the clef signs.

"It's written awfully small and packed together, compared to what I remember learning," George said finally, straightening up from the table. "I'd have to refresh on some of these symbols, but I think I could figure it out."

Relief flooded Jasper's face. He blew such a large breath out, it rustled the music pages and sent one fluttering to the floor.

Jasper gathered the music sheets and thrust them toward George. "Can you learn them?" His voice was low and earnest. "Bring 'em back and show us?" He stared hard at George, his eyes all fire and hope.

"I…uh…yes, I can try," George stammered. "I don't have a piano at home, but I'll...I'll see what I can do."

Jasper clapped him on the back so hard, George stumbled forward.

"I knew it," Jasper said, triumphant. "I knew it. Something's changin'."

George sat for a long time that night in his attic. He did not open his laptop, or even a notebook. He did not turn on the lamp. He only sat and stared out the solitary window, watching the moon make its silent course across the sky.

A hundred and fifty years.

Was it possible? Things did not always have to make sense to be true.

But how?

How is a useful question in its own right. *How* helps a person understand the world around him and the place he has in it. But there was no basis of understanding for this circumstance. George sighed and clasped his hands behind his head. It all felt like a hallucination now that he was back in his own home. But there were the music pages sitting on his desk, and the image of Jasper's face—distrusting at first, but then so hopeful, so insistent—burned in his memory.

How had he gotten caught up in this mess? And why had he agreed to help? He knew the answer to that one. He felt something for these people. Just sympathy, perhaps, or curiosity. But George knew, as he watched the moon disappear over the window frame, that it was more than that.

There was a realness, a genuine humanness that drew him. He believed their story. And in a way he could not quite figure, he was part of their story. The feeling of it lodged in him like a misshapen pebble, big enough that he could not shake it, but small enough that he couldn't quite get a clear view of it either.

But why, of all things, in a situation like theirs, were they concerned about an old piece of music? He supposed a drowning man would grasp at any straw, no matter how small, but all that excitement for a song? George thought back to Aunt Pam's lesson with the opera station. *Music is a part of being human.*

But why this particular song? Surely they had others.

George stood and massaged his tired eyes. After a hundred and fifty years with no change, he figured he would probably do anything for some new music too.

He took one last look at the moon, now half hidden behind the trees. Liese's voice played again through his mind. *Do you ever think the trees talk to each other?* Oh, his Liese. What would she think of these neighbors?

He paused to look at the photo on his desk. The moonlight reflected off the glass, making Liese's face hard to distinguish. George hobbled down the attic stairs. He leaned heavily on the railing to keep weight off his bad leg. The joints gnawed like a wrench on a rusty pipe. He couldn't help groaning with relief when he climbed in bed.

14

GEORGE

CIRCA 2023

George about had a heart attack when he got in his car the next morning to go to town. Hanna was sitting in the passenger seat, twisting her braid around one hand and poking at knobs and dials with the other.

George slid into the driver seat before he saw her, then startled so hard that he bashed his head on the ceiling. He swore and jumped back through the open door, but his lame leg did not follow fast enough. George crashed sideways onto the dirt floor. He shot up, red-faced and stuttering.

"Wh—what the...?" he demanded, glaring at Hanna through the driver door.

"Sorry, Mr. Morgan."

She looked sheepish, but George was not about to let her off that easy.

"You can't just keep showing up at all hours of the day," he snapped. "Looking in windows, messing with my car. You've got to knock it off, Hanna. This is my home."

She toggled her braid and stared at the floor. "Sorry, Mr. Morgan," she repeated, more quietly this time.

George sighed. "It's alright." He smoothed his hair and brushed dirt off his jeans. "What were you looking for? You just curious?"

"I thought..." She pulled her lips tightly together, then looked up at George. "I thought maybe you could try takin' me outa here in your drivin' machine."

George stopped wiping his jeans. "I thought you said there was no way out."

"There ain't. At least, we ain't never found one yet, but..." She took a deep breath. "Well, maybe a machine would be different. We don't got machines like this in Green Meadows. Maybe it would…I dunno. Work, somehow." Her gaze dropped back to the floor. She twisted her braid over her finger. Dust drifted in little clouds where her shoe scuffed the bare dirt outside the car.

"I…" George began. He rubbed his forehead, then lifted both hands and let them drop to his sides. "Hanna, I can't take a fourteen-year-old girl by herself for a ride in my car. It wouldn't be right."

"I ain't fourteen," Hanna snapped. "I'm a hundred and sixty-four."

George's reply stuck in his throat. Finally he relaxed and chuckled. "Not much better." He grinned. "I don't normally drive old ladies around either."

Hanna shot him a look, then grinned also. "Just pretend I'm your granny," she said, patting the driver seat. She giggled, then sobered. "Please, Mr. Morgan. Just once. I have to know if it works."

"Oh, all right." George climbed back into the car. "It's worth a try, at least, huh?"

He started the engine. Hanna's eyes shot wide open. She clutched the sides of her seat.

"Don't worry," George said, glancing at her. "It's louder than a wagon, maybe, but I bet it rides much smoother."

"I wasn't born in the woods to be scared by an owl," Hanna snapped, though her knuckles were white as death on the seat fabric.

George arched an eyebrow but said nothing. He backed slowly out of the barn and cranked the wheel around until the car faced the end of the driveway and the road.

"Where do you think the boundary is?" he asked, turning his attention back to Hanna. "The boundary of the time stop."

She shook her head. "Your property line, I reckon. That's the end of Green Meadows." Hanna still held the seat edges as if they were the only thing keeping her mind from outright exploding. "We've never gotten full out of Green Meadows in any direction."

"Well, let's find out."

George shifted the gear into drive and rolled toward the road. Next to him, Hanna's breaths came in quick, tense gasps.

"Here we go," George said, picking up speed.

He had no idea what to expect. If one of the cottagers was with him, would it keep him from leaving, too? It was a weird idea, and not one he actually wanted to consider.

The station wagon churned forward. George's palms were sweating on the steering wheel. He glanced at Hanna. Her eyes were squeezed shut. It looked like she was holding her breath.

Turning back to the windshield, he saw that they were almost at the end of the driveway. The road came closer, closer.

George took one more quick look at Hanna. She was still there, rigid as a bolt, hands clamped to the edges of the seat.

"Almost there," he said. His voice was steady and soothing, the same voice he might use for an injured puppy.

He looked up as the car passed the edge of the driveway and crunched onto the gravel road. George whooped and swung the wheel to turn the car toward town.

"How about it," he called, jubilant.

He turned to see Hanna's reaction, but she was gone.

George slammed the brake pedal. The station wagon slid to a stop. Twisting in his seat, he craned his neck back toward his cottage. Hanna sat at the end of the driveway, her knees pulled up as if she were still in the seat, her hands clenched on tufts of grass. George gaped for a second, hardly believing his own eyes. She had been in the car, then she was out. Like teleportation in those 80s sci-fi movies.

Hanna stared at open air.

The thought passed through George's mind, like a feather on the wind, that he had never seen a look so immensely sad.

A second thought followed close on its heels. *It's real.* Everything the cottagers had said. The time stop, the being stuck...all of it was real. He thought he had believed them before. But now...

"Hanna," he called, shoving the door open and clambering to get out. She shook her head.

"Hanna," he said again, jogging toward her.

Her look cut him off. It was like solid granite took the place of raw emotion. Her gaze, in an instant, was cool and removed.

"Worth a try," she said, her voice stolid. She stood and brushed off her skirt. "Thanks, Mr. Morgan."

With that, Hanna turned and walked back to the forest. She did not look back once, and George couldn't think of a single thing to say to her retreating form.

15

LUX

CIRCA 1873

Lux woke at dawn the next morning. He was an early riser by habit, a practice ingrained from his boyhood. He liked getting up early. He had hated it as a child, but now he savored the discipline of warming up his mind and muscles while all else was quiet. It was the best time to practice. It was structured. Resilient. It kept him strong.

"We are not like other people," his mother had often reminded him through his younger years. "We know things that very few others do. To learn, you must practice. To practice, you must forgo the shallow comfort of excess sleep."

Lux was glad for it now. He was close. Surely he would finish his training soon. Then he could leave Green Meadows, make his own way.

Thirty minutes of muscle work in the silent hotel room. Pushups, squats, stretches, he kept at it until his muscles burned too fiercely to continue. Then thirty minutes of mind work.

He recited the Code first, whispering the words to the empty room.

"The Code of the Gifted. For the enduring sustainability and safety of all those Gifted by birth, instruction, or any procurement of the Gifts, heretofore referred to as the Gifted, as passed down through the teaching and governance of the Magister, through whose discovery and knowledge the Gifts have been procured for the good of all."

Lux closed his eyes, bringing to mind the words taught him so diligently by his mother, drilled into his mind from the time he was old enough to talk.

"Article 1. The Magister is the highest authority concerning all matters pertaining to the Gifts, the Gifted, and the Code. As the Magister protects the safety and well-being of the Gifted and aims for the highest good of all members of the Gifted as well as the benefit of the world at large through the proper use of the Gifts, so shall the Gifted protect the safety, well-being, and respect of the Magister."

Lux recited the remaining four articles, then turned his mind to the Gifts themselves.

Relax, concentrate. Still all other thoughts. He focused his attention on various objects about the room, stretching his hand toward them, willing them to lift, pivot, veer, in response to the power pulsing through his veins.

Briefly, he considered the fire. The coals burned low. Lux lifted both hands, braced, focused. The heat rose in his blood, coursing through his wrists, hands, the ends of his fingers.

The coals brightened. They glowed orange, red, white, then flames burst from their depths, filling the hearth in seconds with flickering tongues of fire.

Lux sat back, breathing hard. He grinned. This was getting easier.

By the time he left the hotel, the streets once again bustled with activity. Vendors settled carts into place, their wares clattering and bouncing over the rough cobbles. Shop owners drew back curtains and propped doors open. The train whistled the early morning arrival of new passengers.

Lux climbed into the waiting carriage in front of Barker's Hotel. He would accomplish the business piece of his journey first.

The carriage brought him to a large brick building with *Cayman Wholesale* painted in white letters across the top. Lux stepped through the door. It was dim and dusty inside and smelled like dirt and cigars. He heard the grunts and shuffling of a few men loading sacks onto one of the many rows of shelves up ahead.

To Lux's left, a portly, bald gentleman stepped out of an office. He brushed the front of his jacket with hurried strokes and smoothed the ends of a carefully-kept mustache.

"Good morning, sir. How do you do?" The gentleman shook Lux's hand.

"Very well, thank you. Mr. Cayman, I recall?"

"That's right." Mr. Cayman dipped his head in a polite bow. "What can I do for you?"

Lux returned the bow, then removed an envelope from his pocket. "My name is Lux Crane. We exchanged letters about a food order."

"Ah, of course, Mr. Crane!" The gentleman ducked into the office and motioned for Lux to follow. "It's all ready to go," he said, sweeping his ledger book aside and laying a page on his desk for Lux to examine. "We can have it out on the three o' clock train tomorrow if you'd like."

"Let's do the morning train, the eight o' clock," Lux said, picking up the paper. "I'll be riding on that one and can oversee the loading and unloading firsthand."

"Very good, sir." Mr. Cayman pulled a watch from his pocket and glanced at it. "Is all to your specifications?"

Lux finished reading and looked up. "All correct. I'd like to see the goods, please."

"Of course." Mr. Cayman bowed again. "This way."

He led Lux out of the office and through the warehouse. Shelves lined much of the floor space. They were filled with all manner of dry goods and animal feed, all labeled in neat lettering. Where there were not shelves, stacks of crates and barrels stood like miniature mountain ranges. Mr. Cayman and Lux skirted around these, taking the main walkway to the back of the warehouse.

"Drought's pretty bad further west, eh?"

"That it is." Lux ducked to avoid a rope and pulley. "We're glad you can still get crops in over here."

Mr. Cayman grunted in agreement. "There must be quite the water store underground in these parts. Drought doesn't seem to touch us."

Wouldn't that be nice, Lux thought. His mother's words came to mind. "Water is too dangerous because of what it can do, Lux. If it were to reveal us..."

He frowned. There was something to that, but he did not have time to consider. They stopped in front of teetering stacks of crates, sacks, and barrels.

"Here's your lot," Mr. Cayman said, sweeping a hand in front of the load. He pointed out the oats, wheat, beans, sugar, and various other food stores while Lux cross-checked them on the order sheet. When Lux had signed off on the order and shaken Mr. Cayman's hand, he departed.

Lux had the carriage driver drop him off several blocks from the hotel. He tilted his face toward the warmth of the sun and inhaled deeply, then straightened and leaned against a nearby wall, studying the passersby. Most of them looked harried and distracted, as though they walked in a haze of tasks that nipped at their heels like a high-strung dog.

Lux watched them, his gaze somber and mind deep in thought. *Water here. Not enough water in Green Meadows. Crops here, drought there. She won't teach me the ways of water. She's afraid of what it can do. Why?*

After several minutes he stirred and set a steady pace along the sidewalk. The business portion of his trip was done for now. It was time to visit Auntie.

Lux had happened upon Auntie's bookshop in one of his earlier trips to the city.

His mother had not allowed him to go any further than Hillsboro until he was nearly eighteen, but the need for supplies had forced her hand. The current drought was not the first Green Meadows had experienced, though it was certainly the worst. They were short on food a few years ago, too.

She did not trust Reuben to go and would never go herself. She sent Lux with strict instructions and a final whispered warning: "Keep your head down and don't mingle. The Magister has eyes like a hawk."

Small wonder that he had walked around with his throat in his mouth, that first trip.

But he had found Auntie.

Lux liked books. It was a built-in feature of a lonely childhood. His mother read, too, and had read aloud to him when he was growing up. They had a decent library at home, but she had often voiced her wish for more books.

"Something new to read," she would say, pacing restlessly around the library, "would do us good, wouldn't it?"

Lux had been determined, on that first journey, to bring back some books. He had tracked down their supplies, then gone in search of a bookstore. There, he had happened upon his little aunt.

She had recognized him first. He hadn't seen her since he was five or so, but he sensed the familiarity even before she dropped her tea on the floor, burst into tears, and flung her skinny arms around him.

Lux did not tell his mother. Once, when he was seven, she had nearly snapped his head off when he asked when Auntie would come to visit. He would not ruin things now.

He had gone to the bookshop on every trip since. Only a few trips, but such relief. These visits with Auntie were always his favorite part.

Lux pulled open the door to the shop, setting off a tinkling bell tied to the opposite handle. He stepped inside and closed the door behind him. The smell of old books met him with comfortable contentment. His shoulders relaxed.

Lux removed his hat and surveyed the wooden shelves crowded with volumes, a bedraggled plant wilting in the front corner, and the clock ticking on the wall and only...Lux checked his pocket watch...two hours and twenty-three minutes off the correct time.

"I'll be with you in just a moment," a crusty female voice called from somewhere among the shelves.

Lux grinned. "No rush," he hollered back. "It's just me."

He heard the scattered thudding of books falling to the floor, then a clip-clip-clip of hurried footsteps. A tiny, withered-looking woman with a fluff of ash-colored hair on her head, a vibrant purple shawl over her shoulders, and a pair of spectacles on her nose came dashing around the corner of an especially tall shelf. She ran with remarkable speed to Lux and threw her skinny arms around his waist.

"My Luxy boy!" She crowed, her face split in a wide, toothy smile.

Lux loved Auntie's voice. For all its aged raspiness, it still held a hint of the lilt his mother's voice carried. Auntie's was sturdier, though. More matter of fact.

"Hello, Auntie." Lux laughed and returned her embrace, stooping low to reach her.

"Come!" The woman grabbed his hand and led him toward the back of the shop, winding around shelves and crooked stacks of books posted like cairns among the aisles. "What brings you here, Luxy? What's the errand this time?"

"Food supplies. The drought's ruined all the cottagers' crops. Mother's ordering in a load to keep everyone fed and the stock alive."

"Ah, I see." Auntie chuckled and shook her head. "My sister. Such a puzzle."

She pulled Lux through the door of her office and pointed to a cushioned chair checkered with greens and blues.

"So," she said, as Lux sat down. "How are things?" She poured two cups of tea from a pot in the corner, handed one to Lux, and sat down with the other at another chair that she pulled from behind a crooked wooden desk.

"Fine. All is fine. Except the drought, of course, but we'll make it through without much trouble."

"How's your mother?"

Lux shrugged as he took a sip of tea. "Good, I think. It's always hard to tell with her." He propped the cup on his knee. "She does a lot for the cottagers. Seems to satisfy her in some way, though I don't think Mother is ever truly satisfied with anything. I've never totally understood it."

"Understood what, Luxy?"

He shrugged again. "Why Mother, with all her Gifts, went to Green Meadows. And not just went there, but stays there."

Auntie swirled her tea and watched Lux.

"She barely even uses her power at all," Lux continued. "She does more basic kinds of tasks. Banking their money, bringing in food, that kind of thing."

"Well that's part of the point, isn't it? Not to be showy? It'd be against the Code for her to do anything obvious."

"Of course. I don't mean she should break the Code. There are ways enough to be subtle. I just mean...it's like she..." Lux hesitated.

"Like she what?" Auntie's voice sounded like dry leaves rustling over each other. She cocked her wrinkled head and looked at Lux.

"Like she's wasting them. Her powers. Like she's really doing nothing with them, after all her dedication to learn them in the first place."

"She's teaching *you*, isn't she?"

"Yes, slowly." Lux shrugged. "Sometimes I think..." He shifted in his chair. Auntie waited. "I don't mean anything against her, I just...sometimes I think she doesn't intend to finish my training at all." He shrugged again. "And I have things I want to do. With my own life, I mean."

Auntie took a long, slow slurp of tea, her faded brown eyes boring holes into Lux's. "And what, Luxy, do you want to do with your life?"

The way she asked the question made Lux pause. He looked at her, then dropped his gaze and fiddled with his tea cup.

"I'm not sure. Something big. Something meaningful. As soon as my training's done, I want to move to the city. There's more to do here."

Auntie chuckled. "A work doesn't have to be big to be worthwhile, you know."

Lux waved away her remark. "Maybe. But I can hardly see myself spending the next thirty years helping cottagers with their banknotes." He looked at Auntie. "I could come here and live near you, learn from you."

Auntie burst out laughing. Her wrinkled face looked fit to split, and her eyes flashed with merriment. For a second, Lux saw a glimpse of the loveliness that must have existed once in the face of that tiny, shriveled woman. It surprised him.

"Learn from me?" Auntie wiped tears from her cheeks and chuckled.

"Well, why not? You have Gifts too, don't you?"

"Not a smidge." Auntie grinned and swallowed more tea.

"Wait, but..." Lux scrutinized his aunt's expression. "What do you mean, not a smidge? Did you..." He sat back in his chair, surprised. "Did you break the Code?"

"Ha! No. But I never cared a fig for the Code."

"Never—" Lux stood abruptly. His voice dropped to a whisper. "What do you mean you never cared for the Code? Auntie, that's dangerous talk."

"Oh sit down, Luxy." She waved a hand toward his chair. "No one is going to come stomping in here and punish you."

"But—"

"Sit down."

Lux sat. Auntie drank the last gulp of tea and nudged her cup aside.

"Auntie." Lux watched her closely. "How did you lose your Gifts?"

She looked at him and smiled. It was a sad smile, this time.

"That," she said, "is the result of an incident between me and your mother."

Auntie didn't bother waiting for Lux to look any less taken-aback. She took a deep breath and leaned into her rickety chair.

"Your mother was a lot like you, once. Full of energy and ambition. We both were, I suppose, in those days, but hers had a different flare to it. There was a..." Auntie pursed her lips and thought for a second. "There was a fire in her. A hot, blazing fire, like flames in a dry prairie, quick to devour. My fire was the quieter sort. The crackle of flames that warm, but don't bite. Not that I was always right, mind you." Auntie winked at Lux. "I had my fair share of missteps. But I...I understood something that your mother didn't."

She paused, thoughtful.

Lux shifted in his chair. "What did you understand?"

Auntie smiled, but otherwise ignored his question. "Your mother's drive was well-intentioned at first, but at its core was fear. Fear of the Code, fear of the consequences, fear of not doing enough. I tried to tell her otherwise, but...well, I was older, but only by a couple years, and she didn't want me telling her what to do."

"Only by a couple years?" Lux thought of his lovely, graceful mother next to his shriveled little aunt. He had always assumed Auntie was the elder by at least a couple decades.

Auntie chuckled, but again did not bother addressing his remark. She folded her bony hands and went on.

"She thought she knew better; always had. I should have seen it coming. She wouldn't let anything get in her way." Auntie sighed. "We fought. I tried to reason with her, but she...well, she had found a way to take my Gifts, suck them away as her own."

Lux jerked as if ice water had been thrown on his face. *Took? Stole the Gifts from her own sister?* He opened his mouth, but no words came out.

"I don't think she realized what she was doing. I don't know that she saw it as taking my Gifts. She'd been getting more and more irritated at me. She didn't like that I wasn't afraid of the Code. I wasn't like her, and she knew it. She was always afraid. I wasn't."

Auntie paused and crinkled her forehead. "Well, anyway, there was a night we disagreed. She said she was leaving, and she didn't want me to come. I argued with her." Auntie looked at Lux. "You were only a little boy at the time. You and she were all I had left."

Lux felt sick. He stared openmouthed at his hardy little aunt.

"She wouldn't be reasoned with. She got angry, and then she took my Gifts." Auntie shook her head. "She loved me still, as small as it may have been. She didn't realize what her theft would do. When she saw how I withered like a sunbaked raisin, she stopped."

Lux did not move. His gut roiled.

"I remember the way she stared at me. Horrified, terrified, guilty...oh, so guilty. She ran from the room." Auntie looked at Lux. She smiled sadly. "She left me there at the house, took you to the train station, and went away. I've never seen her since."

Auntie pulled her shawl more snugly around her shoulders. "I've always loved her, though." She nodded her head slowly up and down. "Always loved her."

"Even then?" Lux's voice was strained.

"Ah, Luxy." Auntie met his eyes with gentle warmth. "Fear is a beast. A ravenous beast. Your mother has been much devoured." She shook her head. "She's my sister. I've known her since she was only an invisible little thing kicking behind our mother's skin. Bonds like that don't just disappear."

"But she—"

"She did. But she didn't realize, didn't really know, what she was doing."

They were silent for several minutes. Lux stared at nothing, his brows furrowed. Auntie watched him. She tilted her pruny face to one side, then spoke.

"Of what, exactly, are you afraid, Lux Crane?"

Lux's head snapped up. He stared at her. A thousand unnamed answers crowded into his mind. They churned like monsters in a pit waiting for him to fall in. They were always present. Always hungry. And he wasn't sure he even knew what to call them.

"I...I don't know."

Auntie grinned, pushing the wrinkles by her eyes into tight little swoops. "You'd better figure it out, Luxy boy. You'd better figure it out and decide if it's worth all the running."

Running. He felt like he had been running his whole life. Running and hiding. But from what?

Auntie stood and pushed her chair out of the way. "Come," she said, stepping around the side of the desk. "You asked what it is I understood. I think I have found a way, finally, to explain it."

Lux stood. "What is it?"

"Ah, it can't be told with words, Luxy. It's much too beautiful for that. No, not with words. But it can be heard. I will play it for you."

Lux did not let her play it for him. He was too afraid. The song—only a few notes of the song—terrified him with a power he did not even begin to understand. He begged Auntie to stop, and she did.

She watched him, eyes sad but still kind. Auntie's eyes were always kind.

"When you stop running," she said, "come find me, Luxy. I'll play it for you, and then you'll understand."

16

GEORGE

CIRCA 2023

George steered his station wagon into the Hillsboro Public Library parking lot. He had watched Hanna until she disappeared around the edge of his cottage, then returned to his car and headed straight for town. He had work to do. Maybe he couldn't drive the cottagers out of their prison, but he could learn the song. That, at least, was better than nothing. First, though, he had questions to answer.

George parked the car and climbed out. He had always liked libraries. They were one of the only places in town he felt comfortable. Quiet. Studious. No one probing for conversation. He pushed through the revolving door and stopped at the information desk.

It was clean and tidy. There was an I LOVE READING mug full of pens, and next to it, a stack of matching bookmarks. A four-inch plastic cat stood nearby, wagging its solar-powered tail in slow, steady strokes.

"Maps of the area?" George asked the lady behind the desk. "City, county maps, survey maps, anything of the sort. Especially older maps, if you have any."

The lady smiled and pushed her glasses up over smoothly combed, grey hair. She wore a dove-grey sweater, and her glasses were connected at the ends with a string of brightly colored beads.

"Doing a research project?" she asked in a half-whisper.

"Of sorts."

She flinched at his unadjusted volume, but smiled again and led him toward the maze of shelves. They passed the middle grade and children's sections, skirted through rows of graphic novels, past politics and history, and finally to a dusty corner near the back windows of the building.

"You should be able to find what you need here, hon," the lady said, in a complete whisper this time. She gestured to a shelf full of reference books and folded maps. "Holler if you're looking for anything else. Don't actually holler, of course, but don't hesitate to come ask." She chuckled softly and turned to leave.

"Thank you," George said. Another flinch, and the tidy, sweatered figure disappeared into the maze.

George skimmed the shelf for maps of Hillsboro. There was no one else in that aisle, so he pulled a map and spread it on the floor. He lowered himself stiffly to one knee to see it up close.

It was a city map, a fairly recent one. He found Chili's and Walmart, ran his finger along the highway to where County Road 7 branched east, and traced it to where a very thin line turned north. That would be the dirt road by his house. The road stopped at a dead end. George lingered for a second where the road line finished. He had not yet driven to the end.

George studied the map where his property lay. It did not show his cottage, of course, but he could pick out the approximate location. Behind his property, where the Meadows and the forest should have stood, there was nothing.

Just a blank spot in the midst of streets, highways, and civilization.

He rifled through the shelf and found a topographic survey map. Wincing as he maneuvered his bad knee, he spread this map next to the other and once again located his property. There was the road.

And behind it, nothing.

George's finger rested on the patch of empty green. His study of several more maps produced the same result. The space was there, but nothing more. Mapmakers drew roads around it, but none through. Even the oldest maps he found from Hillsboro's early days showed nothing different, except for one, which included a few triangle-shaped trees and the label, Private Property.

George folded the maps along their creases. Checking each label, he slid them back into their places on the shelf.

He stretched the kinks out of his legs and found a vacant computer near the front of the library.

He didn't have internet access at his cottage. Didn't want it. He only used it on the rare occasion anyway, to check email or look up manuscript submission information.

George clicked open the internet browser and typed out the county website. He ran a property search of his address. There was his uncle's name as the owner. Apparently the county had not updated the records yet. There was nothing else listed under Property History.

He clicked out of the county site and searched an online satellite map. This one caught George's eye.

Amidst the forest were patches of treeless green. There were three of them grouped near each other toward the center of the wooded section.

"Meadows," George murmured. "Not just one. That's why they call it that."

The map showed nothing else, though. No buildings, no roads, no civilization of any kind. Just empty land and dense trees.

George closed the internet browser and limped back to the information desk.

"Did you find what you were looking for?" the grey-haired librarian asked.

"Yes, I did." George scratched his head and glanced around the room. "I need a different topic now. Basic piano instruction?"

The woman chuckled. "You have quite the variety of interests at hand." She rose from her chair, letting her glasses hang around her neck from their bead string. "Right this way."

George drove to Hillsboro Community College in search of a usable piano. They had a performing arts hall, and he knew they offered some sort of preliminary music degree. He figured there would be a practice room or two around, hopefully with a piano.

He pulled into the parking lot and climbed out of the car. It was a beautiful day. Cloudy but warm, just a hint of chill in the breeze. He gathered his things and closed the car door, careful to avoid a smashed Burger King wrapper as he stepped away.

Near the performance hall's double doors, George noticed a man watching him. He looked remarkably old… though his eyes were bright. Thick, sagging wrinkles webbed through his face. He was hunched and small, as if his flesh had dried partway to jerky.

George nodded politely. The old man stared hard, pulling his forehead wrinkles into deep crevices.

"I say, what's happened to your leg?"

His voice had a distinct cadence, almost a brogue, though George couldn't quite place it. But it was dry and chalky, the way a sand crab's voice might sound if it could talk. George almost cringed. He caught himself just in time and forced a polite reply.

"Oh, uh..." George said, stopping mid-step. He gestured to his gimp leg. "I don't know, actually. Birth defect. It's always been that way."

"Ho, now. I see."

It wasn't a question. Even if it were, George would not have known how to answer. He tipped his head once more, in lieu of reply, and reached for the door.

"Where're you off to?"

George paused with the door half open. *Is the guy lonely, or what? Doesn't he have someone else to talk to?*

"Uh, just...inside," he said, trying to sound friendly. He did not want to be rude, but the way the man looked at him, the way he talked...

Disturbing, George thought. *That's the word for it.*

The old man watched him. His eyes were beady and intent. A slow smile split the wrinkles on his face and spread like butter. Quite suddenly, he stood and hoisted a walking stick.

"Well now, enjoy yourself," he said. He grinned at George, turned, and walked away much faster than George would have thought possible at his apparent age.

George stepped inside and watched the door until it closed. Goosebumps ran up his arms. He shook the feeling away and went in search of a practice room.

He found several in the basement. One had a tucked-away piano, a battered thing with a crooked lid and a rich, pleasant sound. George closed the practice room door. He sat on the creaky piano bench and spread Jasper's song sheets on the music rack.

He opened an old blue book titled *Music Theory for Beginners* and began to read. He was surprised at how much he remembered. Each page dislodged a memory from his piano lesson days. Sitting on a hard bench next to Aunt Pam, banging out songs from the dog-eared lesson book, counting along as she pointed to the notes, "One, two, and three, four, one, and a two, and a three, and four."

He remembered straining to reach the pedal and could almost hear Aunt Pam's voice saying,

"Learn the notes first, George-o, and then add the feeling. You can't draw the emotion out of a song 'til you give it the respect of learning the mechanics."

He had loved watching Aunt Pam play the piano. When she sat down and clanked the key lid back, George would lay his book or homework down and watch from his usual corner of the old pinstriped couch.

She would wag her bleached-blond head side to side, her plump shoulders bouncing to the rhythm of Scott Joplin and Irving Berlin, face lit with one of her big smiles, eyes on the page half the time and screwed tight shut the other half.

George was not one to dance, but his thin fingers and chewed nails would always pick up the rhythm and tap it out on his knee.

She never played for very long. It happened in spurts. Aunt Pam could be in the middle of mopping the floor or paying bills, invoices spread out over the table and checkbook in front of her.

With no indication why, that George could ever find, she would lay her pen down, push back from the table, and strut to the piano. If George was nearby, she would wink at him. He would grin back, and she'd go to playing like it opened some secret passage of joy in her soul.

After five or ten minutes, she would close the piano lid and mosey out to the yard to light a cigarette, humming whatever song she had just finished.

Then there was Liese, and she...

George closed the music theory book. For several minutes he stared at the battered piano. Then he stood, gathered his things, and left.

Several days passed before George tried again. He had told Jasper to give him one week to work on the song. Time dwindled fast, and he had little to show for it on either the music or his novel.

Thoughts of the cottagers—as George had begun referring to them—and their song sheets distracted him from the unfinished manuscript on his laptop. Simultaneously, his pursuit of progress on his writing kept him from buckling down to figure out the music.

Finally, after an exasperating morning of pacing the attic and forcing a few sentences into his fledgling novel, George flipped the laptop closed and left the house.

He drove to the community college and hurried to the little practice room. It was mercifully empty. George laid the music sheets once again on the piano rack. He scraped the piano bench over the floor, swung his bad leg out at as comfortable an angle as possible, and sat down.

For the next two hours, he poured over the pages with a pencil, muttering note names and periodically consulting the old blue library book. Slowly, a tune emerged. Clunky and unrefined, but a tune nonetheless. George pulled the melody from the battered piano, struggling to unite rhythm and resonance through unpracticed fingers.

Crude as his abilities were, he relished the sound of the hammers hitting their strings, each note filling the little room with a timbre that spoke to the deep places within him, like a breath blowing life to a dwindled flame.

George picked through the tune again and again, until he was sure he would not forget it. When he had finished for the last time and stood, he let his hand linger for a moment on the piano lid. A longing whispered in his soul. Just a whisper, like the feeling one gets when he remembers something long forgotten, something true and good.

Someone knocked on the door. George flinched and looked over. "Yes?"

"Just seeing if you'll be done soon," a student's voice called. "All the other practice rooms are full."

George looked back at the piano. The feeling had vanished. His bad leg ached. "Yeah...yeah I'm done."

He gathered his belongings and opened the door. The student, a scrawny young man with glasses and a trumpet case, looked at George in surprise when he exited.

"Oh, sorry, sir. I hope I didn't interrupt."

"No, no, I was just finishing."

George climbed the stairs out of the basement. As he turned the corner toward the front doors, he heard a sandy cough from somewhere in the foyer. Glancing sideways, he saw the shriveled old man sitting on a bench, watching him. George turned away quickly.

"Pleasant day now, don't you think?" the crab voice called.

George cringed. He gave a halfhearted wave and pushed through the doors.

Outside, clouds still covered the sun. A wind blew in gusts, cool and threatening rain. It rustled leaves tinged with yellow. A delivery truck rumbled by, spewing exhaust. George wrinkled his nose and limped to the parking lot.

He had the tune for the song. Tomorrow, he would find Jasper.

17

LUX

CIRCA 1873

Lux waited for the pounding in his head to lessen. He must open his eyes. But not yet.

He forced calm through his aching body. What had happened? He was supposed to be on the eight o' clock train. The train with the food. He had watched the groceries being loaded. He had checked off every sack and crate. He had gone back to the station, then to the vendor cart with the man selling sausage rolls. He bought one to eat on the train. He turned the corner toward the station, then...

Lux swallowed back nausea. The tall figure, the dark jacket and trousers, slicked, dark hair, the pale face, and the one finger that stretched, pointed...

Then a splitting pain through his head. Darkness.

All of this flashed through Lux's mind in an instant. He listened. There was the rumbling of carriage wheels, the spray of gravel. His body swayed, but only barely. He was cramped. His back was pressed against one surface, his knees pulled up and stuck against another.

Slowly, carefully, Lux opened his eyes.

"I wouldn't move if I were you."

That voice. Too smooth. He recognized it immediately. The back of Lux's ears prickled. He shifted his eyeballs to see the face watching him from above. Grey eyes, bright, amused. High cheek bones. Square jaw. Thin mouth.

Cyrus, the same Cyrus he had seen all those years ago in his mother's parlor, sat on one of the carriage seats. The seat was pale blue velvet, slick and unworn. Cyrus' long legs stretched across the empty space to rest on the opposite bench. He leaned forward just enough to see Lux's face.

Lux himself was lying on the floor, wedged between the two seats. His jacket was gone.

"Where are we going?" Lux's voice was even and controlled. Perhaps, he thought, almost as smooth as Cyrus'. But not too smooth.

Cyrus smiled. "I didn't expect to see you in the city." He leaned back and rested his head on the carriage wall. "I've searched for you for a long time. You and your mother."

Lux's heart rate quickened.

"I suppose you know exactly where she is," Cyrus continued. "Probably out in the middle of nowhere. In some backwoods village, is she?" He tipped his head forward and grinned at Lux. "I'm right, aren't I." Cyrus chuckled. "I should have known."

He leaned back again and crossed his hands behind his head, as if this was nothing more than a relaxing drive.

Lux ticked through possibilities in his mind. His mother had gotten in trouble. She had offended this Cyrus fellow. She had defied the Magister? Broken the Code? *Not likely. Not Isabella Crane.*

"She never did register you," Cyrus said, not turning his head.

She *had* broken the Code. This was new. But she had always emphasized the Code. She had harped on it again and again. The Code was the law of the Gifted. The Code was made for order and safety. The Magister enforced the Code. Never, ever break the Code.

Lux said nothing. The less said, the better. He would find out what was happening soon enough.

"You'd be better off sleeping," Cyrus said. "We'll be there soon."

He tilted forward. "You'll need your strength." He flicked one long finger toward Lux. Again the splitting pain, the darkness.

Lux woke. They were not moving anymore. In fact, he was not in the carriage at all. He shifted his aching head and looked around.

He was slumped against the wall in a dim hallway. A few lamps flickered on the walls. There were doors, all closed. The air was musty, almost sour on his tongue.

From the dark end of the hall, he heard murmuring voices, then footsteps. Cyrus stepped into view and eyed him.

"Get up, Crane." His voice was edgy. "Time to go."

18

LUX

CIRCA 1873

Lux levered his aching body off the floor. Cyrus stood a few paces ahead with both hands jammed in his jacket pockets. He cocked his head toward the end of the hallway and waited.

"Crane, get a move on." Cyrus' eyes were cold and unmoving.

Lux gave the hall one more sweeping glance, and followed.

There were few lamps lit, but Cyrus seemed undisturbed by this. He led Lux past a dark staircase, through hallways lined with shadowy pedestals and sculptures too dim to make out. They stopped in front of a set of double doors. Orange light stretched across the floor from the gap underneath. Cyrus knocked. There was silence for a moment, then the doors peeled open.

Lux squinted in the sudden brightness. He stepped into a large, tall-ceilinged room that smelled of wood wax and old cigars. With the exception of two windows, the only wall ornaments were a few landscape paintings, each magnificent and heavily framed. To Lux's right, a fire crackled in a stone hearth.

To his left, a man sat at a vast, cherrywood desk bathed in lamplight.

"The Crane boy." The man leaned back in his chair. He looked to be in his early thirties, with glossy brown hair and a short beard, but with the gravity in his blue eyes of one much older. He set a half-smoked cigar on an ashtray and hooked his thumbs into the pockets of an exquisite vest.

"Now this *is* a surprise. I wouldn't have guessed from his look. Would you, Cyrus?" The man's voice was deep and rich. He did not smile. He only perused Lux from head to foot with an inquisitive stare.

"Well I hope," the man said, pushing himself up from his chair and walking toward Lux, "that you will be useful to us after all this trouble."

He stopped in front of Lux. Lux forced himself to keep eye contact. He could smell cologne and chewed cigar paper.

"What is this about?" Lux had no trouble keeping his voice even. Years of training had taught him not to betray emotion, regardless of how uneasy he might feel.

The man grinned. Lux could hear saliva stretch over shiny white teeth.

"About?" The man chuckled and stepped back. "You aren't going to play dumb with us, are you, Crane?"

Lux took a slow breath. "I don't know what you want."

The man's laughter burst through the room. He circled back to his desk and leaned against its front with his arms crossed.

"Crane, your family is a real dilemma." He shook his head and split into another grin. It looked forced. "Your mother's more clever than I guessed, I'll give her that."

Lux's pulse quickened.

"Does that bother you?" The man chuckled. "It's a compliment, boy."

Had he noticed something as subtle as a pulse? *Surely not. No one could detect that from across the room.* Lux forced himself back to full calm.

"Not easy to impress the Magister," the man continued. "She's a feisty woman, that Isabella. Practically disappeared into thin air."

Was this the Magister? It couldn't be. His mother told him the Magister was essentially a legend. Few ever saw him.

The man uncrossed one arm and smoothed his cropped, chestnut beard. "She didn't *disappear*, of course. We all know that's not part of the Gifts."

He winked at Lux. "She's evaded us a long time though. Took off to who-knows-where and took you with her, still unregistered. She didn't even tell me about you, if you can believe that. Cyrus here told me."

Lux glanced at Cyrus. Cyrus did not look back.

The man sighed dramatically. "She's done it this time though. I let her little running-away escapade slide for awhile. She'll turn up eventually. Hiding is just hiding. No one stays hidden forever; it's simply not in our nature. Especially not for the Gifted. But this..."

All trace of humor oozed away. "This is full-out treason."

Treason? As far as Lux knew, his mother had not done anything but be a beneficiary to the cottagers for the last dozen years.

"I don't know what you're talking about." Lux kept his eyes fixed on the man's eyes across the room. The Gifted knew the power of eye contact. The ordinary did not, which was part of why they missed so much. Eyes tell all. Or most, at least, if you know how to use them.

The man's eyes flashed with sudden, hot anger.

"You're a fool," he spat, jolting upright and slapping a hand against the desktop. "You think we don't know it was you and your wretched mother? You connive and scheme right under our noses and think we won't see it?"

Lux almost laughed, but checked himself. The very idea of he and his mother scheming anything the least bit interesting was preposterous. But the people in this room were more powerful than himself. He would be a fool, if he pushed them too far.

"My mother has always respected the Magister and the Code," he said. "She'd be the last person to commit treason."

Would she? The conversation with Auntie flashed through Lux's mind. His mother had betrayed her own sister. Whom else might she be willing to destroy?

Still, she had never broken the Code—other than not registering him, apparently. And she had been kind to the cottagers. His mother was a complicated woman, but not given to treason. She feared the Code.

The man's boiling anger cooled as quickly as it had come. He relaxed, crossed his arms, and watched Lux from narrowed eyes.

"A liar and a fool," he said finally. Again that shiny grin. "You'll come around."

With a brisk shift, he returned to his desk chair and sat. "Get him out of here, Cyrus. I'll deal with him later, when he's had a chance to ponder what's at stake."

Cyrus motioned Lux to the hallway.

"Who is he?" Lux asked once the door closed behind them.

Cyrus glanced at Lux. "Let's go."

19

LUX

CIRCA 1873

The room was irritatingly small, but not otherwise uncomfortable, except for the lack of windows. There was a bed, a chair, a lamp. On one wall was a painting, framed in gilded gold, of a stag on a green hill. Nothing else.

A housefly wandered over the painting. It hopped short, buzzing flights from one corner of the frame to the other, nosing its feelers along the oiled landscape in between.

Lux watched the fly for a moment, then reached a hand toward it and focused his Gifts. His blood warmed and tingled.

Light, light, light, light, light, came the minuscule buzzing voice. *Air and light. Feasts of death and dung.*

Not here. Lux sent the thought to the tiny fly. *Out. That way.* He moved his hand gently, and the fly came, following the curve of his movement to the door and the slim gap underneath. The fly buzzed through it and disappeared.

"Now it's my turn," Lux murmured.

He stepped silently to the door. He heard no signs of anyone nearby. Lux studied the lock, focused, and flicked a hand at it, willing the bolt to slide.

Resistance met his efforts like a brick wall. He staggered, surprised.

He tried forcing the door's hinges.

Nothing.

He should have known they would have some way figured out to keep him prisoner. Why did his mother not teach him these things?

He tried again, but to no avail.

From the other side of the door, he heard a snicker. Then the bolt slid, and Cyrus opened the door.

"Melding metals. Pretty effective, isn't it? I wasn't sure what all you could do, but not that one, it seems. Makes our job easier."

Cyrus glanced around the room. He motioned for Lux to give him the chair. Lux didn't move.

Cyrus sighed. He extended one hand toward the chair. It slid over the floor and stopped next to him. Cyrus settled it in front of the door and sat down.

"Let's not make this any more difficult than it needs to be, shall we, Crane?"

"What is *this* supposed to be?" Lux said, allowing irritation to seep into his tone.

Cyrus chuckled. "Well, what it's supposed to be," he said, stretching his long legs out over the floor, "is you explaining where the Arbor Pearls are. But you insist on hesitating."

"The what?"

Cyrus' eyes narrowed. "The Magister won't stay patient forever."

"Was the Magister the kindly gentleman I met earlier?"

"You push your luck, Crane."

"I don't know what I'm pushing, but it isn't luck." Lux's voice hardened. "I've never heard of whatever pearls you said, and I don't know how any of this involves myself or my mother. What do you want from me?"

Cyrus pulled his legs back and leaned forward. He stared hard at Lux. Lux stared back, their eyes locked in silent battle.

Cyrus' eyebrows slowly lifted. He shook his head. "She really didn't tell you, did she."

"Tell me what?"

"Anything." He shook his head again. "Anything of importance." Cyrus shifted in the chair and stretched his legs out once more. He sighed. "You might as well sit down," he said, waving a hand toward the bed.

"I prefer to stand."

Cyrus shrugged. "Have it your way." He looked curiously at Lux for a moment. "You aren't what I expected, you know. From what I saw of you as a kid."

Lux did not answer.

Cyrus watched him, brows knitted, then continued in his usual even, smooth speech. "What did Isabella tell you about the history of the Gifted?"

Lux gritted his teeth. He did not want to have this conversation. Not with Cyrus, of all people. But he did want to hear an explanation. What *had* his mother not told him? Crucial pieces, apparently, unless Cyrus was lying through his pasty cheeks.

He had to admit that Cyrus seemed less grating at present. He wasn't laughing at him. And he hadn't knocked him out with his finger trick in awhile, so that helped.

Lux sighed. "She told me that the Magister was the first of the Gifted. He discovered the Gifts, learned the ways of movement and nature and how to harness them. He understood the potential for benefiting mankind, but he also knew it was a knowledge that couldn't be trusted with just anyone. People would twist it, turn it to evil means.

"The Magister, wanting good from the Gifts, and not evil, began by choosing a select few to share the Gifts with. He instituted rules, the Code, to keep order among the Gifted and their use of power.

"Members of the Code have different levels of Giftedness, depending on their training and natural abilities. Some of the most highly Gifted have learned to prolong their own life. The Magister is, of course, one of these, and will thus remain the leader of the Gifted indefinitely."

Lux eyed Cyrus' dark hair and unwrinkled features, still as unblemished as they had been in Lux's childhood.

"He's not the only one with that ability," Lux said with a note of sarcasm, "though the long-livers are few."

Cyrus' mouth edged a hint of a smile. "Few indeed. Anything else?"

"That's pretty much it. The Gifted have gone on to the next generation, teaching their children and keeping with the Code. Any who choose to deviate are strictly punished."

"As they should be," Cyrus said, straightening suddenly and grinning at Lux. "But your mother, it seems, has not been punished, though she failed to register you as a member of the Gifted, and now has, apparently, committed a crime of severest consequences."

"What is it that you think she's done?" Lux crossed his arms.

Cyrus, to Lux's surprise, sobered. "That's the question, isn't it?" He looked away for a brief second, then turned back to Lux. "But first, to fill in your gaps in the history."

Cyrus stood and paced the small length of wood plank floor in front of the chair.

"The Magister, as you mentioned, discovered the Gifts. This was a quite literal, tangible discovery, contrary to what you may have thought. What the Magister discovered were the Arbor Pearls." Cyrus stopped pacing and looked at Lux. "He found them on a mountain in a thunderstorm. Crawled into a cave for shelter and crawled out with the means to master the very laws of nature."

"With pearls?" Lux's eyebrows rose.

"They aren't pearls, exactly, though they have some appearance of such. There are three of them, each about the size of a walnut, but perfectly round." Cyrus' eyes took on a soft glint. "They are their own. Something other. The shimmering loveliness of a pearl, but with strands of beauty to a depth that is hard to name. Like liquid light in rivers of the smoothest ivory."

"Pearls with gold?"

"No, no. Not gold." Cyrus looked almost offended. "It's more than that. They have color, but not color. Threads tinged with a light I have never seen in any other object on this earth."

He turned to Lux. "The Arbor Pearls are what the Magister used to learn the Gifts. He unlocked some of their secrets. Only bits, mind you; their power is surely beyond what we've yet discovered. He learns from them still, including Gifts not trusted to most."

Like long life, Lux thought.

"The Magister," Cyrus went on, "has kept them under careful protection all these years. Much of the Code is designed to guard the Arbor Pearls."

"And they're missing?"

Cyrus set his jaw. "They're missing."

Lux sat, finally, on the edge of the plump bed. "And you think I have something to do with it?"

"Well, your mother, more specifically, though I admit we haven't quite known what to expect from you. She's hidden you away, of course. Who knows what all she's taught you by now."

Not enough. Lux was surprised by the sting of bitterness that came with that thought.

"Your mother was never one to be entirely trusted, though the Magister couldn't pin her on anything in particular. She was powerful. Quite powerful. She learned quicker than most, figured out things she shouldn't have known. The Magister was wary of her, if anything, but he had a certain...fascination, shall we say, with her abilities and her quick wit."

Cyrus broke into a wry grin. "She outsmarted him; for the time being, anyway. Disappeared before he knew to be properly careful of her. But now..." Cyrus' jaw tightened. He shook his head. "Isabella has bitten off more than she can chew."

"You think she stole the Arbor Pearls?" Lux sounded incredulous, even to himself.

"She's the only reasonable suspect," Cyrus fired back. "No one else in the Code even begins to have the skill to get past the Magister and access the Pearls. She's been gone for fifteen years. Why else would she have hidden away, and what else would she have been planning all this time? Unless she turned you into her secret weapon. But no." Cyrus shook his head again. "No, no, I can see it in your eyes. You really didn't know. Besides, Isabella liked to do things herself."

Again the pang of bitterness. Lux pushed it away.

"But," Cyrus said, his voice suddenly brusque. "You can tell us where she is. That much is certain."

He took a step toward Lux. Lux stood, arms tense.

"Calm down, Crane," Cyrus chuckled. "I'm not going to fight it out of you here and now." He flicked a hand, and the chair slid back to its original spot by the wall.

"The Magister will see to that. He has ways of getting the information he needs, no matter how well-meaning the holder."

Cyrus stepped to the door and opened it. "Sleep well, Crane. You'll need it."

The door closed. The lock clicked and fused. Lux heard the distinct rasp of metal combining. So Cyrus knew the ways of metal. Lux, on the other hand, did not. He could move small pieces, coax a normal lock, but he could not change the metal itself. It was a more advanced knowledge, one his mother had not yet taught him. There would be no escape that way.

Lux stayed where he stood for a long time. Cyrus had given him much to think about. One thing at a time, though. For now, he had to get out of here...wherever here might be.

20

CYRUS

CIRCA 1873

Cyrus stepped away from the door. He waited, aware that Lux would still be listening from the other side. It was strange to see the boy grown up. He had a milder temper than Cyrus had expected, considering his parentage. *What was Isabella thinking, not telling the kid anything?*

He shook his head. Isabella's decisions were not his problem. Well, actually, a lot of them *were* his problem, but not this one in particular. Hopefully.

Cyrus sighed and left the hallway. He took the long way through the mansion to the Magister's quarters. He wanted time to think. This was a strange predicament.

It was only by sheer luck that he had seen Lux by the train station. If that new trainee, Preston, had not taken a wrong turn, they would have missed him. Cyrus had recognized the resemblance to Isabella immediately. He'd had Preston pull the carriage toward the alley where there were not many passersby, climbed out, and waited for Lux to turn the corner.

That look of confused recognition when Lux saw him...well, that confirmed it immediately.

So now, after all these years, Lux Crane was locked in a room in the Magister's mansion.

Life was full of the unexpected.

Of course, Cyrus had expected to find them eventually, though Isabella had held out longer than he thought possible.

He pushed open another door, climbed a narrow staircase, and knocked at the top.

"Come in."

Cyrus entered. The Magister slouched in a pristine velvet chair, staring into the fire. His vest was unbuttoned, his hair disheveled. He had one elbow propped on the arm rest, chin resting on his closed fist.

Cyrus closed the door. He pulled another chair nearby and sat down.

"Well?" The Magister's voice was brusque.

"He's harmless."

"Harmless?" the Magister scoffed. "No one is harmless."

"I mean he's uninformed. He doesn't know a thing about the Pearls. Isabella hardly taught him anything that matters."

The Magister stared at the fire and said nothing. "But he's Gifted," he added finally.

"Yes, he's Gifted, but he can't do much. Some basics, I'm sure. He's clever; that's obvious. Collected, confident, steady. He's clearly been trained, but not to anything advanced."

"That wretched woman," the Magister muttered.

Cyrus eyed him. "There was a time you didn't think so."

"There was a time when I was an idiot," he retorted. He looked sidelong at Cyrus, then returned to the fire.

Cyrus propped one foot on the hearth. The heat seeped through his shoe. He flicked a hand toward the flames, and they crowded to the other side of the grate.

"He'll still be helpful," Cyrus said, leaning back in his chair. "He knows where his mother is, and that will get us to the real information."

"It had better."

The Magister said nothing else for a moment, then he straightened and propped an ankle over one knee. "Someone cut down the Arbor Tree."

Cyrus' head jerked up. "The Arbor Tree? Who?"

"Don't know yet. I saw it two days ago. Went back to the cave to look for any trace of the Pearls, but only found a dead tree. Someone chopped it clean through. The whole thing's lying there broken on the ground. It must have happened weeks ago."

A chill ran through Cyrus' back. "Not Isabella, surely."

The Magister's jaw tightened. "Hard to say, anymore. She was always desperate."

"But loyal. Other than…"

The Magister raised an eyebrow and looked at him. "You were saying?"

Cyrus acquiesced with a nod. "Still. Chopping down the Arbor Tree? Seems like something a villain would do, not a scared woman."

"They can be one and the same, you know." The Magister laughed grimly. "Isabella wasn't always predictable."

Cyrus thought of Ada. His chest clenched.

"If not her," the Magister continued, "who else could it be? Not her son, it appears, from what you've said."

Cyrus shook his head. "I don't think so. Not Lux. He didn't even know about the Arbor Tree an hour ago." *Who else?* He had no idea. This was a new turn.

The Magister strode to the liquor cabinet across the room. "Either way," he said. He popped a cork free and poured whiskey into a glass. "Find out from the kid where they've been hiding."

He took a long swig and grimaced. "Where'd Gertie get this stuff?" He turned the bottle up and read the label.

Cyrus shrugged. "Who knows where Gertie gets anything?" He stood. "I'll find out. About the kid, not the whiskey."

The Magister chuckled. "Fair enough." He held up the bottle. "Want some?"

"Nah. I need my wits about me." Cyrus straightened his jacket and turned to go.

"Cyrus."

He stopped and looked back.

"Find out now." The Magister took another swig and emptied the glass.

Cyrus nodded. As he pulled the door closed, he saw the Magister hurl the empty glass into the fireplace. It splintered into a thousand melting pieces.

21

GEORGE

CIRCA 2023

George crunched over twigs and leaves, aware of his presence disturbing the wild peace of the woods. He was almost to Jasper's place before he realized that he had no idea if the man would actually be there. An uncomfortable prickle started in his stomach. He could have just waited a couple more days and let Jasper come find him instead, avoiding being the one to make the awkward, unannounced visit.

George sighed. As a teenager, he might have changed his mind and turned around. But he was thirty, hardly an excusable age to be a coward over something as normal as a conversation.

Thirty. How had he become what he was? He thought about what it might be like to have a life different from his own. Most men his age had multiple kids by now. They had established jobs, families, marriages maturing into longevity. If they were still married, anyway. If they were divorced, well, that meant one or the other or both had, at some point, stopped paying attention to how good they had it.

George kicked a stick out of his way. Man alive, he had made his share of mistakes with Liese. But divorce had never been an option. They got married young and kept their love like a well-tended fire. Kept their commitment fierce as life itself.

George sidestepped a rock sticking through the dirt. And now he was alone. Had been alone for five years. He had moved on, sure. He'd had to. Time does not stop for tragedy. But did he really want it this way, now? Did he really want to live by himself for the rest of his life? Holed up in his house, trying to keep the neighbors away? Those questions had bugged him since his run-in with the cottagers. He was not sure yet how to answer.

It wasn't that he was miserable. That much was clear. He had grieved, yes, and still did in some ways. But life had moved on, and he had kept people, as much as possible, at a distance.

A quiet, simple life, free from corporate business, scheduled on his own terms—that all appealed to him. Spending his time writing; that was certainly a plus. But if he had a choice, would he choose loneliness? Or was he just afraid of being close to anyone again? Afraid of being vulnerable?

George kicked at a pebble.

No. He wouldn't think about that. There had been enough loss. He was better off alone. George sighed and turned his mind back to the task at hand.

He had reached Jasper's lane. He turned the corner, and the Rainwaters' cottage came into view. George slowed his pace and looked around. The quiet beauty in the morning light was almost breathtaking. Sun filtered in soft rivulets through a misty blanket of fog. Everything was hushed, as if the earth still slept, and George trod the waking hours with the sun.

He couldn't fully enjoy it, not with his mind such a morass. His leg hurt again. He levered it forward and moved on.

There was no sign of anyone in the yard. Not even a dog or a rogue chicken. George hesitated, then climbed the porch steps and knocked on the front door. No one answered. He knocked again.

From behind the cottage, George heard a muffled clatter. He looked around the deserted front yard once more, then hobbled down the porch steps and around the side of the house.

Down a short slope, the trees broke into a wide, open clearing. At the edge of the clearing stood a garden, and in the garden crouched a woman. She had her hands in the dirt and her back toward the cottage where George stood.

A shovel and rake lay in the dirt next to where the woman's long skirts brushed the ground. As George hesitated, she pulled a sweet potato from the ground, brushed the dirt from it with a careful hand, and placed it in a nearby bucket.

Again George felt the urge to retreat. Coming to find someone unannounced was bad enough, but getting stuck talking to the wife instead? George rubbed his forehead. It was starting to ache. *No use stalling,* he lectured himself. *Might as well get it over with.*

He took several steps closer to the garden before saying, "Excuse me, ma'am."

The woman looked up in surprise. "Oh," she said. "I'm sorry." She brushed her hands on her skirts and stood, rather heavily, George noticed, with a hand to the small of her back.

"Is Jasper expecting you?"

"Uh, no," George stammered. "Well, maybe. Not today specifically, I guess, but in general."

He took in the woman's appearance, trying not to stare. She looked young, mid twenties, perhaps. Her eyes were deep brown, kindness mixed with a layer of wan fatigue. She had a cinnamon colored braid hanging over one shoulder and unruly wisps of hair in scattered tendrils around her cheekbones. She was slender, except for the round pregnant belly clearly conspicuous under the drape of her dress.

"You're the new neighbor, aren't you?" She brushed a hand across her forehead and left a smudge of dirt in its wake. "The one in Lux's old place?"

"Uh, yes. Yes, it seems so."

She nodded. "Jasper told me about you. He's in the cellar unloading potatoes. He'll be right back." She smiled and pushed hair away from her face. "I'm Lillian. Jasper's wife, of course."

"George," he said, extending a hand.

Lillian reached to shake it, but saw the layer of dirt on her own palms and fingers. "Maybe not," she said with a gentle laugh, pulling her hand back and wiping it again on her skirts. "Oh, here comes Jasper."

Jasper rounded the opposite corner of the house, pushing a wheelbarrow. He sped up when he saw George.

"Welcome, George," he boomed, dropping the wheelbarrow and giving George a hearty handshake. "I see you've met my Lillian." Jasper put an arm around Lillian's shoulders and squeezed tenderly. She leaned against him, her face all contentment and soft delight.

"I have, thank you." George felt a knot begin to form in the base of his throat. He coughed to clear it.

Jasper let go of Lillian and stepped toward George.

"Did you figure it out? The music?" he asked, lowering his voice to a hush, though there was not another soul in sight.

George nodded. "I've got the main tune. Not any of the chords and such, but the melody part."

Jasper clapped his hands together in a resounding crack, and his face split in a wide grin.

"I knew it," he hollered, then looked around quickly and lowered his voice again. "Can you show it to us? I'll gather Harlan and Hanna and some of the others." Jasper's face brimmed with eagerness.

"Er, yes. Yes, of course."

Jasper smacked George on the back. He let out a whoop and turned to Lillian. "See, Lill? Things are changin'. I can feel it."

Lillian's eyes were wide and bright. There was a light in them that had not been there before. She wrapped her arms around herself and grinned.

Jasper hooked his thumbs through his overall straps. "Come on, George, I'll walk with you as far as the road and then mosey out and round up the rest of 'em. We can meet back here in a couple hours."

George said goodbye to Lillian and headed back toward the forest lane with Jasper.

"Is..." George began, when they'd rounded the corner of the cottage. He hesitated. "Has she been pregnant all this time?"

"Since time stuck?" Jasper sighed. The brightness left his face, and his shoulders sagged. "Sure has."

"I'm sorry," George said after a moment.

"Our child, always there but never seen." Jasper took a deep breath. He ran a hand over his dark hair, then shoved it into his pocket. "That's been the hardest part."

George felt the knot tightening in his throat again. Neither of them spoke anymore until they got to the lane. The men shook hands.

"See you tonight, George. Let's say seven o' clock."

George nodded. "I'll be here."

By the time George arrived back at Jasper and Lillian's cottage that night, a dozen guests had already gathered in the living room. There were six or seven chairs in a semicircle, most filled with people. Other guests stood near the fireplace or sat on a long, wooden bench against the wall. There were several men and women, as well as a few children. The youngest was a girl who looked to be about seven years old.

An oil lamp burned in the middle of a small table. That was the only light other than the fire. The room was warm with so many bodies. A bit stuffy. George tugged at his shirt collar.

Some of the guests talked in low voices, others sat stiffly or just gazed at the fire. They all looked up when George entered. Eyes widened. Mouths fell open.

"Here he is, gents. And ladies," Jasper added to the women among the group. He introduced the new faces, then, "You know the Stones, of course, and Lillian."

Harlan nodded. Hanna tilted her head and grinned, almost a smirk. Lillian smiled. The rest murmured incoherent greetings and stared at George, some with fear, others with thinly-masked puzzlement. George gave an awkward wave.

"Well, George, let's get to it, eh?" said Jasper.

He led George to an empty chair and sat his own bulk into one next to him. While George fidgeted with the music sheets to keep his hands busy, Jasper produced an instrument from somewhere George did not see, and plucked a few strings.

It was a guitar of sorts, though with a shorter, rounder body, and a slightly thinner neck. At the sound of the strings, the company in the room shifted, as if a breeze stirred life among a stand of stagnant grass.

Elsewhere in the room, a tall, gangly man named Tom brought out a violin. Peter, a potbellied fellow with three children and a nervous-looking wife, brought out another guitar, this one much smaller than Jasper's, and a man named Marcus, a silent man with small eyes and a jet-black beard, produced a smooth, wooden box that stood as high as his knees. Hanna, much to George's surprise, pulled a thin, wooden flute from the pocket of her dress and readied her fingers over the tone holes.

George could feel the expectant tension in the room. Not even Jasper smiled now. Every eye stared at George, every gaze a spectrum of fear and hope. He cleared his throat and shuffled the music sheets with clammy fingers.

"Well, um..." George cleared his throat again. "Let's see. I have the note names written out here." He turned the pages to face them. "If I just start at the top, um..."

He glanced up. The group stared blankly at the page of markings. George swiped a hand across his brow.

"Um, well...let's see."

"Can you hum it for us?" Jasper asked.

George looked up. Jasper gave an encouraging nod. "Uh, yeah. Yeah, that should work. I remember how it goes. I...um...well, can you give me a note to start on?"

Jasper plucked a string. George hummed a few measures to himself. "A little lower."

Jasper plucked a deeper tone. George jogged his finger along the notes and hummed again. "That should work." He took a deep breath. "Alright, let's start at the top. I'll hum the tune, and you follow along. I'll go slowly, but let me know if...well, if you need me to back up. We'll do a few measures at a time." He cleared his throat once more. "Here we go."

It was tentative at first. George's voice was a bit shaky, and the others pulled notes from their instruments as if their fingers could not quite communicate the way they intended. Marcus tried to keep a simple drum beat on his wooden box, but gave up and listened until everyone could stay at a consistent pace for more than a few measures at a time.

Slowly but surely, the sound steadied, and a tune emerged. George slapped the beat against his good leg and hummed each section. Jasper, Tom, Hanna, and Peter worked out the notes until they could play them all together. They had figured out the first third of the song pretty well when Jasper said,

"Now that we got the tune, let's go from the top again. Tom, you take melody. Peter, you and Hanna and I will put some variation in there, spice it up a mite. Marcus, you too."

They started again. Peter, Jasper, Hanna, and Marcus fumbled to find a suitable accompaniment. The sound of dissonant tones against Tom's violin melody grated on the ears.

Their faces were sheer concentration. Hanna looked fierce, almost angry. Eyebrows clenched, they persisted with hands, fingers, breath, and bow until all at once, it clicked.

The room swelled with the song. Every face lifted. Every eye widened.

George felt his heartbeat quicken. His chest burned with sudden urgency, a desperate search for...for what? He felt as though another presence surged through him. A joyous one, so alive in its own right that it swept like fire through his soul, burning away the old cobwebs and shadows and leaving a light so bright he could scarcely breathe.

All around him, George saw the same fire in the people gathered. Their eyes gleamed. Mouths opened in wordless wonder.

Lillian straightened in her seat on the couch, her cheeks full of color. Peter and Marcus bowed their heads as they played. Their shoulders, knees, and feet moved in time to the music. Tom and Jasper also dipped and swayed, as if the waves of sound coursed right through their veins. Hanna's face softened and glowed. She tilted her chin toward the ceiling.

They all smiled. Real, genuine, life-filled smiles. Peace not known in many, many years.

Over and over they played that first section, pausing where they had left off learning the tune only long enough to glance at one another for the beat and start back at the beginning.

The onlookers sat, enthralled, some with eyes closed and faces tilted upward, feet tapping and grins blazing. Others watched the musicians, mouths open and tears spilling down their cheeks. No one wiped them away. No one, as far as George could tell, even noticed.

George looked from one person to the next, that strange longing burning through him, his whole being enveloped by the music.

Jasper's front door crashed open.

"ENOUGH!" roared a voice.

The warmth and light of the room vanished. George turned in time to see a man, as burly as Jasper and almost as tall, storm into the room. He had greasy, half-grey hair and a shadowy beard. His shirt sleeves were rolled up past his elbows, and he had both fists clenched tight. He filled the room like thunder.

George saw, more than heard, the effects of the man's presence. His ears had gone fuzzy.

People scattered like ants. The man pointed one fist toward a chair and unclenched his hand. The chair splintered and clattered onto the floor. He was shouting.

Peter's wife grabbed the hands of her children and bolted through the kitchen and out the back door. Peter ran close on her heels, his guitar held tightly in one hand. Marcus dove over a couch, took hold of his wife's arm, and disappeared through a doorway.

Voices yelled. The intruder bellowed and swung his hands. More chairs exploded at their joints and crashed to the floor, though he never touched a single one.

George clambered back and crouched by the wall. He saw Lillian grab Jasper's guitar and run to the bedroom. Jasper slammed the bedroom door closed and stood in front of it, yelling curses at the raging man and brandishing a broken chair leg like a battle axe. Tom, too, grabbed a piece of splintered wood and swung it dangerously, eyes blazing.

George's eyes darted right and left. His brain reeled.

"George..."

His ears cleared. He looked up. Harlan crouched a few feet away, beckoning him. Hanna had disappeared through the open front door. She stood by it, one hand out toward George and Harlan. Harlan ran for the door, and George followed.

The music.

George jerked to a halt and turned back. The music sheets still lay on the table in the middle of the room. George glanced at the man shouting only a few yards beyond. His fists were clenched and swinging, his attention all on Jasper and Tom.

George lunged to the table, grabbed the sheet music, and ran, forcing his maimed leg along as he followed Harlan and Hanna out the front door and into the night.

22

GEORGE

CIRCA 2023

George stopped partway down the forest lane, breathing hard. He folded the music sheets and stuffed them into his shirt.

"What the hell was that?" he demanded.

Hanna and Harlan slowed next to him.

"That," Hanna said, leaning both hands on her knees, "was Reuben."

"The groundskeeper?" George sputtered.

"That's the one." Hanna spat. "Practically the devil hi'self."

"Hanna." Harlan gave her a reproving look.

"Well it's true. Almost."

"He wasn't always like that."

"Well he is now!" Hanna whirled on her brother, eyes flashing. "Lots of things weren't always like they are now, but that doesn't make 'em any better." Her voice rose in pitch as she went on. "And all we've got after bein' stuck for two straight lifetimes is a stiff-as-a-board, crippled bachelor who can barely get two words out edgewise and would be beat all to pieces if Reuben ever got ahold of him for even a second. George Morgan can rot, for all I care. I don't know what everyone's so excited about. Nothin's changed, and nothin's goin' to!"

She yanked the wooden flute out of her pocket and hurled it to the ground.

"Hanna!" Harlan reached for her arm, but she twisted away from him and ran, sobbing, up the lane.

"I— I'm sorry," Harlan said, turning to George. "I don't...she just..." He held his hands out, palms up, then thrust one toward Hanna's retreating figure, as if to complete a thought he could not quite explain.

"It's alright." George bent down and picked up the flute. He dusted it off and handed it to Harlan.

George looked back toward Jasper's house. The lane was empty. "Shouldn't we go help them? Will he hurt anyone?"

"Tom and Jasper will see to him," Harlan said. "They won't let him do any more damage than he's done a'ready. We should move along, though, get out of sight before he comes out."

Harlan turned and walked down the lane, his gaze following his sister, now far ahead.

"Come on, George," Harlan said over his shoulder. "Don't worry about Jasper, he can hold his own. We'll sort it out tomorrow."

George hesitated. He took a few more deep breaths, then followed the Stones away from Jasper's property.

His leg hurt terribly. He didn't run often. Or ever, really, unless there was danger. Ah, irony. So much for a secluded, peaceful cottage.

It's better this way.

The thought surprised him. George slowed for a second, letting it settle in his chest like a seed in newly tilled soil. Better this way. Better to have the cottagers, to be part of their strange story, than to be alone.

"You alright?" Harlan asked, turning to glance at him.

"I'm good. Coming."

George gritted his teeth against the pain and caught up to Harlan. At his own path, he paused.

"Thanks for what you did tonight, George." Harlan said, nodding to him. "And don't worry about Hanna, she'll calm down." Harlan opened his mouth as if he were going to say something else, then closed it, nodded to George once more, and jogged onward.

George watched his retreating form. The forest felt suddenly quiet. Quiet and lonely. He hurried through the forest and into his cottage, locking the door behind him.

Someone knocked the next morning. George set down the coffee pot and headed to the front door. He reached for the handle, then paused. *Considering recent events,* he thought, snatching a quick peek out the window.

It was only Jasper.

"Morning," George said, pulling the door wide enough for him to enter. "Come in. Everything alright?"

"More or less." Jasper removed his hat and stepped inside. He pulled his boots off before walking gingerly into the living room, like a giant in a lily field.

"Coffee?" George asked.

Jasper's eyes widened. "You've got coffee?"

"Well of course, I—" George took one look at Jasper's face and didn't bother explaining any more. He went to the kitchen and poured coffee into a clean mug. When he returned, Jasper was leaning over a table lamp, squinting at the bulb.

"What in the name 'a..."

Jasper stood and darted his gaze to the floor lamp in the corner. It was an old lamp—shiny brass base, pole, and an off-white shade with a dent on one side. George had bought it years ago when he moved into his apartment. He got it for practically nothing at a thrift store and had not bothered replacing it. It still lit the room, after all. Not pretty, but he didn't notice that anymore.

Jasper was staring at the lamp like it was the eighth wonder of the world. "You light your whole house like this?"

George chuckled. "Yes I do. Had to pay an arm and a leg to get the wires run out here." He handed Jasper the coffee. "You've never seen it at all? Electricity?"

"Not out here. I recollect hearin' it talked about from a travelin' peddler once. Some newfangled thing they was workin' on in the big cities, but..." Jasper looked around the room, felt the couch cushions, surveyed the rows of books on the shelf by the wall.

"Well I never," he said, running a finger over the books and shaking his head slowly.

George watched as Jasper paused for a moment at a small, framed picture of him and Liese that sat at the end of a book row. It was a wedding photo, the only one George still had. Jasper studied it. Then he stirred suddenly and stepped away. He looked into his mug, inhaled, and sipped his coffee, grinning like a kid with a bucket of candy.

"I suppose coffee beans don't grow around here, huh?" George said, moving pointedly away from the bookshelf and photo.

"No coffee, no tea leaves. It all ran out a long time ago." Jasper took a long swig and smacked his lips. "A fellow misses the real stuff."

George could have sworn he saw the man's eyes roll back into his head. "I can imagine," he said, chuckling. He pulled a chair nearby and lowered himself into it. "So..."

"Last night." Jasper sighed and sat on the edge of the couch. It groaned under his weight. "I've got to think where to start."

He closed his eyes for a moment, then cleared his throat and began. "Reuben, you recollect, is groundskeeper for the Lady, but also more. The Lady stays in her mansion. Reuben does her biddin', you understand. Enforces her rules."

George nodded and sipped his coffee. "Go on."

"Reuben is the only one she trusts. No one really knows why. Or if they once did, they don't remember no more, but everyone knows that the Lady is in charge, and that means Reuben is in charge."

"Why is the Lady in charge?"

Jasper sighed and scratched his chin. "Cause all our land belongs to her. Most of the animals, too."

George straightened. "What? Why?"

"There was a bad drought. A real bad drought." Jasper drained his coffee. He set the mug aside and leaned back into the couch cushions. "This was all before the time stop, of course. We all owned our parcels fair and square. We had them mortgaged to the bank, paying them off crop by crop." Jasper shrugged. "The Lady is the bank. Was the bank. Still is, I guess."

Sheesh, George thought. *The woman must be extremely wealthy.* "And the drought?" he asked.

"Knocked us all on our backsides." Jasper shook his head. "Just life, sometimes. We had to do somethin'. No one's crops were growin'. We were all in a bad way. The Lady is richer than any of us knows, I imagine. She had food stores shipped in from far off. Made sure we made it through those tough years. But in return..."

"She got your land and stock."

Jasper nodded. "Wasn't much we could do to kick against it. We didn't have a choice." He sat back up and looked at George. "She's not all bad. She was fair in those days. Kind, even. Did what none of the rest of us could do, and made sure we survived. We all got to stay on our land and work the fields again when the rains came back."

George glanced at Jasper's hands. They were powerful. Work-worn and leathery.

"She ordered in seed, too," Jasper went on. "Got all the folks back on their feet. The deal was that each family would sit down with Lux and figure out how much time and how many crops would suffice to pay off their debt. But then…well, something changed. The Lady..."

Jasper pursed his lips in thought, then continued.

"She got strange. Stopped comin' around town as much. When we did see her, she looked brooding and suspicious. Stopped talkin' to most people. Tom brought a vegetable order up to her house once. Saw her through the upstairs windows, pacin' like a coyote. Arms all folded tight, face set like a flint rock. She didn't stop the whole time he was unloadin'. Just back and forth. Back and forth.

"Then folks started seeing stranger things, too. Bunches of clouds all piled up next to her windows, or trees all bent over one day and straight as a ramrod the next.

"Robert Baines swore he saw the Lady lift a felled tree once that had blocked the lane to her house. Tossed it out of her way as if it were no heavier than a chunk of firewood."

George raised an eyebrow. "Right."

"No, I mean it." Jasper held both beefy hands up like he was surrendering to the police. "Saw a couple of 'em myself. Wouldn't have believed it otherwise, maybe, but enough people see somethin', and I guess you just accept it after awhile."

"Piles of clouds, throwing trees," George crossed his arms and slouched against the chair back. "You're pulling my leg, Jasper. That's fairy tale stuff."

"I..." Jasper furrowed his brow in confusion and looked at George's leg. "What?"

"You're joking. The Lady has, what? Magic powers?"

"Yep." Jasper shrugged. "Call it what you will. She's no ordinary woman." He smirked. "C'mon, George. I ain't hornswogglin' you. We're stuck in time, for goodness sake. And you saw Reuben last night."

George remembered Reuben breaking furniture left and right without putting a finger on it. Hanna too, teleporting out of his car when it crossed some invisible curse boundary. *Fair point.* It wasn't far-fetched.

"This just gets weirder and weirder," George said, more to himself than to Jasper.

"It was just oddities we saw at first," Jasper continued. "But then she brought on Reuben. Taught him some things, I imagine, and he's none too nice about it.

"Anyone does something the Lady doesn't like, Reuben makes 'em pay for it. Breaks fences, splinters barns. Once he wrecked a chicken coop over the heads of Tom's hens. That was after time got stuck, so it didn't kill 'em, of course. None of us can die, natural or otherwise, but they were beat up pretty bad. Took 'em months to start layin' again."

Jasper shrugged his massive shoulders. "I guess you could say we're all frightened of her in one way or another. And of Reuben, but Reuben's really just the mouthpiece for the Lady. She makes rules, and he makes sure people keep 'em."

Jasper took a gulp of coffee. "Anyway, she brought Reuben on. Then not long after that, Lux disappeared, and that broke her right to the middle, I reckon."

"Who is Lux?"

"Her son."

George's head snapped up. "Her son? I'm living in the house that belonged to the Lady's son?"

Jasper nodded.

"But...wasn't her son rich, too? Why'd he live in a little cottage at the far edge of the whole place?"

"We aren't sure. There was a big to-do about it though; we know that. Rumors of Lux and the Lady arguin', then the news that Lux had moved out of the mansion and into his own cottage. An old homesteader had lived here before, but he had moved back east, left the place empty."

Jasper chuckled. "No one knew how to treat Lux at first—him livin' like the rest of us. I'm sure he found it awkward, but he tried hard. He was kind, Lux was. And there was something about him in those days...something deeper and livelier. Like he knew a thing or two we didn't, and he was tryin' to show us. He was the one who brought the new song. Said he wanted to teach us to play it."

Jasper's forehead creased. "He never got the chance. There was one night when Lux went back to the mansion. Tom saw him go. He lives close to the Lady's estate. Saw Lux walkin' up to the big house. The next morning, Lux was gone. Dead."

"Dead?" George's eyebrows arched. "How?"

"The Lady said he just died all a' sudden, right there in her house. She was torn up somethin' awful. Tom heard her screamin' all the way from his own property. He ran to see what had 'appened, see if she needed help. Reuben caught him just before he got to the door. Told him Lux had died."

Jasper was quiet for a moment. He stared at the floor. "We looked all over for him, in case there was a mistake, or…somethin' amiss. Never found anything though. And there was no reason to disbelieve the Lady. She was grievin' like any mother would. He was her only child."

George waited. "And then?"

Jasper roused and looked up. "Then, well, the Lady broke. She loved Lux more than anything in the world. She holed up in her house. Mourning, we figured. But it never stopped. Few have seen her since." Jasper pulled in a deep breath and let it out as a sigh. "Somewhere in there, time stopped working."

"That's when it happened?" George sat up straight. He leaned forward. "That's when time stopped?"

"Yep. No one knows the exact day. It happened over the course of a week or so after Lux died. A sort of pallor came over everything. It's hard to know how to explain it. It was like…like the light was still there, but its warmth was gone." Jasper grimaced. "We could feel it in our bones."

He crossed his arms and looked at the leaves rattling outside the window. "We noticed the truth of it in the animals first. Calves and lambs never born, chicks never hatched." He shook his head. "It all just stopped. Took years to really confirm it, but..." He lifted both hands in the air, then let them drop into his lap.

Jasper stared at emptiness for a second, then turned back to George. "You know the rest from there. Except... well, the Lady banned the song. And all songs. She hates 'em."

"Why?"

" 'Cause Lux is the one who brought the new song to begin with. We had our own music, of course, just folk tunes and such, but Lux brought this new one he had down on paper. He'd started showin' a few of the music-inclined folks how the note markings worked. But then he was gone, and the song was lost.

"I think for the Lady they go hand in hand. She couldn't stand any music after that. She gave strict orders, through Reuben, that no one better dare play any instruments, least of all any of the song Lux had started. And, as you saw..." Jasper shrugged. "That still holds."

George thought for a moment. "How did he know we were playing the song last night?"

"You mean how did the Lady know. Like I said, she's powerful. She hears things, sees things, controls things, and sends Reuben to bring down the rod." Jasper shook his head. "No one knows for sure what all she can do. Maybe she heard us playing all the way from that big ol' mansion of hers. Maybe she heard a rumor. Maybe she just felt it in her gizzard and sent Reuben to find out what was goin' on."

Neither of them spoke for a few minutes. George sat with one elbow propped on the armrest of the chair, his chin resting on his hand, and his forehead creased in thought. Jasper picked at a loose thread on his shirt cuff and stared at nothing.

Finally George shifted straighter and asked, "How did you come by the song, then? You said Lux's music was lost."

Jasper grinned. "I found it."

"Where?"

Jasper's mouth opened and closed. He looked at George, then down at the floor. His hands fidgeted with the edge of the couch pillow. "Well," he said, clearing his throat. "To tell you the truth, I found it on your property, just a few weeks before you moved in."

"What? How?" George heard the surprise in his voice.

Jasper coughed. "I was just lookin' around. I've done it before too. Didn't know anyone owned it, of course. It'd been empty for so long." Jasper shifted on the couch. "We all get restless with the years not movin' forward, and just...well, anyway."

George squinted at him. "But where'd you find the music?"

"In the barn. It was in a metal box hidden in the wall." He looked at George, eyes round and seemingly quite embarrassed. "Honest, George, I didn't know anyone owned the place."

George chuckled. "It's alright."

Jasper relaxed and nodded in appreciation. He picked up his empty coffee mug, looked inside, and set it back down.

George took the mug to the kitchen.

"I got the music off the table last night before we left," he said, returning with the full mug in one hand and the pot in the other.

"I saw you grab it. We're all grateful." Jasper's eyes lit up at the steaming mug. He took it and nodded his thanks.

"So everyone's alright?" George asked, lowering himself into his chair. He passed Jasper the coffee pot and kneaded the side of his crooked knee. It still ached from yesterday.

"Of course. Reuben did a lot of threatenin', but that's about it. Well, that and he busted up half my fences on his way out." Jasper's voice hardened. "He can be a real brute, Reuben can, but he knows better than to take on me and Tom together, and in my own house too, with Lillian right there behind the door. He knows I'd beat the tar out of him before I'd let him anywhere near hurtin' Lillian."

George did not doubt it. He sat silent for a moment, then pushed himself up and crossed to the window. Clouds hung low overhead. A few raindrops spattered on the window glass, unsettling bits of dust that had collected over the previous weeks.

"So, let me put this together." George shoved his fists deep in his jeans pockets and stared out the window. "A drought happened. The Lady took everything in payment for food, then she started to go off the rails. She taught Reuben some kind of magic. Lux moved out, he and the Lady weren't getting along, and he died.

"Time got stuck. No more music allowed. A hundred and fifty years goes by, then you find the sheet music in my barn, and then I show up a few weeks later, knowing nothing about what's happened, but able to help teach you the song. Is that correct?"

"Yep," Jasper said. "You can see why there was a lot of excitement when you came."

"And what now?" George asked without turning back around. He wondered at the strange predicament of the cottagers. Bold but fearful. Restless but accepting. Going on through the years and years of sameness, because what else was there to do? They had families. Farms. Undwindled hopes.

Surely, George thought, *surely there's a way out.* A way to break the curse, or whatever it was that had them trapped in the flow of time.

The music, at least, was a change. A way to push back against their circumstances, a way to spring newness and beauty into the bleak cycle of their lives.

And the fire...the longing...George could still feel the memory of it, like warmth seeping from drenched coals. He wanted to hear it again. The song. He wanted to hear it through to the end.

Behind him, Jasper chuckled. "What now, eh? Well..."

George turned from the window. Jasper grinned, a glint in his worn, green eyes, and George could see the same embers lodged there, the same yearning.

"I guess we find a better hiding place."

23

GEORGE

CIRCA 2023

That night, Reuben returned to Jasper's land. He came after moonrise and destroyed the barn. He did the same at Tom's place. George heard the news from Harlan, who stopped by long enough to say that Jasper was as mad as a March hare.

"Hanna and I are helpin' him get the fences back up. He'll have to have a barn, too, before weather gets cold."

George shook his head in disgust. "Can't anyone stop him? Reuben, I mean?"

Harlan shrugged. "They'd have to stop the Lady; she harbors him. And no one's about to take her on. She's no ordinary woman."

"So I've heard."

Harlan rolled and unrolled the rim of his hat. "People have tried, you know. It's just...well, it seems no matter what we do, Reuben and the Lady are as much a part of this thing as any of the rest of us. It ain't changin' 'til it changes at the roots, I expect."

"Until the curse is broken, you mean."

Harlan shrugged. "I expect so. Curse, or whatever it is."

George leaned against the door frame. Harlan stood, pensive, on the front porch, rolling and unrolling his hat brim.

"Do you think there's a way to break it? The curse?" George asked.

Harlan did not answer at first. He let the brim of his hat flop back into place and watched an ant scurry along the porch railing.

"It seems like there's got to be," he said finally. "It happened for a reason. Just because we don't know what it was, doesn't mean there wasn't one." He looked at George. "Maybe if we could find out the reason, find out why it happened, we could undo it somehow. Fix what got broke."

George nodded and shifted his shoulder against the door frame. The tune from Lux's music began playing in his head. He remembered the fervent urgency. The fire. The wonder.

He straightened. "Tell Jasper we can meet in my cellar." He said it quickly. If he waited too long, he knew he might change his mind.

Harlan blinked. "To keep learnin' the song?"

George nodded.

"But..." Harlan cocked his head. "You sure you want to get yourself mixed up in this more than you already are? What if Reuben comes here?"

An image flashed in George's mind of Bent Davis, one of the middle school bullies who had made George's seventh grade year a misery. He remembered telling Uncle Barry about Bent one evening in the garage while his uncle pulled parts out of a broken-down Mustang.

"Well, George-o," Uncle Barry had said, wiping grease on a rag and looking at George with one of his crooked grins. "If you can't outrun him, you're gonna have to outsmart him."

George blinked the memory away and turned to Harlan. "I'll figure something out."

That night, a stream of cottagers arrived in groups of two or three, knocking timidly at the door and hurrying to the cellar with not much more than a quick hello and wide-eyed glances at George's lights and furnishings.

George felt strange seeing guests in his home, especially so many at once. They included the same group from Jasper's place, even Lillian, who whispered to George on her way through that Jasper had urged her to stay home, but she wouldn't miss this for the world. She said it with a flush in her cheeks, and George guessed that she too still felt the lingering warmth of the song.

Besides the fourteen from before, there were two new faces.

"Benson and Greer," Jasper explained. "Bachelor brothers. They work for Tom."

George accepted all this with a nod. His hands fumbled a little as he closed and locked the front door and looked around for any missed details.

He, George Morgan, had fourteen people in his cellar, invited there of his own accord. He shook his head. What had he become in a few short weeks? He had barely touched his novel. His notebooks collected dust upstairs, and when he did open his laptop, he only managed to clunk out a few sentences. The neglected plot felt dull and forced, devoid of whatever interest he once thought it held.

So much for a quiet place to work, he thought to himself, pulling the front curtain across its window. Somehow, this was better. He headed for the cellar, wondering what a good host would do. Should he offer tea? Crackers? He had some crackers in the cabinet.

Don't be an idiot, George thought. They had come here for safety and music, not refreshments.

He clumped awkwardly down the cellar steps and pulled the trap door shut behind him before surveying the group collected below. It was a tight fit. Tom, Jasper, Marcus, and Peter sat near the center with a lantern and their instruments. Hanna sat against the back wall next to Harlan, her face pale and stern, her arms crossed over her chest. Her flute was nowhere in sight. George sent her a quick, tight smile. She looked away.

The rest crowded around as best as they could, some sitting along the dirt walls, others standing in corners. George stood by the steps and shuffled the music sheets into the correct order. He looked up. Every eye watched him, tense and expectant. They looked resolute. Hungry. Afraid. Brave.

George cleared his throat. "We stopped about..." He ran his finger over the page, skimming the notes. "Here."

He took a deep breath.

"Alright, let's get started."

They picked up where they had left off, George once again beating the tempo on his thigh and humming the tune in its proper rhythm. The musicians followed along, picking out the next section of the tune, repeating it over and over until they knew it by heart.

They had added all but the last third of the tune to their memory when Jasper said, "Should we give it a go?" His eyes glinted.

The others nodded. Everyone shifted in their places. George sat on the steps, his heart pounding. Already he could feel the thrum of the song, the burning embers sparking to life. The anticipation in the room was palpable.

"Alright," Jasper said. "Here we go. One, two—"

"Wait." George held up a hand.

No one moved.

A faint sound filtered through the trapdoor. George climbed the steps and pushed it open just an inch. There it was again. A knock on the front door. His chest tightened. He hesitated, shivering in the breath of air that seeped through the opening.

"Is anyone else coming?" George whispered to the group below.

Jasper shook his head. All were deathly silent.

Again the knock sounded. It was firm. Demanding. But not violent.

"Stay here," George said, and hoisted himself out of the cellar.

"George, wait!" Jasper hissed. But George lowered the door, leaving the pantry in darkness.

24

GEORGE

CIRCA 2023

George was not sure whether he was being foolish to answer the door. It couldn't be Reuben, or he would have just busted right in. Wouldn't he? George hesitated. The knock came again, louder this time. Hoping he was not about to get his face bashed in, George turned the knob and pulled.

"Oh," he said in surprise.

On the step stood a middle-aged woman in a sweeping, black velvet dress. She had silver-tinged auburn hair piled in careful curls on her head, framing a long face with stern, though graceful features. She stood tall and proud, her eyes narrow and bent on his, her jaw set and her mouth in a firm line.

She was both frightful and beautiful. George could see at once that this was a woman used to being in charge.

"Oh?" she repeated, raising her eyebrows.

"I—I'm sorry," George stammered. "I'm not used to guests."

"Shocking," she said, her eyes grim and, as far as George could tell, not a bit shocked.

"How can I help you?" George did not know how on earth he should address this woman. *This must be the Lady, surely.* "Would you like to come in?"

"I'd prefer that to the porch." She had not moved her eyes from George's. "Is this your home?" Her speech was soft, though commanding, her accent a Mid-Atlantic lilt.

"It...yes, yes it is, your majes—" George broke off, embarrassed.

"I am not a queen, Mr. Morgan," the woman said, with a flicker of amusement in her expression. "But I would like to ask some questions. And I'd like a cup of tea, if you have one in your possession."

"Oh. Alright. Uh, not a problem. Come on in."

George moved aside and held the door wide. The woman swept into the living room and looked about, eying each feature with shrewd intrigue.

George glanced outside, but it seemed she had come alone. He closed the door and hustled to the kitchen, pleading silently that the group downstairs would not make a noise.

"Here you are," George said a few minutes later, handing a mug of plain black tea to the woman in his living room.

She was sitting on the edge of the sofa, looking very out of place with George's simple furnishings. Her eyes brightened when she saw the tea.

"I brought some milk and sugar," George continued, setting the milk jug and a small pot and spoon on the side table. "Not sure how you like your tea."

The woman eyed the plastic milk jug but said nothing. She scooped a small mound of sugar and stirred it slowly into her mug, watching the swirling brew. She took a sip, closed her eyes, and swallowed. The lines on her face softened, taking away some of the grimness. She sighed, smiled, just barely, and opened her eyes.

"Thank you, Mr. Morgan. Your name is Mr. Morgan, isn't it?"

"Er...yes ma'am. George Morgan. How did you know?"

"I know many things, George." She took another sip of tea. "My name is Isabella Crane, though I suppose you know that as well."

"N-no ma'am. Pleased to meet you, though."

Isabella gave him a sharp glance. "Most here call me the Lady. It's a ridiculous name, but it stuck. Lady Crane would be far more appropriate. Where I come from, titles mean something. For those who aren't common, anyway; and I," she added, glaring at George, "am not common."

George shrugged. He was not sure how to respond, but he preferred not to let on what he had or had not heard about her. He thought about the group gathered under his pantry, then quickly pushed the thought away. *Stay in the present, George. Don't mess this up.*

"Do you know, Mr. Morgan, that my son once lived in this house?"

"Your son, ma'am?"

"My son. My only child. He died soon after."

Despite the chilled strangeness of this woman and all he had heard of her, a tinge of empathy crept into his chest. He knew how it felt to lose people.

"I...I'm sorry. That must have been terribly difficult."

"It was. Still is." She smoothed the folds of her dress. "Look, Mr. Morgan, I don't want to infringe any longer than necessary on your time. I'll get straight to the point. I'm quite aware of some unpleasant incidents of late. Reuben asked to use his methods to find out your role in all this, but I preferred to come myself." She gave him a long look.

George shifted in his seat but forced his eyes to stay glued to hers.

Isabella broke her gaze and looked about the room. "I have much...insight, shall we say, into what goes on in Green Meadows, but my view, oddly, is a little obscured when it comes to your being here and what, precisely, you have been doing." She looked back at George. "Have you been helping the cottagers learn music?"

George creased his forehead. "Music, ma'am?"

"Stop answering my questions with other questions, George. It bothers me." She took a long drink of tea. "Songs. Musical songs. Have you been teaching them?"

"I don't know much about music, ma'am. My aunt played the piano, but I only ever learned enough to know I wasn't much good at it."

"And whom, pray tell, is your aunt?"

"Pamela Morgan. Was. She died a while ago."

"I see."

Everyone had died. *Also terribly difficult,* George wanted to say, but he kept it to himself.

"You're not from around here, are you, George." It was a statement, not a question.

George shrugged. "I guess not, depending what you mean. I've only lived here about a month." Had it really only been a month? His previous life seemed a different existence.

Isabella studied him for a moment, taking in his gimp leg, limp-collared shirt, and faded hair. George's skin squirmed. His eyes begged to stare at the floor, the wall, anything but the strange, examining woman, but he steeled himself and gazed calmly back.

The Lady set her cup on the side table. She folded slender hands into her lap. They looked starkly pale against the midnight dress. "I'll be clear, George, so as to make things simpler for both of us. That song is not an ordinary piece of music. My son dabbled in things he shouldn't have. Took unnecessary risks. The song he brought has power to it. Dangerous power. I told him to leave the song alone, to get rid of it, but he refused."

She sighed and rubbed her temples with delicate fingers.

"Clearly it did not turn out well for him." She fixed her eyes again on George. "You must keep that song away from the cottagers. They don't know what they trifle with. I have...experience, shall we say, with extraordinary things. This music will bring only death, as it did to my Lux." She glared at George.

Isabella closed her eyes and clenched her teeth for a moment, then opened them again, her composure regained.

"That's all I came to say," she said, standing suddenly and gliding toward the front door in a swirl of velvet skirts.

George clambered to his feet and followed. "I hope I didn't upset you," he said as she pulled the door open.

Isabella turned to face him. "That remains to be seen," she said, her voice as cold as stone. "Good evening, Mr. Morgan."

With that, she marched around the back of his house. George went to the window and watched as she approached Reuben at the edge of the woods and disappeared with him down the footpath.

"What in the world?" George muttered.

He scratched his head and let out a long sigh, wondering for the hundredth time how he had managed to end up in the middle of such a mess.

"George?"

George whirled. It was Jasper, standing in his kitchen doorway.

"She's gone, is she?"

George nodded.

"You did well, George. Thanks for protectin' us."

Protecting? George blinked. He didn't know what he was doing. Liese had been his to protect. He had failed on that one.

Everything suddenly seemed unsure. He didn't know whom to believe. George wondered how much Jasper had heard. Was the song really that dangerous? It was powerful; that much was certain. George needed time to think. He needed to figure this out.

"I think we'd better call it quits for tonight," George said, not meeting Jasper's eyes. "No saying for sure if she'll come back."

Jasper said nothing for a moment. He stood there, not moving. His hulking frame filled the doorway.

He could break me like a twig. George didn't linger on that thought. Not for long, anyway.

Jasper did not look dangerous, though. He looked like a pillar. He looked weary. And something else. *Guarded? Disappointed?* George couldn't tell.

"Alright, George," Jasper said finally. "If that's what you want. It's your house. I'll let the others know."

"Jasper..."

Jasper turned, his eyes questioning.

"I...it's just..." George opened his mouth, closed it again, then sighed and said, "Might want to wait a bit before starting home. Reuben's with her. Maybe he's walking her back to her house."

Jasper nodded, slowly, and disappeared into the pantry. George heard the trapdoor scrape open and the sound of low voices. He wished he was alone in his bed.

He stepped to the window and lifted the curtain edge. Not much, just enough to look out. He didn't want to see the faces of the line of people exiting his front door.

As they left, though, trailing silently through his back yard, he watched. George did not move until the last cottager faded into the forest.

25

CYRUS

CIRCA 1851

Six months after the Crane sisters joined the Gifted, Cyrus noticed a change. Two changes, actually.

First, Isabella was, quite clearly, in love with the Magister. It was not a surprise. The Magister had been enamored with her from day one, and Isabella savored the attention like many a woman would.

But it changed.

Cyrus practically saw it happen, like watching a sunflower move to follow the sun. Isabella actually loved him. The Magister. Not an infatuation. Not a fling. The roots went deep and dug into the bedrock of her heart.

Cyrus noticed it one evening when the sisters had come at dinnertime. There were many members of the Gifted at the mansion that night. Some were new trainees; others, veterans of several years.

They had all eaten the meal together, as often happened at the mansion. Even the Magister joined. He rarely mixed with the other members, regardless if Isabella was present. More often than not, he would eat privately and invite Isabella to join him.

It was all part of keeping the Gifted well afraid of him. Cyrus and the Magister had carefully arranged it to be so. Even Isabella, Cyrus knew, was afraid. Her fear lay well beneath the surface.

Only Ada seemed to stick with no more than a healthy respect. The Magister would have known this if he had taken the trouble to notice Ada more carefully.

Dinner, then, was awkward. But no more than expected. The dozen or so Gifted besides the Crane sisters ate with rigid movements and tense smiles. Many of them openly gaped at the Magister sitting at one end of the table.

A few tried to show off, using their Gifts to pass dishes and pour wine, glancing at the Magister to see if he had noticed.

Cyrus gritted his teeth.

The Magister said little, only looked passively at his guests, like a king quite sure of his command.

Isabella sat on one side of him. She talked to him quietly, but not overmuch. Cyrus noticed and appreciated her discernment. It seemed she knew his boundary lines around others and wouldn't push him too far.

Ada sat next to Isabella and, as usual, observed all that happened—and her sister, in particular.

Ada actually smirked when a guest looked for approval and missed his wine cup. Wine splashed on the tablecloth. The guest flushed as red as the stain.

Isabella glared at the poor man. Ada looked down to hide a smile, then flashed him a compassionate shrug.

The defining moment, though, was something small. Something only Cyrus could have noticed.

The Magister, tired of company, turned to give his usual signal that it was time to send everyone away. It was a simple signal. He would, without visibly moving his hands, twist the ring on Cyrus' right pointer finger. As far as Cyrus was aware, not even Isabella knew of this long-time habit.

But this time, before the ring began to move, Isabella put a hand on the Magister's arm, pushed her chair back, and stood. The guests immediately moved their own chairs and began gathering up their things to go, aware that if the Magister's favorite was finished, they had better be finished too.

The Magister's eyebrows rose in surprise. He looked at Isabella. She looked at him. Cyrus saw both. He knew, like he knew the feel of wind, that Isabella Crane loved that man. She had noticed the shift of mood before he had time to communicate it. She had noticed, accepted, and acted.

His friend had realized it too. Cyrus saw that just as clearly. How would this fare for Isabella? Cyrus did not know.

His friend was awfully strict with his hold on superiority. He would never consider another his equal—not even for love.

But that look...

Cyrus filed the memory away. He would examine it later and see what conclusions it held. The second change Cyrus noticed was more unexpected, though he had hoped for it.

As the guests filed out of the dining room, and the Magister disappeared through an opposite doorway, Cyrus felt a touch on his arm.

It was Ada. Little Ada Crane was looking at him. Her brown eyes were bright and quizzical.

"You really care about him, don't you." She said it quietly, just to Cyrus. "You really are his friend."

Cyrus stared back in surprise. He was starkly aware of her statement. Aware of her simple beauty. Aware of her touch on his arm.

"Yes," he said. "I do. And I am." He cocked his head. "You didn't think so before?"

"I wondered." She let go of his arm and tied her hat strings. "But I thought maybe it was more formality. Just a business partnership."

She tipped her head back so Cyrus could see her eyes again. His heart rate quickened. "I've been trying to see who you really are. Where your loyalty lies."

Cyrus held his breath. "And?"

"Still figuring it out." Ada grinned at him. "But I like what I've found so far."

She dropped a polite curtsy, turned, and left the mansion.

Cyrus swallowed hard. He was on Ada's mind, after all.

He went to the table and started gathering up the dishes for Gertie, just to have something to do.

Ada Crane. What all had she seen in him?

I've been trying to see who you really are. Where your loyalty lies.

Where was his loyalty? To his friend, yes, but what if everything fell apart? What would he do then?

Was it the Pearls that kept him here? Was it for want of power that he stayed, training and directing the Gifted under careful scrutiny of the Magister?

Was it the effects he saw on the city? There were better crops, less accidents, fewer tragedies. The work of the Gifted did have an impact.

But the Magister. His hold over the city grew. His control was expanding. Cyrus saw it, and was wary. But he stayed.

Was it his own position of authority that fed a subconscious ego?

He tossed dirty napkins into a pile. *Damn it all.*

What would Ada Crane think if she knew who he really was? That his deepest loyalty was to himself?

26

LUX

CIRCA 1873

Lux tried every panel of the wall, looking for loose boards. Nothing. He tried every piece of the floor. Still nothing.

Time felt meaningless in a room with no clock and no window, but he knew it was ticking fast. How many hours until nightfall, then morning? How long did he have until the Magister used the "methods" Cyrus had referred to?

Out. There must be a way out.

Lux again checked the floor, the walls, the door. He moved the bed, the table, the stag painting, all to no avail.

He looked at the ceiling. It was smooth plaster, except for an ornately-carved wood design right in the center, as if it had once housed a chandelier. That seemed odd for such a small, out-of-the-way room. The carving lay flat against the ceiling, protruding about a hand's breadth from the plaster in thick swirls of carved vines and leaves.

It looked skillfully made—a subtle decoration that was beautiful, once noticed.

It was worth a try. Lux focused his energy on the wood. He braced his hands in thin air and rotated, willing the carving to shift.

It did.

It shifted so quickly that he almost lost control. The whole carving came loose from the ceiling and tilted dangerously, almost clattering to the floor before Lux balanced it and lowered it to the bed.

He hefted it. It was lighter than he had expected. Hollow, in fact.

Lux looked up. Where the wood piece had been, he now saw a hole wider than a man's shoulders. There was thick threading carved into the edge's opening. The base of the wood carving had the opposite threading. It must have been made to work like a giant screw.

Lux brought the chair and stepped onto it. He could just reach the edge of the opening with his fingertips.

He would have to jump for it.

He did not waste time wondering what was up there or hoping nobody would hear him. He would be as silent and quick as possible. There was no other option.

Lux bent his knees, steadied himself, and leapt.

One arm dashed against the edge of the opening. It stung like fire, but he managed to grab the ledge with both hands.

He dangled for a second, then took a deep breath and heaved his body upward.

Lux clambered into the ceiling. It smelled of dust and old wood. Something skittered off to his right, and he repressed the urge to flinch. Not a rat, he hoped. Rats were liars, and mean to boot. He had never gotten along well with them.

He stood slowly, feeling about him to get an idea of the space. There was a low, rough ceiling, just high enough for him to hunch with his knees and shoulders slightly bent. In front and behind him were wood plank walls. To his left, past the opening in the floor, another wall blocked any exit. To his right, there was open air. He hoped that meant it led somewhere helpful.

He felt as far as he could with one foot. The floor was a series of joists, close enough together to walk on fairly easily.

Lux looked down through the opening. There was the chair, the bed, the carved wood piece. He would have to put the room back to normal. There was no doubt Cyrus would figure out soon enough where he had gone, but with any luck, Lux could at least leave him wondering for a few minutes.

It occurred to Lux that Cyrus might know about this passage, or attic crawl space, or whatever it was. Maybe he put Lux in this room on purpose, just to laugh at him when he caught him crawling through the ceiling like a piece of vermin.

Oh well. He was out of options and running out of time. He had to take the risk. If he got caught, he was no worse off than he had been.

Lux turned himself onto his knees and leaned over the opening. Swiftly, silently, he maneuvered the chair back to its place and straightened the bed covers, using his hands like a puppeteer with invisible strings. Then he raised the carved wood piece, brought it slowly to the opening, and settled it back into its threaded grooves.

All was pitch black. Lux waited, panting. The physical toll it took to use the Gifts still surprised him. He was stronger now than when he was younger, but he still felt the energy sap, especially with larger objects and more precise movements.

He thought of the splitting headaches Cyrus had given him. What toll must it take to manipulate something living? What kind of stamina did his mother have to steal Auntie's Gifts as she shriveled like a prune?

Lux shuddered and pushed the thought away. This was not the time or place for those ponderings.

He couldn't see a thing. The air around him was stuffy and intensely dark. Sweat beaded on his scalp and crawled down the back of his neck. *Move*. He must move.

Lux pulled himself to a crouch, turned right, and shuffled through the dark.

It seemed like hours, creeping through the ceiling like a misplaced animal. He felt clumsy and stiff. Sometimes he dropped to all fours and crawled to give his back and thighs a break from crouching. When his knees couldn't take it anymore, he went back to the aching stoop.

Sweat dripped from his forehead now. It ran into his eyes and trickled down his back. The air was heavy and thick. Every breath of it suggested panic.

Lux did not panic. He was well-trained enough for that. Panic threatened, though, like a hornet nest in the back of his mind.

The tunnel turned several times, first left, then right for a long ways, then left, then right again. Once, it branched. Lux waited and listened. Both ways were silent, both just as dark. There was no knowing which led where. For all he knew, he would come to a dead end down either one of them and have no idea how to get out.

There must be other exits, like the wood decoration back in the bedroom. But how would he find them? He didn't know what to feel for. Any notch under his feet could be a carefully-placed panel hidden from the view of people below.

Lux swore under his breath, turned right, and hoped for the best.

After countless minutes, though in reality it may have only been a quarter of an hour, Lux rounded another corner and heard singing.

He halted and forced his breathing to lengthen and slow. He listened.

The sound was coming from up ahead. It was too muted to discern much of its bearer. Lux shuffled forward as quietly as he could, straining his ears to keep ahold of the sound. It ebbed and flowed, but remained at the same general distance. Lux approached, and the song grew louder. Finally he stopped. It was below him.

He could hear it more clearly now, muffled but audible. It was a woman's voice. Not pretty, per se. It crackled and broke like rotten machinery, but held to a general tune. The words, when he could catch them, went something like this:

O'er light and water, soil and sky,
A voice like the crash of the seas,
Singing the song of the birth of the world,
Leaving the mark in the trees.
The trees, the trees,
Leaving the mark in the trees.

Lux could not remember if he had ever heard the song before. It sounded familiar, but in a far-off way, too vague to be trusted as a memory.

He did not care one way or the other. He only wanted to get out of the muggy passageway as soon as possible.

The singing continued for another moment, then petered out. Lux hoped the woman, whoever she was, had left the room. There was no other sound he could detect.

Sweat stung his eyes. The air choked him. It was so thick. So stifling. He forced himself to breathe. *In...out.*

Lux stepped aside and felt where his feet had been. There was a thin line in one of the joists. He followed it. It continued across the others in, yes, a circular pattern.

He listened again but heard nothing. Hoping the woman had left the area, Lux willed the circle beneath him to rotate and come loose. Using the Gifts, he lowered it slowly until he could see below.

There was a wooden countertop covered with yellow batter and a smattering of baking supplies. The floor was of grey stone. Other table legs were visible nearby, but Lux couldn't see far enough from where he was to discern much detail.

He let the ceiling piece settle on the floor, turned onto his stomach, and pushed his legs through the opening. There was very little room on the counter between bowls, spoons, and batter. He lowered himself down until he was dangling by his hands.

The countertop was still too far to reach with his shoes. Lux maneuvered his feet, trying to aim his drop to cause the least amount of mess and noise.

The next instant, a flurry of green feathers and grey beak exploded in his face, crying, "Peep away, Peep away!"

Lux crashed onto the counter in an eruption of cups, spoons, spices, and sticky batter.

27

LUX

CIRCA 1873

Lux rolled sideways, shoving spice jars and bowls out of his way in a desperate effort to get off the counter and onto his feet.

Someone kept smacking him with a stick. *Not the green-feathered thing, surely.*

He leapt away from the counter and stood. Yellow batter dripped from his shirt. The smell, mixed with his sweat, made him think of musty socks and lemon bars.

His back and shoulders throbbed from the repeated smacking and from where they had landed on a myriad of baking supplies.

He looked wildly about him.

"Out, out, out, out, out," called the squawking, green-feathered form that had shocked him seconds before.

Lux saw now that it was a parrot. The bird hopped from foot to foot on the countertop, wings outspread. It appeared to be trying very hard to look intimidating. The attempt seemed pathetic now that Lux was standing on solid ground instead of dangling from the ceiling.

An old, hunched woman stood on the other side of the counter with a wooden spoon clutched in one hand. She was broad-shouldered and plump, with loose grey hair hanging about her neck and a fierce scowl on her sagging face. A smattering of whiskers trembled in the folds of skin under her lip.

"Who ye be?" she demanded.

Her voice was wet and gravelly. Lux grimaced.

The parrot hopped onto her shoulder and pumped its head up and down. The woman scratched the feathers under its beak.

"Such a good boy, aren't ye, Peep," she said, crooning to the bird like one might to an infant. "Always helping old Gertie."

Lux grimaced a second time.

The woman cleared her throat. "I said, who ye be? What're ye crashing into my kitchen for, ruinin' the pound cake, eh?"

"I'm sorry," Lux said. He wiped cake batter and sweat out of his eye. "I tried not to hit anything."

"Ha! Tried not hit anything, eh? Ye hit the whole kit n' caboodle." She shook her head and looked with annoyance at the scattered mess.

"Sorry," Lux said again. He shrugged. "The bird—"

"Peep, peep, peep," called the parrot, bobbing its head proudly.

"Such a good boy, Peep," crooned Gertie. She scowled again at Lux. "Peep saw ye hangin' outa the ceiling like a new-skinned hunk o' cow beef. What did ye think he'd do, eh?"

Lux opened and closed his mouth like a trapped fish. "I..."

He looked at the mess, the scowling old woman, and the wretched parrot. Peep cocked one eye at him and preened in triumph. Lux glared back. If it weren't for the woman watching, he would have a thing or two to say to the stupid thing.

"Well?" Gertie demanded.

Lux shrugged. "Sorry," he said again.

"Sorry my eye," Gertie mumbled. She dropped the wooden spoon and peered up at him. "Who the heck are ye?" she said. Her voice stuck, and she coughed one wet cough. Peep hopped off her shoulder and started pecking at a smear of cake batter on the counter.

"I'm..." Lux paused to consider but could not find any reason to lie to the woman. He hated lying as a rule, anyway. "I'm Lux. Lux Crane."

Gertie's eyes sharpened. Her mouth dropped open. "Crane," she said, her voice low and gurgling. "Ye lyin' to me, boy?"

"No, ma'am."

She stared hard at Lux, then waddled around the counter, grabbed his chin with one clammy hand, and examined every inch of his face.

Lux saw bits of dandruff by the roots of her hair and a smear of bird poop down her shoulder. He forced himself not to cringe.

"Crane," she said again, letting go of his chin. She stepped backwards and looked up at him. Her eyes were soft now, soft and wondering. "Isabella's boy?"

Lux's skin went cold. He hoped this was good news to the old woman. "Yes, ma'am."

"Well I'll be," Gertie said. She leaned one hand on the counter for support and shook her head.

"What's Isabella's boy doin' in my kitchen ceiling, eh?"

Lux looked at the gaping hole he had just come through. He wondered if Gertie knew anything about the passageway, the Arbor Pearls, the accusations against his mother...any of it.

She knew who his mother was, at least, and she didn't seem upset about it. That was a start. He decided he had better stick with the simple truth. He turned back to Gertie.

"Trying to escape."

Gertie watched him for a moment. Her little eyes bored into his, and her whiskers stuck out all directions.

Finally she heaved a great sigh.

"Well, ye'd better get cleaned up, eh? Ye look like a dung heap and don't smell much better."

"Gertie, I—"

"No arguin' with me, boy," she said, jabbing one finger at him. "This here's my part o' the house, and I won't have no skulking, stinking boy tryin' to sneak outa here like a half-dead weasel."

She waved him toward a door at one end of the kitchen. "Come on, Lux Crane. Get yerself cleaned up. We'll talk about escapin' later."

"But the Magister—"

"I told ye, this here's my part o' the house. I can't fiddle faddle things this way and that a' way like the master does, but I have my own tricks. He won't bother ye here while I've got anything to say about it."

She pointed at the ceiling. "Put that back first, eh?"

Lux gave up. He returned the ceiling piece to its place and followed her through the door. She left him in a washroom with a piece of soap and a tub of water after demanding his clothes to clean.

"Won't take long," she said when he hesitated. "Ye don't want to run around the city covered with grime and pound cake mixins,' do ye?"

Lux gave her his clothes. He washed from head to foot, wrapped a blanket around himself, and stepped out of the washroom. He found Gertie in the kitchen wiping the last of the cake batter off the floor. His clothes hung in front of a crackling fire.

The kitchen looked almost exactly like his mother's kitchen at home. Some of the finishings were different, but the layout was the same. The arrangement of the counters, ovens, fireplace, all of it.

Coincidence? He didn't know.

Lux shook himself back to the present. Smells of stewed chicken and spice cake permeated the room. Lux's stomach rumbled.

Gertie was singing while she cleaned, her voice even more disjointed now that it wasn't muffled by the ceiling. Peep, standing on the back of a chair, bobbed his head to the tune.

Well I'll sing ye the song o' the cat and the crow
And the lady who discovered the pair.
She found 'em in the cellar far down below
When she tried to go out for some air.
And the cat and the crow, and the lady down below,
Well they all had a grand ol' time
With the carrots and potatoes, the onions and tomatoes,
And the best of the cellar's wine.

When she paused, Lux cleared his throat. "Sorry again about the mess," he said.

Gertie popped her head up. "Fine, fine," she said. "Not a problem." She heaved herself up from the floor with one hand on a chair and the other on her lower back.

"Gertie's not too spry anymore," she said wryly.

She patted Peep's head and rinsed the dishcloth in a bucket of water. "Yer clothes will be dry in a jiffy." She bustled to the stove. "Sit down there by the fire and have a bite to eat."

Lux obeyed. The thought of Cyrus looking for him pushed at his mind, but he couldn't very well go traipsing out a window in nothing but an old blanket. He hoped Gertie was right about him not being bothered here.

He pulled a chair to the fireside and sat. Gertie waddled over and put a bowl of chicken stew in his hands. It was rich and delicious, and he told her so.

She beamed. "Ah shucks," she said. "Gertie's been makin' stew for plenty o' years. It's nothin'."

Lux ate two bowls' worth and set the dishes aside. "Gertie," he said after a moment, "what was that song you were singing before?"

"The cat and the crow?" she asked. "Just a bit o' nothin'. That tune's been around for ages."

"No, no," Lux said, "not that one. The other song. The one you were singing before I fell out of the ceiling. Something about a mark in the trees."

"Ah, that song." She eyed him. "How long were ye sittin' up there?"

Too long, Lux thought. "Not long," he said. "But I heard part of it. I hadn't heard it before. Where's it from?"

"It's the song o' the Maker's worlds." She squinted at him. "Ye know the story of the Maker's worlds, don't ye?"

Lux shook his head.

Gertie sighed. "Grown-up lads without the brains that actually matter," she muttered. "Well, I'll tell it to ye," she said, wiping her hands on her apron. "Put yer clothes on first though, just in case. We don't want anyone knockin' on the door with ye half in yer skin."

28

LUX

CIRCA 1873

"The way it was told to me," Gertie began, "is that the Maker of all th' worlds used a different bit of his heart to form each one. For one, he laughed. That's a world o' such brightness that no human bein' could live there for th' sheer beauty of the Maker's mighty pleasure.

"For another, he cried out the sorrow of all the hurt that people would give him, for all ages. That's a dark world, unfit for people's survivin'. Th' Maker's sorrow has depths we can't begin to understand.

"For another, he roared his anger, trappin' it on a world far away from his beloved creatures, lest it burn 'em all away. That world's all fire and blazin' white heat. It would melt yer very soul if ye came within fathoms of it.

"For this world, the Maker sang. He made a song o' such beauty and power, kindness and mercy, rightness and freedom, love and blessed goodness. He weaved 'em all together to give life and wholeness to his creatures.

"Most have forgotten th' Maker's pattern for the worlds. He knew it would be so. He left a mark in each one, a reminder to us of his almighty imprint over all that's made.

"The story says that th' bright world has a sparklin' river. Not water, but light. It's said that the rainbow of th' Maker's promise came from that river.

"The world o' sorrow has a bed of stones as hard and bright as the clearest diamonds, for th' Maker's beauty still comes outa hard-pressed pain.

"The world o' fire has a river gleamin' of pure gold that never burns, for th' Maker's wrath is just, but his heart is kind.

"This world has a set o' softer stones, made from th' Maker's song. They capture a glimpse o' the beauty and mightiness too big for our human understandin'."

Gertie smiled. It was a lovely smile, in spite of her worn, sagging face.

"They say that th' Maker put the stones in the care of trees that would grow for all the worlds' ages. That's a lovely thought, eh? Trees that won't die 'til the world itself falls to ruin and newness." She pulled herself out of her chair and tottered to the counter.

Lux watched the fire. *Stones and trees.* Stuff of legend, yes? *And yet...*

"I knew yer mother, you know." Gertie glanced at him, then turned back to the pile of bread dough she was twisting into fat buns. Peep nipped at the dough and rubbed his feathery head against Gertie's hand.

"I didn't know 'er well," she continued, "but I used to see her when she'd come to th' mansion. She was all fire and passion, but nervous too. She never seemed at ease." Gertie dropped buns onto a baking sheet and slid them into the oven. "She was close to th' Magister." She watched Lux carefully. "Worked side by side with 'im back in those days."

Lux glanced up, then turned back to the hearth. "She never told me that," he said, then added in a lower voice, "She never told me lots of things."

Gertie paused by the oven, looking at the young man who sat straight and dismal by the fire. She opened her mouth to speak, but closed it again. Finally she moved to the counter and began wiping up sticky remnants of bread dough.

"Well," she said, more to herself than to Lux. "Isabella must've had 'er reasons."

Someone knocked hard on a door beyond the kitchen, the opposite end of the kitchen from the washroom.

Cyrus' voice rang clearly. "Gertie, open up now, or I'll pop the door myself."

Lux's head jerked up. He jumped to his feet. Gertie waved him toward a doorway at the back of the kitchen.

"I'm comin', I'm comin'," she called. "Don't get yer knickers in a wad, I'll be right there."

Lux was rushing toward the doorway. Gertie grabbed his shirt collar and pulled his head close to hers.

"Go through th' pantry window," she whispered.

Her whiskers tickled his ear, and her breath smelled like old fish and putrid tea. Lux fought the urge to pull away.

"Hop into th' neighbor's cellar. Ye can get through to his kitchen and find a way out. My friend Mabel and me used to visit each other that way when we were girls." She shoved him toward the pantry and waddled quickly away.

"Gertie?" Cyrus' voice carried a clear warning tone.

"I'm comin'," she called, sounding entirely nonchalant. "I've got dough on my hands, just wipin' it off." She did not look back at Lux.

He ran past the ovens and into the pantry. It was a full-sized room, really. There were drawers of all sizes and rows of shelves, all stacked with sacks, jars, and lidded crocks. Barrels stood like sentries along one wall.

A single window let in light from the back corner. Lux moved the curtain and slid the glass open, thankful it did not squeak.

He could hear Cyrus in the other room, snapping at Gertie, and Peep chattering like a broken record.

Gertie's voice rose above both. "What're ye doin' practically smashing my door to bits, eh? Dinner ain't ready yet, and even if it were, ye don't need to be barrelin' in here like a starvin' puppy."

"Quiet, Gertie. Have you seen a man come through here?"

"A man? I'm a bit old for courtin', don't you think? Unless that's why yer here, eh?" Her voice took on a crooning tone with a hint of jest. "Ye miss old Gertie?"

Lux almost chuckled as he stepped out the window and slid it closed behind him. Gertie had called this place a mansion. Hurried as he was, he glanced up now to see for himself. Brick walls towered several stories high, ending in a roof with complex layers of rooflines and gables. A mansion indeed, but in the middle of the city.

It looked startlingly similar to his mother's mansion back in Green Meadows; only, hers was built of wood. The thought bugged him, but he did not have time to consider.

Toward the front of the house, across the street, he could see stately brownstone buildings with balconies and turrets.

All of this he took in at a glance. There was only a short distance between this side of the mansion and the neighboring house, a much smaller, though still elegant building of grey brick and dark roofing.

Lux skirted a row of witch hazel bushes and found the cellar door. It sat at an angle against the foot of the house.

The wood was faded, but the handle and hinges looked clean and well-oiled. Lux wondered at Gertie's comment. Had she really been at this mansion since girlhood? *Perhaps her growing up was not all that different from mine,* he thought, thinking again of his mother's mansion in Green Meadows. At least Gertie had a friend, though, even if she did have to sneak through cellars to visit her.

Lux pulled open the cellar and climbed inside. His feet found purchase on a packed dirt floor. It took a moment for his eyes to adjust. The cellar was clean, but it did not look to be often used. There were empty crates in neat rows on the floor and a few bunches of dried herbs hanging from the ceiling. Nothing else.

Lux found a steep staircase leading upward. He climbed it and listened.

Silence.

He pushed a trap door open and peered into another pantry. It was similar to Gertie's, though smaller and not as well-stocked.

He heaved himself through the opening, closed the trap door, and tiptoed to the kitchen.

There were no signs of a cook. In fact, a coffee pitcher and toaster fork on the counter were about the only indications that the place was ever used. Other than a calico cat stretching in the corner, it was mercifully empty.

There was a door on the opposite end of the kitchen. Lux could see daylight through its window. That door would let him out on the far side of the house, away from the Magister's mansion.

As quickly as he dared, he snuck through the kitchen, gave the cat a warning glance, and slipped out the door.

Lux ran without looking back. If he could make the six o' clock train, he could be out of the city tonight.

29

GERTIE

CIRCA 1873

Gertie resisted the urge to give Cyrus a shove out of the kitchen door.

"Good luck to ye," she called to his retreating form.

He glared at her and disappeared around a corner.

Gertie chuckled and closed the door. He did not believe her story about having no notion of Lux's having been there. That was fine. She didn't generally believe him either.

He didn't entirely *not* believe her, so the result was the same. He did not know what to think about what she had said, and she had not said anything to help him in the least, so it all worked out. Lux would be out of the next-door house and on his way to the train station by now. Cyrus wouldn't be able to catch up. She had kept him talking long enough to be sure of that.

Gertie smelled burnt bread and hurried to the oven.

"Dag blasted, nitpickin' fool," she said, yanking the sheet of overdone rolls out of the oven.

"Fool, fool, fool," Peep piped in from his perch in the corner. He had taken refuge there after Cyrus shouted at him to shut up or he would wring his head off.

"Ye got no room to talk," Gertie huffed. "A fat lotta help ye were. Didn't even tell me when th' rolls were done, eh? Too scared to say a tootin' thing."

Peep fluttered off his perch and landed on Gertie's shoulder.

"Ah, git off it, eh? Ye know Gertie can't stay mad at you long." She chuckled and scratched Peep's head.

"Gertie's gettin' too old for this kinda nonsense," she said, pushing the burned buns aside. She started mixing a batch of biscuits. "Isabella Crane's boy here in my kitchen," she murmured. "Never woulda thought it. Not in a whole heap o' lifetimes."

That poor Crane girl used to come to her every now and then. Maybe just for a bit of home. Ada would come too, but Isabella more often. Gertie would give her a cup of tea and listen to her. That seemed to be all Isabella really wanted. She never asked Gertie much about her own life, but that was fine with Gertie. She cared about the girl. Saw her fire, her love, her confusion.

Gertie had guessed she was pregnant. It was too early to show, and Isabella did not tell her, but Gertie knew. She didn't ask her anything about it. She could put the pieces together well enough. She only gave Isabella some tea and listened to her chatter about the Magister, and how much she loved him, and how he trusted her more and more. All the while, Gertie's heart hurt for that girl who had attached herself to such pain.

The Magister did not trust anyone. Even Gertie knew that. She served food, and cleaned the mansion, and saw and heard things that no one else would have guessed.

No. He might love Isabella in a way, but he would never love her completely. Isabella would know it too, sometime. Her heart would break. But she would cling to him anyway.

Gertie shook her head now, remembering. She threw biscuits on the sheet pan and muttered to herself about how broken the world had gotten.

Peep hopped off her shoulder to find a more stable perch.

But now she had met Isabella's son, real as can be and grown into a handsome man. That was something good, surely…though the son seemed almost as confused as his mother had been. Gertie slid the biscuits into the oven, sighed, and plopped into a chair. She was deadbeat tired.

"Peep," she called. Peep squawked and fluttered to the arm of her chair. "Tell me when th' biscuits are done, eh?" She chucked him under the chin. "Don't let 'em burn. I don't 'ave time to make more before dinner."

"Dinner, dinner, dinner," Peep said, bobbing his head.

"That's th' one."

Gertie leaned her head back and closed her eyes. She thought of her girlhood, of growing up in this same mansion, her mother the housekeeper and her father the gardener for a rich man whose business eventually went bust.

She had stayed in the city, working for one family and then another. She had married a good man, but they were never able to have any children. Then her husband died, still almost young, and Gertie was left on her own. Since then she had gone back to keeping other people's houses. It seemed stable. It was what she knew.

She could hardly believe her eyes all those years later when she saw an advertisement for a housekeeper and discovered it was for this very mansion, her girlhood home.

Cyrus had grilled her like anything during the job interview, but she had said all the right things and sworn compliance when he had explained something about never telling anyone what happened here, never speaking ill of the Magister, and so on.

"So keep my mouth shut and leave everyone alone?" she had asked.

"Precisely," Cyrus had said. "Forever."

Gertie agreed without batting an eye. She would have done just about anything to come back here.

It was the only home she had left. She would rather not talk to people most of the time, anyway. Gertie stretched her tired old body and tried to position herself a little more comfortably.

"Isabella Crane's boy here in my kitchen," she murmured again. "Wouldn't 'ave thought it possible. Not after all that 'appened."

She wondered what that boy still had to face. It seemed he didn't know much. Gertie's heart hurt for him, and for Isabella, wherever she was, and for all those who pay the price when someone loves power more than the Maker's own handcrafted people.

30

CYRUS

CIRCA 1852

Cyrus noticed the shift when it happened. The Magister's infatuation with Isabella quelled. He confirmed it soon after.

It had been eighteen months since the Crane sisters joined the Gifted. They had lived at the mansion for the last two of those months. Against Ada's wishes, Isabella severed ties with their previous landlord the moment the Magister offered living space in the mansion's vast rooms.

Now the Magister called Cyrus to his apartment.

"You were right," he said. "She did cloud my judgment." His eyes were brooding and dark. Anger. Disappointment. Tortured desire.

"Get her out of here, Cyrus. Out of the mansion. I don't want her back here."

"Ever?"

"Ever. Unless we call her for a specific task. Don't take her far. She's still useful. But I can't..."

Cyrus waited.

"I can't send her away myself," the Magister finished. "Do you understand? I need you to get her away from me."

"She does care for you."

"Enough, I hope." The Magister shook his head. "I've been a fool, Cyrus. I have to stay in control. Do you understand?"

Cyrus did understand, or at least suspected, perhaps more than his friend did.

"Send her away. That sister of hers, too. I don't want them here. But keep watch on them. They've sworn allegiance to the Code. They'll keep it, if they have any sense to them."

Cyrus did so. He found Isabella and Ada in the kitchen, chatting with Gertie.

Ada's face lit up when she saw him. "Look who's here," she said, brushing cake crumbs off her dress.

Cyrus loved that dress on her. It was deep purple, like the dahlia flowers she always exclaimed over.

"You coming for lemon cake? Gertie just pulled it out of the oven."

Cyrus' heart nearly twisted to pieces. She looked so comfortable, so glad to have him there, and he was about to rip their world apart.

He gave Ada one pleading look. She stopped short. Her face fell. "What is it, Cy?"

That name...he loved it when she called him that. They were friends. It had never become more than that. Cyrus was too wary of his position with the Magister to suggest more, and still unsure of what Ada thought. She was comfortable around him, though. For now, that was enough.

He was about to ruin that anyway.

He cleared his throat. Both sisters stared at him. Gertie bustled away somewhere out of sight. "You have to leave," he said. "Both of you."

"Leave?" Isabella's face turned pale. "What's happened?"

Ada said nothing, only watched him with furrowed brow.

"Nothing's happened." Cyrus stood tall. He clasped his hands behind his back. "The Magister doesn't want you here anymore. I'll take you to a house outside the city. You'll be safe there. And provided for."

The last of Isabella's color drained. "Doesn't..." She swayed. Ada grabbed her arm and guided her to a chair.

"I don't believe it." Isabella's voice trembled. "That can't be true." She stood, her face flushing red. "You're making that up. He wouldn't do that."

"He can't have you here anymore. I'm sorry."

Isabella's beautiful, auburn head shook. Her eyes blazed. "How dare you say that," she said, her voice breaking. "He wouldn't do that. He wouldn't send me away."

"He insists on you both leaving immediately."

"He wouldn't do that!" Her voice rose and shook. "How dare you. You're lying!"

"He's not lying."

It was Ada. She spoke softly.

Cyrus gave her a tortured look. She was watching him with rigid calm. Such pain, and yet confident that he would not tell her anything but the truth.

"I'm sorry," Cyrus said. He said it to Ada, then turned to her sister. "I'm sorry, but it's true. The Magister says that you're still useful, but he won't have you here anymore unless he summons you for your Gifts sometime in the future."

"Useful," Isabella gasped. "Summons me..." She dropped back into the chair. "Summons me like a meaningless servant, not like his—"

"Izzy," Ada said. Her voice held warning.

Isabella glanced at her sister, then at Cyrus. She buttoned her lips up tight and clenched her jaw.

"Take us to the house," Ada said, not looking at Cyrus again. "I'll gather our things."

It had been weeks now since the Magister banned the Crane sisters from the mansion. Cyrus had given them space at first. He helped them settle into the old farmhouse at the city outskirts, then let them be. He kept an eye on them, as the Magister insisted, only checking enough to see one of them come in or out of a door, and so know they were still there and functioning.

Now he went for a real check-in.

Isabella answered the door.

"Oh," she said, clearly surprised. She stood in the doorway, head erect. She would not look him in the eye. "Come in."

Cyrus stepped inside.

"I ordered in a load of groceries. They should be here tomorrow morning." He took off his hat and studied her. She looked tired.

"We have money," she said, throwing him a narrow glance. "Plenty of it. You don't need to buy our food."

"Magister's orders." Cyrus set his hat on a nearby table.

"Well...thank you." Isabella sighed and swiped a silk sleeve across her forehead.

Then Cyrus saw her sway, saw her put her hand to her belly, and he realized.

"Does he know?"

Her eyes jerked to his. She blushed, paused, then, "I don't know. I don't think so."

"The kid might have it in his blood, you know. No one knows yet if the power of the Pearls passes to a child."

She started to look away, but Cyrus dodged and held her gaze. "If it does, you'll have to register him."

Another pause. "I know." Isabella's look turned from pensive to pleading. "Don't tell him. Please. Ada will help me. We'll be fine."

"Why not?"

"I...I don't know if he would hurt the baby. He's not who he used to be, Cyrus. He's gotten so..." She bit her lip. "He's suspicious of everyone and everything. I...I married him, you know."

Cyrus' head snapped up. "Married him? When?"

"Six months ago. Secretly." She raised her chin. "I'm not as unprincipled as you might think."

"And he's sent you away?"

She nodded. A tear spilled from the corner of her eye, but she brushed it off. "He seemed so sure of us being together, before. He said I would help him. Said we would work together. He even..." She glanced at Cyrus. "He even gave me more doses of the Pearls. More than anyone except you."

She cleared her throat. "Once we were married, though, he was more guarded and distrustful. As if he chided himself for becoming attached to someone and worried I might ruin his plans."

"His plans?"

"For the Code, the Gifted, all of it. He wants it all to go exactly right, and I think...I think he worried I would mess it up somehow. If he knew there was a baby, then..." She looked at Cyrus. Her eyes glistened. "I don't know what he'd do."

Cyrus didn't know either. A kid likely would not factor well into his friend's carefully controlled world. A wife didn't, obviously.

"Does your sister know? About the marriage?"

"Yes. She did not approve. She's like that, you know. But she couldn't stop me, and she knew it."

"You'll have to register him," Cyrus reiterated. "If he has any Gifts, anyway."

Isabella sighed. "I know. I have until he's six. Maybe by then the Magister will be understanding. Maybe..." She hesitated. "Maybe I can win back his trust before that."

Cyrus considered. His first loyalty was to his friend. That was certain. But he knew Isabella was right. His friend had changed.

The Magister's paranoia had increased over the years. He was more uneasy. More suspicious. Less focused on the good of society, which was the whole purpose of the Gifted in the first place. And he was absolutely set on being the sole authority. He had a system in place, and he would not hesitate to get rid of anything that disrupted the smooth workings of that system.

Cyrus thought of Braxton, who disappeared after breaking the Code. The Code was strict, and allegiance was allegiance. But Cyrus feared how his friend might react—and who he was becoming.

Cyrus would protect him if he could. And he would protect his friend's wife and child for as long as he was able.

He would not tell them—any of them—that he was balancing their fates. He would have to bide his time.

When he told the Magister about his child, which he knew must happen someday, even if it be decades from now, it would be in a way that would keep himself in the Magister's trust.

And when he protected Isabella's child from his own father, which he knew was also likely, that too would be done carefully. No one would suspect Cyrus of being a go-between.

"I won't tell him," Cyrus said. And he wouldn't. *For now, anyway.*

Cyrus found Ada before he left. She was on hands and knees in the garden, pulling weeds from a bed of flower shoots. Elsewhere, carrot sprouts and cucumber vines stood in neat clusters. Young tomato plants reached skyward in their pots, and mint leaves wafted their heady scent into the sun-warmed afternoon.

Ada did not see him at first. She plucked invaders from the dirt and dug her fingers in to find any leftover roots.

She was singing to herself. Cyrus couldn't hear the words, but he heard bits of the tune punctuated every now and then by a grunt when Ada pulled a particularly stubborn weed.

A strand of hair slipped from the bun at her neck. It stuck to her sweaty face. She swiped it away with one hand, leaving a streak of dirt across her cheek.

Deep in Cyrus' chest, he felt the familiar smoldering. Those embers, the ones he had tried hard to bury, quickened and burned.

This would not do. He had ruined whatever chance there was. *Get it together, Cyrus. She isn't yours, and never will be.* Thus quenched, he took a step forward.

Ada looked up and flinched in surprise. "My word, Cy. You can't be sneaking up on me like that." She laughed without much humor and put one hand to her chest. "You scared me."

"Sorry." Cyrus grinned, enjoying the sound of his nickname. He sat on the edge of a rickety wooden bench left by a former occupant of the old house.

Ada stood and wiped her hands on her apron. "Have you been here long?" There was no accusation in her voice. He couldn't tell if she actually cared about the answer or was just trying to make conversation.

"No, not long." He propped one ankle on his knee and looked around. "The garden looks nice."

"Thanks." She wiped sweat off her forehead and eyed the beds. "I don't quite know what I'm doing, but we'll see how it goes."

She laughed lightly. Cyrus' chest burned.

Ada looked at him, her eyes cool and steady. "You here to check on Isabella?"

"Yes. Well, both of you, but yes." He cleared his throat and sat straighter. "She told me about the baby."

Ada stiffened.

"I figured it out," he hastened to add. "But she confirmed it. I won't tell him." He watched her shoulders relax. "Not for as long as I can help it."

Ada studied him. "And how long will that be?"

He sighed. "I don't know." He would not lie to her. He never lied to her.

Ada nodded. She dropped her gaze to the ground and pushed at a clump of dirt with her shoe. "She really loves him, you know. The Magister."

Cyrus nodded. "I know." He took his hat off and swiped hair back from his forehead. "I've tried to tell him."

"But you'll protect the baby, won't you?" She was watching him again. Pleading with him.

"I'll do my best." It was all he could promise.

Neither of them spoke for a moment. Ada looked out over the garden beds, her expression worried and distant.

Cyrus toyed with his hat. Finally he stood and cleared his throat. "I won't keep you any longer. Just wanted to make sure you're—everyone is okay."

"Thank you." She said it sincerely.

Cyrus met her eyes. He opened his mouth to say something more, then closed it again. *Let it be.* "Goodbye, then. I'll come again soon, bring you girls some of Gertie's lemon cake."

"We'd like that." Ada grinned. "I miss that stuff." She reddened a little, coughed, and edged away. "Bye, Cyrus."

Ada went back to her weeding. She did not look up again. Cyrus paused only a second, then turned and left.

31

GEORGE

CIRCA 2023

George buckled down to his novel again, intent on finishing the next chapters and not thinking about strange songs or conversations for awhile.

It worked, at first. He returned to his routine—early morning cup of coffee, several hours of work at his laptop in the attic, sandwich for lunch, a leisurely walk down the road, a cup of tea, then novel work again until it was either dinnertime, or his mind was too drained to continue.

He lay in bed one night while the wind rustled ever-changing leaves outside, and the clock ticked away in the corner. A week had passed since the Lady's visit. George could no longer help pondering what Isabella had said.

That song he brought has power to it. Dangerous power. This music will bring only death.

Death from music? That didn't make much sense.

Not that any of this really does.

Songs were songs, were they not? Just music. Not a matter of life and death.

A memory hit George like a dump truck. He was eight years old. That was the year his parents died. He was sitting in Aunt Pam's lap, curled against her shoulder. The frizzed ends of her hair tickled his face. Her perfume smelled like one of those flower-scented candles at the dollar store. She was singing.

George concentrated on the memory. This was the first time, ever, that he had remembered it. Most of that year following his parents' death was a blank wall.

He could not remember which song she sang. That part didn't matter. He only remembered that he felt safe.

She sang for a long time. When she stopped, the feeling quelled and vanished. George climbed off her lap and left the room.

That night, he had overheard his aunt and uncle whispering by his open bedroom door. They must have thought he was asleep.

"It's like magic, Barry," Aunt Pam said. Her voice was raspier than usual. "He never lets me touch him. No hugs, no head pats, nothing."

"Can't blame the kid," Uncle Barry answered.

" 'Course not. He misses his mama, poor thing, and I'm not her." She sighed. "I imagine it'll take awhile. I hate to see him hurting like that, though, and not be able to comfort him the way a kid ought to be comforted."

Uncle Barry had *hmmed* in agreement.

"But Barry," Aunt Pam went on. "When I sing, it's like a light flicks on. Doesn't matter what songs, and we both know I'm no Aretha Franklin. Folk tunes, nursery rhymes, the old hymns. I'd sing to him all day if I could, but my voice gives out."

She had coughed a wheezing cough. It was quiet for a minute. George thought at first that they had left his doorway. He was about to open his eyes, but then,

"I see something soften in him," Aunt Pam continued. "That boy crawls up in my lap and stays there as long as the songs last. Just like magic, Barry. I swear, it's like a magic charm."

They had left then, headed down the hallway toward their own room. George didn't remember much past that. Only that he had lain awake in the dark for a long time, wishing the songs could last forever.

George felt the same desire now, lying in the dark in his cottage by the forest. Loneliness sank into his bones. It ached. He listened to the crickets outside the window, then sighed and pulled the covers up higher over his shoulders.

He still did not understand. He didn't understand lots of things. Certainly not why God let some things happen. But he had long since reconciled with his parents' deaths, his crippled leg, and the way he just never seemed to fit in with other people. Maybe he didn't need to know why.

He had reconciled with the death of his wife, too. Mostly, anyway. That had taken a long time.

George rubbed the creases out of his forehead and tried to think. All that stuff was in the past. This was the here and now.

Should he give any credence to what the Lady claimed about the song? There was no saying for sure. He didn't know what to think, but he was too much entrenched to pretend none of his past weeks with the cottagers had happened.

And, George admitted to himself, he cared about the people. Genuinely. Jasper and Lillian and the Stones, anyway, and the others by default. He couldn't just leave them in their cursed existence and act like all was fine.

But if the music really was dangerous…

Well, that remained to be seen.

He needed to figure out what had really happened. What did the Lady know about the song that she hadn't shared with him? She had seemed authentic in her warning. He did not doubt her opinion on the matter, but there was something missing, something about the two vastly different understandings of the music that demanded an explanation.

And, George knew, he wanted to finish that song. Dangerous or not. He wanted to hear the whole thing, experience it all, see what would happen. The light...the vibrant urgency...it was not easily forgotten.

But if it was dangerous for the cottagers...

Wait a minute.

George sat up.

"They can't die," he said aloud.

The curse. The stopped time. Why was the Lady afraid of people dying when they were trapped in time, never growing older even by a day? Would the song kill them all at once? George sat for a moment, staring at the blank wall of his bedroom, his forehead creased in thought. Finally he laid down and jerked the covers back up to his chest.

Tomorrow, he would go find Isabella Crane.

32

ISABELLA

CIRCA 2023

Isabella Crane walked the upstairs hallway of her mansion. There were several upstairs hallways. This was the one in which she usually found herself pacing back and forth in the loneliest hours of the night.

This hallway felt the most like home. Like what home should have been. What it once was, before everything went wrong.

She walked with long, graceful strides to the window at the far end. Turn, swish. Then a slow, even walk to the staircase at the other end. Turn, swish. Repeat.

Her silk robe was comfortably soft against her skin. She had untwisted her pile of hair and let it fall in amber waves over her shoulders. That was what made the swishing sound with each turn. Her hair, less fine than it once was, brushing over silk. Turn, swish.

Isabella kept her gaze on the window at the end of the hallway. This hallway was much like the hallway in her girlhood home. That one, too, had a window. And watercolor paintings. Her mother had loved watercolor. In fact, Isabella had managed to find prints of some of the same scenes that had hung in her family's hallway. She had placed them as near as she could to where their original counterparts would have been.

She paused at the window. Just a millisecond. Then turned.

The staircase was less like her childhood. It was regal and polished, the wood gleaming like gold under the lamp sconces. Her childhood stairs had been pretty, also, but she remembered them as being more friendly, more inviting to little girls sliding down the rails, and less susceptible to dust.

No, this staircase she had copied from the mansion in the city. The Magister's mansion. In fact, almost every other part of the house was modeled after that home she had longed for as a grown woman. Longed for and been denied.

Turn, swish.

The window. How often she and Ada had crowded together by the window long ago. They would look out over the rolling expanse of lawns and trees, imagining fairy castles in the branches and reindeer in the snow.

And the music. Their mother would play cello in the library. They would hear the sound coming through the double oak doors that were always left open. Rich, beautiful songs with a depth that made Isabella's heart ache with a longing she could not name.

Their father played the piano. Sometimes, when he was home early, they would both play. Piano and cello would meld together like two birds of different voice and color, sometimes joyous, sometimes desperately sad.

Isabella and Ada would sit in the hallway and listen. They would lean shoulder-to-shoulder against the wall, heads back, and listen to the music.

Isabella had double oak doors in this hallway, too. There was a piano behind them. She had let Lux learn to play, as a boy. Sometimes she had regretted it when he got older and played better. The pain was too much. She would yell at him to stop. He would, and he'd look hurt, and she would never tell him why.

"I just can't take too much of the sound," she would say. "You play beautifully. I just can't take too much."

She did not tell him that the music reminded her of her father. That it sank into her heart and awakened feelings she had buried deep beneath sorrow and stone.

Isabella squeezed her hands around her arms.

Another turn.

The window. She and Ada, ten and twelve at the time, had been looking out of their window when the rider came galloping over the road, spraying gravel and dust as he pulled to a halt in front of the house.

He came with news. Their father was dead. Accident at the depot. Killed instantly. No suffering.

No suffering. Maybe not for her father. *They* suffered. They all suffered. Isabella remembered the shock, the ripping, crushing emptiness. How could her father be gone in an instant? No more to come through the door and sweep her up like an armful of roses?

Their mother had shrieked. One long, rending wail, and she was broken. She had become a silent shell. No words of comfort for her daughters, no healing embrace, no "We'll get through this together."

Just big, empty eyes and still hands.

She had died a month later.

Isabella, at ten years old, found that death was unknown and dark and terrible. Death struck with no warning. Death took a person's happiness and security. Death was the ruiner of life.

Turn, swish.

The stairway. There had been no more rides down the stair rail for her and Ada. No more laughter for a long time. Only solemn-faced lawyers and neighbors full of pity.

Their parents had left them a great deal of money. Income would not be a problem. It still was not a problem. There was plenty left.

Men in dark suits had sold the house and furniture, set the girls up with trusts and accounts, and sent them to live with a distant relative.

Ada had cried.

Isabella had not.

She pushed all that terrible emptiness down and vowed to hold the reins of her own life. She would make whatever decisions led to greatest happiness. She would spite any who stood in her way. Death was her terror and her enemy.

They had grown up, she and Ada. She was proud, confident, stunning. Ada was quiet, steady, not afraid of anything. Ada had, as far as Isabella could see, healed from the pain of their parents' deaths. Isabella despised her for it.

Then there was the Magister and the Pearls. The sudden rise to love and power. The invitation to a new home. Isabella had reveled in it. Here were heights of happiness and security.

Then the blow of disappointment. New pain. Exiled from the Magister and his house while carrying his child.

She had given birth to Lux, her own son, without his father ever knowing he existed.

Turn, swish.

Five years of secrecy, then she had fled. She had taken Lux and fled to Green Meadows to hide from the Magister. She knew nothing of Green Meadows before then; she only wanted to get away—far enough away that Cyrus and the Magister would not find them. Green Meadows was so small. Unnoticeable. A smidge of existence in a much greater world. It would do.

She had almost killed Ada that night she and Lux fled...almost been the causer of death. It was not on purpose. She was angry at Ada, sure. Angry at her and tired of her patience and optimism. Tired of how unafraid she was.

Isabella didn't want Ada to come into hiding with her and Lux. The older they had gotten, the more she felt repelled by her sister. Ada still liked music and laughter. She acted as though life were serene and simple, and she tried to make Isabella think so too. Isabella couldn't stand it anymore.

They had quarreled, there at the old farmhouse. Ada had insisted she would follow them, claimed she would follow them to the train station and stall them if she had to, even if it meant pulling the rails off the ground so the train couldn't leave.

"I don't care if it breaks the Code," Ada had said. "I don't care if every person on the train sees it happen. You can't leave me behind."

Isabella had scoffed at Ada. She was far more powerful, and they both knew it. But Ada *would* follow them, if she could. Isabella knew that too. So she had taken Ada's Gifts. Pulled them right out of her blood like water from the ground.

But oh, the shriveling...the sight of her sister drying up like a prune there on the kitchen floor—

She would not think about it. That was long ago.

Long ago, yes, but guilt lasts a lifetime. She had almost been the bearer of death to her own sister. Her sister who had never left her. Her sister who had always been her friend.

Everything Isabella had done since then had been to make up for that one terrible act. She became benefactor and protector of the cottagers in every way she could.

Without using much of her Gifts, of course—she couldn't risk Cyrus or the Magister somehow finding out where she and Lux were hiding.

She had held back from teaching Lux the more powerful Gifts. There was too much risk. Even handling water was out of the question. They would endure droughts in other ways. There was too much potential that word would spread of a tiny town in the middle of nowhere that was immune to drought and disease. Cyrus would find them. The Magister would find them.

No. Keeping Lux and herself safe was the most important thing. But she did what she could for the cottagers. It helped assuage her conscience.

Turn, swish.

Then Lux brought that song, excruciating in its power. Only a few notes had terrified her beyond reckoning. It wasn't just the pain of memory, not just the ordinary effect of music. This song was different. It twisted in the core of her being like a storm about to burst the world apart.

She abhorred the feeling. It was otherworldly. Deathly.

Lux had stepped back for awhile, and she felt as though she had lost him. He left their home, his home here in Green Meadows, and moved into one of those peasant cottages. He had a strange light in his eye and was easily excited. She could sense the song in him. It had changed him. He wouldn't be able to stand much more. There was too much power.

Then that terrible night when Lux had come to her, insisting on playing the whole piece. She had tried to stop it. If she could pull the terrible power of that song away from Lux, away from Green Meadows, use her strength to draw it out of Green Meadows the way she could draw water from the ground or sickness from the blood...

She had tried. She waged every bit of her Gifts against it, and almost succeeded. But she was too late.

Death had won again. Lux, her son, the light of her life, was gone.

Turn, swish.

Isabella stopped. The hallway was silent except for her own breathing and the pounding pulse in her ears.

No more music. Anywhere. She had banned it from Green Meadows. Ordinary music was pain. That particular song was death. And now...

She started walking again.

Now George Morgan was here, and he was teaching the cottagers the song. Where, for goodness' sake, had George Morgan come from? She couldn't piece it together. He was not from their time; that much was obvious. He was not Gifted; that was obvious too. He was, seemingly, quite ordinary. And not very intelligent, for that matter.

How did he get here? No one else had gotten in or out of Green Meadows in more than a century. Isabella had tried to make things right, tried to will time back to its correct course, but to no avail.

Now George—an unGifted, middle-aged, crippled man from the future—had shown up out of nowhere and gotten himself involved with the cottagers and the song. It unnerved her. *He* unnerved her. What could he possibly do that she could not?

She didn't know. Right now, she didn't know what to do about it, either, other than to try and intimidate him enough to change his mind. That should be easy enough. How could someone like George stand against someone like her?

She held the reins; George Morgan did not. He could find that out if he dared.

Isabella reached the staircase. She paused, turned, looked back at the window once more, a dark rectangle glinting at the end of the hall.

She clenched her jaw and turned away.

33

GEORGE

CIRCA 2023

George started into the forest early the next morning. He hoped he wouldn't run into anyone he knew. He wanted to sort things out with the Lady before he met up again with the cottagers.

He made it past Jasper's place without incident. It occurred to George that he did not actually know how to get to Isabella's estate. From what the others had said, her house was by far the largest and fanciest. He assumed it would be easy to spot.

The familiar prickle in his stomach squirmed to life and urged him to go back to aloneness and normalcy. Those were comfortable. Predictable.

George distracted himself from it by imagining the town somewhere ahead. He had often wondered what it would be like to step back in time and see how life worked in previous eras. Now the past had stepped forward to meet him instead.

A mile after Jasper's, the trees opened into a broad meadow, and the town came into view. It was much like he had pictured, though perhaps a bit larger.

More than half a dozen shops lined the main street. George saw a tailor, two general stores, and a feed supply, among others. The buildings were simple wooden structures. Some had two stories, others a false front with a tall facade of wood and windows made to look like a second level.

Sheesh. He had read about stuff like this in pioneer books. It was eerie to see it in person. Fascinating, though.

People had tied horses and ponies to hitching posts along the street. Women wore long dresses with pleated skirts. Men had overalls, or trousers held up by suspenders. Some wore suits with short neckties, more like handkerchiefs in a fancy knot.

Small children walked with parents or scuffed bare feet in the dirt. Older kids seemed to be doing much the same jobs as many of the adults. Boys pushed carts and carried loads. Girls in calf-length dresses bustled in and out of stores with baskets on their arms.

No school? Maybe it wasn't the season. Or maybe, George realized, kids had no need for more school after the first five or ten years. A hundred and fifty sounded like straight torture.

An array of cottages sprawled from the edges of town onto several other dirt-packed streets that crossed the meadow and disappeared into the far edge of the forest. Chickens and goats meandered through yards. People walked here and there, attending to their daily duties in and out of houses, gardens, and shops.

The townspeople gaped at George as he walked by. A few women shrieked. One dropped a basket of blueberries. They rolled, unnoticed, into the dirt.

He heard gasps and whispers scattering from every shop, yard, and street corner. George did his best to appear nonchalant and polite, which mostly came out as a stiff, hurried gait and a tight-lipped smile cast to various passersby.

"Where does the Lady live?" he asked a young man who stood pale and wide-eyed by a pile of grain sacks.

The boy pointed further up the street and to the right. When he spoke, his voice sounded tighter than a water balloon about to burst.

"Two whoops and a holler that a'way," he said. "Just beyond th' edge of town. Her lane's got a row of poplars on each side and a gate at th' end."

George thanked him and limped on.

"Sir, you sure you wanna..." the boy began, but George waved without stopping, and the boy trailed off.

George found the lane just as the boy had described. Tall poplar trees lined both sides, like sentries stationed in two long rows. The lane was long enough that George could only make out some white pillars that marked the front of the Lady's house where the trees narrowed beyond clear vision.

He tried the gate. It was not locked. George pushed it open and closed it carefully behind him before starting up the lane.

He had no idea what he would find, and very little idea of what he would say to the Lady if he could gain an audience with her.

Good morning, Ms. Crane. Remember how you showed up unannounced at my door a couple weeks ago? I'm here to return the favor.

George rolled his eyes and hobbled on. Oh, how he despised awkward conversations. Yet here he was, walking right into one of his own accord. The prickle in his stomach acidified, but George pressed on. He was determined to see this through.

Memories of the song danced through his mind, urging him forward. He wanted, beyond anything, to taste that burning beauty again. But he must find out the truth first.

George slowed as the mansion came into full view. It was, in its own right, a mansion. The white columns lined a wide, beautiful porch. Just the edge of the sprawling, three-story house with balconies, towers, and windows. George gawked. The cottagers said it was big, but this was beyond what he had expected. *Why did Isabella come here, of all places, to live in riches?*

Behind the house, a stone wall rambled across a meadow toward, he assumed, another edge of the forest visible beyond. He could see several arched doorways set into this side of the wall. Gardens, perhaps?

"What d'ye think ye're doin'?" a voice growled.

George jumped and whirled toward it. His bad leg stuck mid-turn. He stumbled, but caught himself before falling completely. Pain shot from hip to foot. George steadied himself and stood.

Reuben waited near the left corner of the house with a rake held in one meaty hand. George swallowed and forced his voice to sound calm.

"I came to see Ms. Crane."

"Did ye now," Reuben rumbled, stepping nearer. "And what makes you think she wants to see you?"

He scanned George up and down in a glance. George did the same to him. He was taller than George, and paunchy. Stubbled beard, greasy hair, small, pale eyes.

When Reuben looked back to his face, though, George could see a hint of confusion. He knew Reuben was aware of his being in Green Meadows, but from the wary expression, George guessed he did not know what to expect.

George hoped he could use this to his advantage. Perhaps Reuben, for all his bark, was as thrown off by George's coming as the townspeople.

George looked him square in the eye. "Because she came to see me first." His voice had surety this time. He felt a flicker in his gut, an ember of confidence flaring into flame. He thought again of the song. The last prickle of unease shrank to almost nothing.

He stepped toward Reuben. "She came with questions. I have answers."

Reuben's eyes narrowed. He didn't speak. His grip on the rake tightened, and George had the fleeting thought that maybe the man would impale him right there. Fear washed over him, but George shoved it away. This fire, this surety, must keep burning. It must.

George kept his eyes fixed on Reuben's. As much as Reuben tried to hide it, George saw the discomfort in the man's face. Here was someone used to bullying as needed to get his way. But George, beyond all expectation, unsettled him.

"Wait here," Reuben grumbled finally. He propped the rake near the front door and stalked inside.

George took a deep breath and let it out slowly. *This is going rather well,* he thought. He hadn't had to run away, and he had not been stabbed with the rake. Both good signs.

Reuben returned moments later and jerked his head toward the stairs inside. "Come with me. Take yer shoes off," he added, eying George's dusty tennis shoes. "She don't like dirt tracked in."

George glanced at Reuben's feet, now devoid of work boots, and nodded. He left his shoes on the front porch and followed the man inside. Reuben lumbered up the stairs. George came after him, hauling his still-aching leg like it was full of concrete.

To his relief, the Lady was in a room just beyond the top of the stairs. Reuben stopped by the doorway, glared at George, and twitched his head in the Lady's general direction. George saw her seated at a small table by a window that overlooked the back grounds. He nodded once at Reuben and stepped inside.

The room looked unexpectedly cheerful. Or at least, it could have been if not for the scowling woman. White lace curtains hung along the edges of the windows, and pleasant sunlight streamed through the room. Ornate sofas and chairs were arranged near a stone fireplace. There was no fire.

"Mr. Morgan. What a surprise," Isabella said, not looking at George. She looked anything but surprised. Sullen, perhaps, only partially masked by obligation of polite hospitality.

"Good morning, Ms. Crane." He looked back at the doorway. Reuben was gone.

"Lady Crane, please, Mr. Morgan. I have already told you once, that where I come from, titles mean something."

"Where do you come from?"

She glanced at him now—a shrewd, narrow glance. "None of your business."

"Fair enough," George muttered, and then continued more loudly. "Look, Ms. Crane. Lady Crane, sorry." He started to rub his forehead, then shoved both hands in his pockets. "I thought more about what you said. About the music, I mean." George cleared his throat. "I wanted to talk with you about it."

Isabella sipped from a porcelain cup. "I don't care to talk about the song, Mr. Morgan."

"Well I'll at least answer your question then. Yes, I've been helping the cottagers learn a song, and yes, I believe it's one that your son brought."

Isabella set her cup back on its saucer and wiped the corners of her mouth with delicate movements. She shifted in her seat to face George, and studied him for a moment.

"Why are you telling me this now?" she asked, her voice calm, but her eyes cold.

George set his jaw. "Because I have questions too."

"Is that so." The Lady turned back to the table and resumed sipping.

"What will happen if people play the song?"

"I already told you. Death."

"How do you know?"

Isabella did not look up. "Don't test me, Mr. Morgan."

"I'm not trying to test you, I'm trying to find out the truth."

"The truth?" She gave a short, harsh laugh. "Truth comes in many layers."

George shrugged. "I don't agree."

"You don't agree?" Isabella shot him a look of pure disdain. "What you agree or don't agree with, Mr. Morgan, means nothing to me." She laughed again. "Do you know why I haven't finished you yet? Why you're still here?"

"Because of your burning curiosity?" George said, not bothering to hide the sarcasm in his voice. Could she kill him? He wasn't sure. From what Jasper had told him, she probably could, but the idea seemed silly, standing here by her tea table.

"Because I feel sorry for you." The Lady looked him up and down. She shook her head in mock pity. "You're embarrassing, crippled, and out of place. You don't belong here." She spat the last four words out like bitter herbs.

George pondered the effect of those words. They did not sting the way he would have expected. Instead, beyond all reckoning, he felt compassion for this woman. She looked fragile, like a once-beautiful tree that had been poisoned with long years of...what? *Sorrow, surely.* She had lost her son, after all. But what else? *Lies? Disappointment?*

Get to the point, George.

"It's not about me. I'm just wondering about the song." George kept his voice steady. "Why do you hate it so much?"

"How dare you question me!" The Lady's voice dripped with venom. "My reasons are none of your business."

"The song *is* my business," George said, his voice rising now. "I didn't ask for it, but it's my business whether you like it or not, and I need to know the truth."

"The truth," she scoffed. "What do you care about the truth?"

"Just tell me what happens," George demanded. "How do you know it causes death?"

Isabella set her cup down hard. It clattered against the saucer and sloshed onto the white tablecloth.

"Because it killed my son." She turned toward George, her eyes blazing. "It was that stupid song that killed my

Lux. He came to tell me again how marvelous it was, how beautiful, how much good it might do. I told him it was dangerous, but he wouldn't listen. I told him there is power to such things, told him not to dabble with magic outside his expertise. He wouldn't listen. He called me afraid.

"Of course I was afraid." Isabella stood now, her thin figure leering, her fists clenched. "I was afraid for good reason. I know power of the extraordinary, but this was something different. Something terrifying. I begged Lux not to do it, but he insisted. 'Just once, Mother. Just listen to it one time. Let me play it all the way through for you just this once.'"

Isabella sat down, trembling. She picked up a handkerchief and twisted the embroidered corner. "He didn't make it all the way through. I thought of every possible means to stop him, to save him. There was one way that might work. That might combat that terrible power. But before I finished..." She took a shuddering breath. "He was gone."

"You stopped time," George said quietly. "You stopped time to force his hand."

"I stopped the music," Isabella shot back. "I pulled the song out, flung it away from here. Away from Green Meadows." She glared at George, then looked away. "I didn't know it would stop time."

Isabella turned her back to George. She stared out the window. "I was too late anyway."

George pondered this for a moment. *Pulled the song out?* It didn't make sense. "Pulled it out of what?"

"Everything." She did not turn around. "Almost everything. I only pulled part of it. I didn't complete it entirely. Lux was already gone. That song—" She turned back toward George. Her voice hardened and dripped with bitterness. "That song is like poison. It..." She raised her eyebrows. "You really are daft, aren't you? Do you understand any of this?"

George shrugged.

"Music," the Lady said, as if she were an exasperated teacher explaining a math problem to a child, "music is not just sound. It sinks into people, affects them in ways that other things can't. Most music is harmless, but this song..."

Her eyebrows narrowed. "This song is riddled with power. It is like infection in a wound. I tried, don't you see? I could sense the song sinking into the whole village like a poisonous gas. I pulled it out, flung it away from Green Meadows. I tried to pull it away from Lux, but he had already drunk too much."

Isabella threw the handkerchief onto the table. She picked up her tea.

George thought hard. He was pushing the Lady's patience, but there was one more question that he had to ask.

"Why didn't you undo it? Why have you left it stopped?"

Isabella said nothing for several minutes. Then, as if rousing out of a dream, she stirred and looked at George. "I can't. I've tried."

She stared at him in disgust. "And now you want to risk the lives of us all. My life. Was Lux's death not enough?"

Isabella's eyes pierced like daggers. *If looks could kill,* George thought, amazed that he did not feel more afraid of her.

"That song," she spat, "is death." She stood and faced him. "And what would you know of death?"

George's teeth clenched. It took effort, monumental effort, not to speak.

"If you do not cease your endeavors to have the cottagers play that song…" Isabella continued. She spoke every word as if it cost her great effort. Like all her insides were raging flames, and she was only barely holding them back from consuming George there on the spot. "If you choose not to cease," she said again, "I will cut off your tongue, your fingers, and every other means you have. You will not kill me, you hear?" Her voice rose in pitch and volume. "You will not kill me!"

The last sentence was almost a shriek. Isabella reached one hand toward George. He took a step backward. His movement seemed to flip a switch in whatever chaos was roiling in her mind.

Her hand stopped short. Her face slackened. Shaking, she sat back down in her chair.

George let out a long breath.

Isabella propped her head on one hand and closed her eyes. Strands of fading auburn brushed her cheeks like autumn leaves on tired branches.

At last she sighed and picked up her porcelain cup. "Go now," she said, her voice once again even. "Do not come back."

George watched her for a moment, then nodded. He turned to go. At the doorway he looked back.

"Thank you for your time, Lady Crane."

She only flicked her hand toward him, as if he were a fly she wanted gone.

George passed Reuben on the way off the porch. Reuben glared at him, but said nothing.

So many questions, so few answers. He had a headache, and his leg felt like someone had run it through with a screwdriver. George hoped he wouldn't see anyone he knew on the way home.

34

CYRUS

CIRCA 1858

Cyrus set out for the old farmhouse. It was time to check in on the Cranes. He went by at least once a month, though only at night now that Isabella's son was old enough to retain memories.

He wanted as little direct contact as possible with the kid. The less Lux knew at this age, the better. They still did not know what kind of abilities he would have, though he clearly had some. Isabella had been training him since toddlerhood.

He was five years old now, almost six. Almost to registration age.

Cyrus hired a cab and settled into the seat. The carriage wheels clattered away from the mansion, and the cityscape began to roll by out the window. He pulled his hat low, though it was dark outside other than what glow the street lamps and windows offered.

Isabella was being stubborn. Cyrus didn't blame her. She was afraid. But still, did she really think she could keep putting off registering the boy? He doubted it.

She would cave soon; she would have to. Not registering Lux as a member of the Gifted would be a direct breaking of the Code. Isabella would not break the Code. Cyrus didn't believe she had the capability to go against the Magister, even if she wanted to.

Still, he was getting nervous. She was waiting too long.

Cyrus wondered what the Magister would do when he learned he had a son. A son whom Isabella, and Cyrus himself, had hidden from him all this time.

He will be furious.

Would he be glad though? Proud of a progeny? Cyrus hoped so, but his friend was getting ever more unpredictable. The Magister's insistence on control consumed him. He had gone and married Isabella, then sent her away. He had never entirely gotten over her, either. Just made the calculated decision, after the fact, that would best serve his power and stuck with it.

It was too bad. Isabella would have served him faithfully.

But a kid...there was no saying.

Cyrus pushed away the thought that he had made his own calculated decision not to tell the Magister, and that he had carefully crafted an explanation that would, most likely, keep himself in the Magister's favor.

This was not about him. He was looking out for his friend's own good, best he knew how.

Cyrus glanced outside. They were passing the edge of the city. Only a few more minutes now.

And what of Ada? She had given up on him years ago. He could see it in her eyes, the rare times she was around during his visits. She treated him with polite indifference, nothing else. No more "Cy," even by mistake.

He was the messenger, the bearer of bad news that had assisted his friend and hurt her sister. Any hopes she may have once had for him were buried beneath that unfortunate truth.

Cyrus groaned and rubbed his eyes. It had all seemed so simple once…before the Crane sisters walked across the bridge.

The carriage stopped. Cyrus climbed out.

"Should be about half an hour," he told the driver. "Just wait for me at the corner over there near the main road. I won't be long." The carriage pulled away.

Cyrus turned toward the house. It was dark. That was unusual. He ascended the steps, flicked a finger. The lock slid back. Cyrus opened the door, cautiously at first.

There was something wrong. All his senses told him so.

"Isabella?" He surveyed the entry. It looked normal—same neat bench in the corner, same fern.

Cyrus passed through the entry, checking in doorways as he went. The parlor was dark and quiet, the dining room deserted.

"Isabella?" He listened. Nothing. "Ada?"

The house smelled stale. No lingering scent of dinner or candle wax, just old wood and dusty linens.

Cyrus' nerves were tight as drum leather. This was not right. This was not at all right. He moved faster now. Seeing the staircase, he took the steps two at a time and ducked through each doorway at the top. Ada's bedroom was up here, and a small washroom. Both were dark and silent.

Cyrus ran back downstairs and through the hall. Here was Lux's room. He looked inside. No Lux asleep in bed. A few clothes were strewn about the floor, and one of the dresser drawers left open.

Cyrus' heart pounded faster.

They had run away. *Surely not.* Where would they hide? The city was all they knew.

Cyrus ducked out the doorway and entered Isabella's room. No one. Some paintings were missing from the walls, and her closet stood empty.

"No, no, no!" Cyrus' mouth was dry as sawdust. *What will the Magister do?* "Stupid," he muttered. "Isabella, this was a stupid idea."

He checked the washroom just to make sure, but it, too, was abandoned. Cyrus strode back to the main part of the house. He crossed the dining room into the kitchen. A single lamp burned low on the table in the corner. Cyrus ran to it. There were scattered table linens and some half-eaten biscuits with an open jar of jam.

Someone coughed. Cyrus nearly jumped out of his skin.

Huddled on the floor, just beyond the table, was an old woman. She was tiny and shriveled. Her veins stood out in stark, wrinkled lines on her neck. Her hair was a fluff of ashen grey. She sat in a ball with her eyes closed, apparently asleep.

Cyrus swore under his breath and crouched near her. He didn't want to touch her at first. She looked too fragile. *What in the blazes is going on?* Had the Cranes hired a maid?

"Ma'am?" He spoke loudly and touched her shoulder. She groaned. "Ma'am, are you alright?"

The woman coughed again. She opened her eyes just a sliver, then squeezed them shut.

"What happened?" Cyrus' voice was urgent. Demanding. "Do you need a doctor?"

The woman shook her head. That was good. She understood him, at least.

Cyrus stood. He crossed the kitchen in three long strides and filled a glass with water from a pitcher. Returning to the woman, he put the glass to her lips and tilted it gently. "Here. Drink."

She did. Timidly at first, then large gulps. She coughed once, inhaled a long, deep breath, and relaxed against the wall, still keeping her eyes closed.

"Better?"

The woman nodded.

"What happened?" Cyrus set the glass on the table. "Where's the family that lived here? Two sisters and a young boy?"

The woman spoke so softly, Cyrus could not hear her at first. He leaned his ear close to her face. "What was that?"

Her voice was gravelly. It shook when she spoke again. "Gone."

"Gone?" Cyrus' stomach dropped. "Where'd they go? What happened?"

"She..." The woman coughed.

Cyrus gave her a drink of water, then leaned close again.

"She took..."

"Took what?" He pulled back with a quizzical look. "Took what? I don't understand."

The woman's chin trembled. Her face...it was so puckered and ancient. Where had they found this poor lady? Maybe she was a charity case. Maybe she had shown up on the doorstep, and they had brought her in to take care of her. It was hard to imagine Isabella allowing such a thing, but maybe.

She opened her mouth to speak again. Cyrus leaned in.

"She took it from me," she rasped. "She pulled it out of my veins."

Goosebumps ran up Cyrus' arms. The lady was crazy. She must be. "But where are they? Where did they go?"

She shook her head.

"Did they tell you where they were going?"

Another head shake.

"When did they leave?"

A pause, then, "Yesterday."

Yesterday. He had barely missed them. Frustration burned in his gut. Fear, too. He had not seen this coming.

He stood so fast that the old woman flinched. Cyrus hurried to the parlor. Isabella lived and breathed for the Magister's approval. She would not have gone far. And Ada would never abandon her sister.

They must be close.

He grabbed an afghan from the back of the sofa and returned to the kitchen. "I have to go look for them," he said, loud enough to be sure the old woman heard him. "I have to find them. Do you understand?"

She nodded.

Cyrus laid the blanket over her shriveled body. "I'll come back for you, okay? I'll be back later tonight. Are you sure you don't need a doctor?"

A tear squeezed out of one eye, but she shook her head. "No doctor." Cyrus hesitated, but the woman said it again, more firmly this time. "No doctor."

"Alright."

He gave her another drink of water and put the glass where she could reach it.

"I'll come back, okay? I'll come as soon as I can. I just...I have to find them before it's too late."

"She pulled it out of me." The woman hunched forward and cried in earnest.

Urgency roared in Cyrus' chest. "I don't know what that means. I'm sorry." He bent quickly and tucked the afghan so it wouldn't slide off. "I'll be back. Just stay here."

Cyrus gave her one last, discomfited glance and ran out the door.

He went to the mansion first, urging speed into the carriage driver with every swear word he could muster. There was no sign of the Cranes there. Mounted on his own horse, Cyrus began a desperate search of every corner of the city.

He asked at the train station, but the ticket master did not remember seeing two sisters and a little boy traveling together.

"There's all blamin' sorts o' people that coulda' come through 'ere," he protested, seeming disconcerted by Cyrus' urgency. "Could be just about anyone in th' whole dratted city in a matter o' two days."

Cyrus checked every car waiting on the tracks. Nothing.

He went to every location he could possibly think of where Isabella and Ada may have sought refuge. Nothing.

The old woman weighed on his mind. She had looked in a bad way. He should go get her, bring her to a hospital just in case. She had seemed—

Cyrus stopped dead in his tracks.

The dress the woman was wearing.

It was dahlia purple.

Cyrus' face emptied of blood and all thought. There was only blankness. A desperate horror. He staggered and caught himself on the wall.

Ada.

Blood surged back through his brain, hot pain and fury. Cyrus leaped on his horse and raced toward the old house.

Maker of all things. What had Isabella done?

35

CYRUS

CIRCA 1858

Cyrus threw open the door of the old farmhouse before he even reached the steps.

"Ada?" He ran inside, calling her name. "Ada, I'm sorry, I didn't realize..."

He rushed into the kitchen and stopped short. The lamp was out. There was no one there.

"Ada?" He fumbled for a match and lit the lamp. His thoughts whirled like papers in a windstorm. *She was here. Where could she have gone? She was in no condition to...*

Where are Isabella and Lux?

Lux.

Isabella.

Gone.

Ada...

His Ada...

No. Not his. She had never been his.

But almost.

Gone.

Where? How could she—

On and on. Mixtures of fury, guilt, and fear roiled, bouncing like burning tumbleweeds through his scattered mind.

Again the mad rush through the house, the search of every corner and closet. He flung clothes aside, ransacked rooms, pulled curtains. He let his Gifts go rampant. Wind ravaged the rooms. Furniture smashed on the floor. He sent his hands this way and that, exposing every possible hiding place. His eyes searched desperately. They took in every detail. Searched for any sign of life.

Nothing. Only a scared mouse and a few displaced bugs.

Back in the kitchen at last, Cyrus collapsed in a chair. He dropped his head in his hands. Never in all his long life had he felt so incapable. So very lost. How had he missed so much?

This was his fault. Isabella and her kid gone, and Ada all but destroyed at Isabella's hand. How blind he had been. None of this should have happened. It was his job to keep an eye on them, and he had failed.

He took a deep breath. Another. It was not all lost. There was logic to this. There was a path to find.

It's your fault.

No. Yes. Not entirely.

You failed.

Then unfail. Figure it out. They didn't actually disappear. Find them.

Cyrus lifted his head and gave his surroundings another weary look.

Ada had barely been able to talk, but she had managed to leave before he got back. The biscuits and jam were gone. Maybe those had helped. He had not offered her any food. The thought bit his conscience. The water glass was empty. She had left it on the table by the...

Cyrus jumped.

There was a small slip of paper sticking out from under the edge of the glass. He grabbed it. It had printing on the back and was frayed on one end. It looked like it had been torn from the corner of a mailer catalogue.

Cyrus unfolded it. There, in shaky handwriting, was a note to him.

Cy, it's not your fault.

He groaned. If only that were true.

Izzy took Lux and fled. I don't know where they've gone. She took my Gifts; almost took my life. I don't know how. Please do not hold it against her.

I have a different life to live now. Not by choice, but so it is. I will find my way. Don't look for me, Cy. You have been guard dog long enough.

—Ada

Cyrus flinched. He stared at the last sentence. *Guard dog*...is that what he had been all this time?

He crumpled the paper and hurled it against the wall. It bounced pathetically and landed on the table in front of him.

He sighed, picked it up, flattened it out, and read it again.

It's not your fault.

It *was* his fault. And he didn't know how to fix it.

One thing was for sure: he would find Ada. He had to make sure she was okay, whether she liked it or not. Maybe he was just a guard dog in her eyes. At least he would be a loyal one.

Cyrus scowled and crumpled the paper again. He tossed it onto the empty biscuit plate, then pulled a matchbook out of his pocket, lit one, and watched the paper burn. When it was reduced to a pile of ash, he flung it into the fireplace.

Cyrus locked the door behind him and left the farmhouse for the last time.

Yes, he would find Ada. But first, he had to tell the Magister that the Crane sisters were gone.

Dawn was breaking over the city by the time Cyrus returned to the mansion. The Magister would be up within the hour. He was always an early riser.

Cyrus, on the other hand, was exhausted. And hungry.

He went to the kitchen. Gertie was there, working by lamplight. She sang quietly, her sleeves rolled up to the elbows, her arms wrist-deep in a floury mass. The room was cool, despite the fire. The smell of warm yeast and butter reminded Cyrus of his boyhood.

Peep hunched on his perch in the corner. He had his eyes closed and one leg pulled up into his belly feathers. Cyrus hoped he would stay that way.

"The trees, the trees, leaving the mark in the trees." Gertie's voice gargled over the words.

"Morning, Gertie."

Gertie jumped and flung one sticky hand to her chest. "Lands alive," she exclaimed, her eyes wide, and whiskers jiggling. "What ye doin' scarin' me half to death, eh?"

"Sorry. I didn't mean to startle you." Cyrus held both hands up, then crossed his arms and leaned against the counter.

"Didn't mean to startle Gertie, ha!" She clutched her dress front, leaving flour and sticky dough bits clinging to the fabric. "What'd ye think would 'appen, eh? Showin' up without warnin' at the crack o' daylight." She turned back to the counter and shoved her fists into the dough. "Didn't mean to startle," she grumbled.

"Sorry," Cyrus repeated. "I should have knocked, I just...didn't," he finished lamely.

Gertie eyed him. "Well that's about th' dumbest explanation I've ever 'eard."

"Alright, alright, you've made your point." Cyrus glanced around the kitchen. "I was just up early and had some time to kill. I was hoping to get some coffee and maybe a bite to eat."

"Hmph." She regarded him with one eyebrow raised. "Up early, is it? Or out late?"

Cyrus glanced at his rumpled, dirty suit. He reached a hand up and smoothed his hair. It felt gritty. "Out late. Same difference. I'm here early, aren't I?"

"Ye don't 'ave coffee at yer own house?"

"No. Look, Gertie, cut the questions, will you? I have enough on my mind right now." He massaged his forehead. "Do you have any coffee?"

"Over there by th' stove," she said, still with a hint of grumble.

Cyrus found the pot and poured himself a cup. The fresh aroma was a welcome salve for his tension.

"Thank you," he said after a long sip. "I didn't mean to startle you."

"Ah, shucks." Gertie wiped her hands on her apron and threw a towel over the ball of bread dough. "No 'arm done."

She waddled to the cabinet and pulled out a tin of shortbread. "Here. This'll tide ye over fer a bit."

He thanked her and took the tin. Cyrus sat by the fireplace, munching shortbread dunked in coffee. He watched the old woman putter around the kitchen.

"Gertie," he said after a few minutes. "You haven't happened to see either of the Crane sisters anytime recently, have you?"

"The Cranes?" She stopped wiping the counter and looked at him, her head cocked to one side. "Isabella and Ada?" Her voice was soft, but her eyes hardened. "I 'aven't seen hide nor hair of either one since ye sent 'em away."

She studied him. "Did ye go and lose 'em?"

Lose them? Cyrus remembered Ada's words. *You have been guard dog long enough.* The shortbread suddenly tasted like chalk. He swallowed and set the tin on the hearth.

"They've left. I don't know where."

"Huh." Gertie wiped her hands. "Serves ye right. Never deserved 'em anyhow." She slapped the rag onto the counter and scrubbed with vigor.

"Gertie, come on."

"I mean it!" Gertie flung the rag into the scrub bucket. She crossed her saggy arms over her chest and faced Cyrus.

Her jaw was set. Whiskers stuck out all directions, quivering like gelatin. "Ye never once deserved to have any piece o' life with those two girls. Ye and th' master gabblin' about with yer secret club, treatin' 'em like pawns on a chess board. Act like ye care about 'em, get 'em to fall in love with ye, then ship 'em off like a litter o' puppies ye got tired of."

Gertie stamped her foot, setting all her ample flesh jiggling. "Of course they left. They've got more sense than ye give 'em credit for."

Cyrus stared at her in surprise. "Gertie, I—"

"Don't bother tellin' me." She turned back to the counter and wrung soapy water out of the dishrag. "I don't want to hear yer excuses."

Gertie scrubbed. Cyrus watched her. She looked like a deflating balloon, rubbing the rag in the same circle again and again. He felt a hint of affection for her. She was a strange old woman, but stout as Irish beer and not afraid of him. It was refreshing.

Gertie let out a long sigh. "Ye're not all bad," she said, folding the rag into a neat square and setting it aside. She eyed him. "Just get a lick o' sense in ye so's yer not messin' with people that trust ye."

"I'll do my best." Cyrus tipped his head to her, then drained his coffee and set the cup by the sink.

"Gertie."

She looked at him.

"Have you seen them?"

"No. And if I 'ad, I wouldn't tell ye anyway."

Cyrus smiled. "I don't doubt it. You don't mind if I check, though."

Gertie rolled her eyes. "Lands alive, ye *are* a snooper. I'll show ye if ye insist on verifyin'. They ain't here."

"No need for that. I can just look around."

She narrowed her eyes. "This is my part o' the house, young man. Ye ain't gonna be touslin' through closets and drawers like ye own th' place. If ye want to search, I'll be th' one showin'."

Cyrus raised his hands. "Alright, alright. Fair enough."

He made her open every cabinet and closet, much to her annoyance, but satisfied himself that neither Isabella nor Ada were hiding under Gertie's protection.

Cyrus retrieved his hat from the hearth. He felt deadbeat tired. The coffee was sizzling through his system, at least. He was awake enough to navigate the wrath of the Magister.

"Thanks for breakfast, Gertie."

"Ah, shucks. It was nothin'."

She waved him away, but not before he saw the look of pity in her eyes. He wasn't on her bad side, at least. That must be a good thing.

Cyrus closed the kitchen door. It was time to face his friend.

36

CYRUS

CIRCA 1858

Cyrus ascended the narrow staircase and knocked on the door of the Magister's quarters. "It's just me," he said.

"Come in." His friend's voice sounded cheerful. That was a good place to start. It wouldn't last long.

He entered the room and closed the door behind him. The Magister was standing by the window straightening his necktie. His hair was wet and freshly combed. He glanced at Cyrus, then turned back to the window.

"Beautiful morning, isn't it?" the Magister said. "Look at that color."

The sun was rising. It cast a glowing swath of pink and orange across the sky. The sun's rim had just crested the horizon and was covering the city in golden light. It was beautiful, though Cyrus didn't take much time to admire it. He sat in a chair near the fire.

The Magister finished with the necktie and reached for a jacket. "What brings you over so early? You aren't usually here 'til breakfast." He paused, one arm of the jacket still dangling free. He studied Cyrus. "You look terrible. What happened?"

Cyrus did not waste time beating around the bush. He knew he would have to spill it anyway. *Might as well get it over with. Carefully.* He cleared his throat.

"Isabella and Ada left. I went to check on them last night. They're gone."

The Magister stared for a moment. His jaw dropped. Closed. Clenched. Slowly, he pulled the jacket off and laid it over a chair.

"Gone?" His voice was quiet. Cyrus could hear the anger simmering like a lava pool.

"Gone. Fled. I looked for them all night. Can't find a trace." He kept eye contact with his friend. It was crucial that the Magister see his unreservedness, his loyalty. "Ada is, I believe, still in the city, though it's possible she went further. She left a note. She..." Cyrus inhaled and let it out slowly. "She said Isabella stole her Gifts and left her there when she fled two days ago. Ada has gone to find her own way. Isabella has gone to hide."

Cyrus saw a myriad of emotions cross his friend's eyes. Anger, shock, compassion, bitterness. The anger remained. Slowly, and with evident control, the Magister put his hand to the windowsill where a spider sat basking in the corner. He opened his palm. The spider scuttled to the outstretched hand and crawled over the fingers, coming to rest in the center of the Magister's palm.

"That wretched woman." The Magister watched the spider hunched in his hand. He clenched his jaw. "She was always out for herself. I never should have taught her so much. You warned me, but I didn't listen." He paced the floor between the window and the fireplace, his palm open, the spider perched still as stone.

"She stole Ada's Gifts? Her sister?"

Cyrus nodded affirmation. "I saw Ada. Briefly."

The Magister stopped. "And you let her go?"

"I didn't realize it was her," Cyrus explained. "She looked all shriveled up. Like a hundred-year-old woman."

The Magister considered this, then resumed pacing. "That's the way it was with Smallguard when I had to take his Gifts." He shook his head, his face rigid. "She did that to her sister, huh? Just because?" His voice rose. "That's why we created the Code, Cyrus. To protect society from people like Isabella Crane. And now she's—"

The Magister picked up a chair with his free hand and hurled it against the wall. It hit with a shuddering crack and splintered into pieces.

Cyrus said nothing. The Magister paced, his face a mask of fury.

"I should have seen it coming," he muttered. "I should have listened in the beginning. Never should've let my head be turned." He whirled toward Cyrus. "Where did she go? Did Ada say anything about where she went?"

Cyrus shook his head. "Only that it was far away. I don't think Isabella told her where she was going. She didn't want Ada to follow."

The Magister stared, then went back to his long, furious strides. "Horrible woman. What does she have planned? She has something in mind. She must. She's more powerful than anyone but you and me. I gave her too much. Taught her too much."

He spun toward Cyrus again. "Does she really think we won't find her? Where would she go? She has high tastes. Not exactly a pauper's daughter. And she's alone, and Gifted. She's a fool to think she can hide from me."

"She's not alone."

The Magister froze. "You said Ada didn't go. She's..."

His face flushed dark red. If it was not for the impossibility of the thing, Cyrus could have sworn his friend's blood was boiling beneath the skin. The Magister looked at the spider. He bent his fingers down and smashed it. Opened his hand. Flicked it to the floor. It quivered and lay still.

"She's with another man?" His voice was low and dangerous.

"No, not a man. She's with Lux. He's her son. And yours."

As fast as the blood had boiled, it drained. The Magister's face turned sheet white. He staggered, caught himself, and sat down in a nearby armchair.

"A son?" He rasped. "She has a child?" He looked at Cyrus, and when he spoke again, his voice was as hard as granite. "You kept this from me. Why?"

"Knowing would only have distracted you."

"That's my call to make, not yours." The Magister's eyes spit fire.

"You wouldn't have had any call to make on it, if I told you. Once you knew, it would be too late."

"Too late?" The Magister snapped, rising from his chair. He took a step toward Cyrus. "Too late?" His voice rose to fever pitch. "It's my son!"

The Magister's hands were clenched, white-knuckled and trembling. One gesture, one simple command, and he could pull the life out of Cyrus and leave him withering on the floor. Like he had done to the spider. Like he had done to Braxton. Like Isabella had done to Ada.

Cyrus looked at him for a long moment. The Magister's eyes blazed blue fury. Cyrus forced himself to stay calm. He knew this time would come. He had anticipated it for years. The Magister needed him too much to do him any real damage. As long as Cyrus didn't push him too far, he would be fine.

You know him better than he realizes. You did this for his own good. Let him see that.

When Cyrus spoke, his voice was quiet and controlled. "Do you *want* a son?"

Just like that, the fury ebbed. Uncertainty flickered in the Magister's face like a spent fire. His shoulders sagged. He slumped in the chair.

"No." He stared out the window. "How old?"

"Almost six."

"But, she'll have to register him." He turned again to Cyrus. "She would have to tell me when she registers him."

Cyrus raised one eyebrow.

The Magister slumped again. "Ah. I see." He leaned his head back and closed his eyes. "She ran off rather than tell me she has a kid. Rather than keep to the Code." He gave a rueful laugh. "It's ironic, isn't it? I helped create the very thing I've worked to protect against."

The Magister rubbed his forehead, eyes still closed. "No matter," he said, standing suddenly. "We'll find her. We will find her, and she can tell me to my face before I suck the Gifts out of her like water through a straw."

"And Lux?" Cyrus asked quietly.

The Magister gave a wry laugh. "I guess we'll see when we meet him. See what kind of Gifts he inherited. See what his mother has taught him." He strode to the window.

"It's her son," the Magister said, clasping his hands behind his back. "Not mine."

"What would you like me to do?"

The Magister waved a hand. "Find them. Ada is done for. I don't care about her anymore. But find Isabella and her brat. She won't stay hidden forever. She can't. And when you find them, her or the boy..."

He turned to face Cyrus. His eyes were hard and set. "Bring them to me."

37

LUX

CIRCA 1873

Lux listened to the train wheels beating their ceaseless rhythm. It would take him back to Hillsboro, which was the closest stop to Green Meadows.

Hillsboro wasn't much compared to the city, but it had numerous hotels, stores, and factories. It was a sight bigger than Green Meadows and fortunate enough to be by the railroad.

From Hillsboro he would have to hire a ride or catch one with a farmer going the right direction.

Lux leaned his head against the window and closed his eyes. Weariness seeped through his body. Thank goodness for strange old Gertie and her chicken stew, or he would have had nothing to go on for the journey home.

He relaxed his aching limbs as much as he could and tried to sleep. They wouldn't reach Hillsboro until morning.

He would get home and warn his mother.

Lux thought of all that had transpired since he left Green Meadows only days ago. What had begun as a simple business trip had morphed into a flight for his life and the life of his mother. Or their safety, anyway. He didn't know if the Magister would outright kill them, but the idea seemed plausible.

And the Arbor Pearls...did his mother have them? *Surely not.* She hadn't left Green Meadows for fifteen years.

But then, she was powerful. Cyrus had said so, as had Auntie.

Auntie. Shriveled little Auntie with her bookshop and her odd habits. Auntie, cheerful and unafraid.

Mother is always afraid.

She feared the Magister; Lux knew that. The Code was strict and held terrible consequences. But what else? Why, with all her power, was Isabella Crane afraid of leaving a cluster of cottages and farms in a rural forest?

And what did he himself fear? Not to leave, of course, though the city always held some fear for him…and, he had to admit, was far more intimidating after recent events.

But always, even in Green Meadows, he had felt unsettled. Always there was the underlying dread. *Of what?*

Something in him, Lux realized, had always known they were in hiding. His mother never outright said it, but he must have picked up on it in her joyless smiles and tight-lipped responses to his questions as a boy.

She told him they had moved for the quiet. But she never seemed at rest, even in the starlit spaces of Green Meadows.

She had built their mansion and hired Reuben, a surly, middle-aged man from Hillsboro, to keep the grounds. Then she became, of all things, banker and benefactor to the cottagers.

It didn't fit. That was the life Lux had grown up in, but it did not fit.

What all had his mother not told him? She never had told him who his father was. Never a word about her falling out with Auntie; that was for sure. She never even spoke of Auntie. Not since Lux was a boy, anyway, before they moved to Green Meadows.

It was always silence. Always secrecy. Always changing the subject.

Lux shifted on the train seat and tried to get his neck more comfortable. He needed to sleep. There was a lot to sort through with his mother when he got home.

38

LUX

CIRCA 1873

Lux found his mother in her breakfast room. She wore a dressing gown of blue silk. Her auburn hair, unfaded apart from a few silver tinges of early adulthood, hung in shining curls over her shoulders. She stared listlessly out the window, with a forgotten biscuit held in one hand.

Lux stopped in the doorway. "Hello, mother."

Isabella startled and dropped her biscuit on the table. "Lux?" She crossed the room and hugged him. "What took you so long? I expected you back yesterday. I thought maybe…" She paused and cleared her throat. "I'm glad you're back. Have something to eat," she said, returning to her seat with a graceful sweep of her gown. Her voice was back to its usual sternness.

"No, thank you."

A knot tightened in Lux's chest. He had found it harder in recent years to stay patient with his mother's condescending tones. They weren't constant, but they did still come. It seemed she vacillated between seeing him as a grown man and as a twelve-year-old boy.

Isabella looked at Lux. "You aren't hungry? When did you get back?"

"Just now."

She perused his rumpled appearance. His clothes were wrinkled, and his shirt torn on one arm. His dark hair, usually clean and combed, lay in limp disarray.

Isabella set down her tea. Her hand trembled. "What's happened?"

"Cyrus," he said, and his mother jolted and knocked her teacup to the floor. It broke in pieces.

She looked at Lux, her eyes sharp and fearful. "Did he..."

"Knock me out, take me prisoner, and drag me to the Magister? Yes. Although I still don't know, actually, if that was the Magister. He never told me."

Isabella put one trembling hand to her mouth. Her eyes glistened. She swallowed hard and smoothed her dress. "What did he look like?"

"Cyrus?"

"The man who might have been the Magister."

Lux stepped into the room and sat on a sofa near the door. "Brown hair, short beard, flawless teeth, fancy clothes. Like a half-snake, half-fox in a rich man's body."

"That's him," she whispered, apparently oblivious to Lux's jab at the Magister's behavior.

She stared at the floor. Lux wondered for a second whether she had forgotten he was there.

When she looked up, her eyes were hard. "What did he do to you?"

"Not much, thankfully. Set me aside until morning. I escaped."

Pain and relief flashed in Isabella's eyes. "What did he say?"

Lux thought for a moment. He had planned, during his wagon ride from Hillsboro this morning, what he would tell her. He couldn't remember it now, though. Conversations rarely go according to plan.

Might as well stick to the point.

"He thinks you stole the Arbor Pearls."

Isabella's face turned white as death. She gripped the side of the table.

"Mother?" Lux stood, but Isabella waved him back. He paused, then sat. His mother took a deep breath and let it out slowly. She turned to her son, looking, Lux thought, absolutely horrified.

Her voice came out as a choked whisper. "Why? Why does he always think I'm against him?"

Lux's thoughts faltered. Whatever assumptions he'd had crumbled like misplaced bricks. He stared at his mother. She looked more fragile than he had ever seen her.

"I...I don't know," he said, trying to comfort her. "I told him it was outlandish. That you were loyal to the Code."

Isabella's eyes dropped. She turned and looked out the window over the sweep of meadow and late summer trees.

"Is that why you wouldn't teach me about using water? Is it because we could make the crops grow? Were you afraid it would help him find you?"

She glanced at him. Nodded. Turned back to the window.

"Do you know what the Arbor Pearls are?" she asked finally.

"I do now," Lux said. "Cyrus told me."

He watched his mother's hair slide over her silken shoulders. He had always loved her hair. As a little boy, he used to play with it while she read aloud. He would twirl it around his fingers and inevitably create tangles. She never rebuked him for it, though. It was one of the only things she never rebuked him for.

"You have the Gifts in your blood by birth," she said. "The Magister got his from the Pearls. So did I. We both passed the Gifts to you."

Lux's insides went cold. "Both?"

Isabella turned from the window and looked him in the eye. "The Magister is your father." She looked away. "And my husband, though he'd likely never admit it."

Never before had Lux felt so entirely shocked and shattered. His mind churned like fish in a feeding frenzy, snapping and grabbing for every speck of life. He forced it back to order. This was what his mother had taught him to do. All his years, she had trained him to stay in control of his faculties, his movements, his Gifts, to keep himself in order and on guard.

The strain this time was almost unbearable.

"Why did you not tell me?" he asked, his voice low and careful.

His mother's eyes hardened. "To protect you," she said. "I won't have you be his pawn."

"Be his pawn?" Lux's voice rose. "Mother, how weak do you think I am?"

"I do not think you're weak," she snapped. "But compared to him, we all are. Still," she added, and her chin trembled. She squared her shoulders. "We'll never be enough for him. Neither of us. Not strong enough, and certainly not trusted enough."

Isabella dropped her hands in her lap and looked away. When she looked back, her gaze was pleading. "Everything I've done has been for your good," she said. "Everything."

"And yours."

She stiffened. "And mine."

Neither of them spoke for several minutes. Lux sat on the edge of the sofa, staring at nothing.

His mother filled a spare cup with tea and sipped it. Finally she set the cup down and cleared her throat. "I've been teaching Reuben."

"Teaching him the Gifts?" Lux's eyes widened. Isabella nodded.

"Mother, why?" Lux almost shouted. He lowered his voice. "He's just an ordinary man. How could he learn them anyway?"

"Blood, son, it's all in the blood." She looked sideways at him. "I didn't explain that to Reuben, of course. He's too much of a dunce for that. I tricked him into getting some of my blood in him." The corner of Isabella's mouth twitched. "It was a simple matter, really. The man doesn't hold his drink well. I gave him plenty of wine and staged an accident. Put a knife just so, and he cut his hand good and deep." Isabella glanced at Lux again. "Then I sewed up the wound for him. After mixing some of my own blood in, of course. I had a clean knife ready and squeezed plenty in." She waved a hand. "The stupid man has no idea why he can suddenly move things without touching them. With my instruction, of course. His powers are small, and I'll keep his abilities very limited, just enough to serve my purposes."

Lux could hardly believe what he was hearing. He stared at her, mouth agape.

Isabella sipped her tea and looked at Lux. "Oh, stop your gawking. Reuben is convenient for me. Loyal as a puppy. He'll do whatever I ask."

"Mother..." Lux lifted both hands, then dropped them at his sides. "What is it you want, really? What are you trying to do?"

"Keep us alive." She stared at him. Her gaze was fixed and burning. "To keep us both alive, Lux. That's all I've ever been trying to do."

Lux hesitated. "Is it worth it?"

His mother's cup clattered on the saucer. Her eyes widened. "Of course it's worth it. How could it not be?"

He shrugged. "We're in a prison of our own making. Isn't that worse than death?"

"Don't say that," she snapped. "Nothing is worse than death. We're safe here, Lux. You don't understand how bad it could be."

Lux turned on her. "If I don't understand, Mother, it's because you haven't told me." His anger flared. He didn't try to quell it. "You limit me on purpose. You say you'll teach me everything, but you don't. You don't tell me why, you don't tell me how, you don't tell me anything."

Lux gritted his teeth. A tirade would do no good. He could see the hurt swirling just above her fear. *Such a puzzle,* Auntie had called her.

Auntie. She harbored no anger at her sister. Lux could not do the same.

"Lux..." Isabella sighed and turned back to the table. "You're just going to have to trust me."

"Like Auntie did?" The words came out before Lux could stop them.

His mother shook violently. Her face paled, then flushed crimson.

"Leave me be," she said, her voice rigid and trembling.

Lux left the room. He would not stay here. He would not hide the rest of his life, holed up in a backwoods village, no better off than the cottagers. He would not become a power monger like his crazy, terrifying father. He would not live in fear of what may or may not happen.

He wanted peace. He wanted to stop running. To stop hiding. He wanted to be free.

39

GEORGE

CIRCA 2023

Later that evening, after his visit with the Lady, George sat on the edge of his bed, lost in thought. He wasn't sure what in particular had sparked memories of his uncle, but he had thought of little else since dinnertime.

Uncle Barry picking him up from his second grade class the day his parents died. Uncle Barry cheering him on in Little League and, later, talking him through the reality of "some people being more gifted at sports than others." Uncle Barry standing at the finicky stove, swearing over a ruined batch of scrambled eggs. Uncle Barry playing teenage George in chess. Uncle Barry sitting in his lawn chair just a few years ago, sipping a beer and retelling stories of how he wooed Aunt Pam.

George chuckled to himself at that last memory, then swiped a hand across his eyes and rubbed his temples.

Rising stiffly, George walked to his dresser and opened the top drawer. It held an odd assortment of practical items and bits of nostalgia. Pens, a few photographs, his college ID, other odds and ends. He rifled through until he found what he was looking for. A thin, leather-bound book.

George picked up the leather volume and carried it back to his bed. This was Uncle Barry's "bits of wisdom" book. As long as George could remember, his uncle had this journal lying around. Uncle Barry wrote all kinds of tidbits in it. Quotes he liked, random questions, things he had seen and wanted to remember. He also used it for the occasional spare paper. Many pages had an address or phone number scrawled across the side—some labeled with a name, and others not.

Of Uncle Barry's few possessions left when he died, this was the main one George wanted to keep.

He opened it now and thumbed through the pages. He had only read portions of it, mostly during his initial grief after his uncle's death. He stopped where Uncle Barry had written, *Recipe for a Good Day: 1 tongue kept under control; 2 ears paying attention; 1 attitude where it belongs; end the day next to Pam.*

On the next page, up in the corner, George saw, *Lost temper. Don't do that.* Further down was a quote that read, *All my life's buried here, Heap earth upon it.—Oscar Wilde.* And on the next page, *A drop of ink may make a million think.—Lord Byron,* with the words *Tell this one to George* and an arrow jotted near it.

George ran his thumb over the words and sighed. He felt tired and heavy. The conversation with the Lady weighed on him, and these memories were not helping. George flipped back to the beginning and made to shut the book…

Then stopped.

Something caught his eye on the front page. George sat up very straight. He read the front bit several times. Slowly, ever so slowly, he closed the journal.

George walked to the front door, pulled on shoes and a jacket, and left the house.

It only took a moment for Jasper to answer the knock.

"George?" Jasper pushed the door open and beckoned him in, but George stayed put.

"We have to finish the song."

Jasper blinked. "I—"

"Now," George said. "We have to finish the song now."

"Now?" Jasper chuckled. "I was going to say I agree, but that makes it even better." He sobered. "What's happened?"

"I'm not sure I can explain it, only...well, I think I know what went wrong. Sort of." George ran a hand over his hair and shifted his feet on the porch. "We have to finish the song. Can we gather the others? They'll all be home, right?"

"I reckon so." Jasper looked quizzically at George, but didn't ask for any more clarification. "You want to go get Harlan and Hanna? I'll gather the rest. Meet back at your house?"

George nodded and hurried off the porch. It had started to rain. Soft drops splattered on his hair and jacket.

"George," Jasper called.

He stopped and turned. Jasper stood watching him, his hulking frame filling the doorway like a gopher in a mouse hole. His expression caught George off guard. There was something in it he hadn't seen there before. Something familiar. Like Jasper saw him for real. Saw him and understood.

"What happened to her?" His voice was quiet. It carried on the rain. "Your wife?"

George's chest constricted. Jasper had never asked about the wedding photo he saw that first day at George's cottage. George had never mentioned it. He didn't want to talk about Liese. But now…

George looked out at the rain. It fell steadily, streaming through the forest like a million silver threads. The lump in his chest rose. It clogged his throat. Icy fingers curled around his airway. They tightened. Burned.

George inhaled a long, ragged breath. He let it out slowly. The fist loosened and shrank away.

"There was a fire," he said, half surprised to hear himself speak. Other than the grief counselor, he had never talked to anyone about what happened. Never wanted to voice it aloud. "Gas leak or something. She was asleep, and..." He paused. Swallowed. "I wasn't there. I...I'd been at work late. It was tax season, and I told...I told her not to wait up for me."

He looked at Jasper. "The house burned so fast, she never even woke up. Fire department got there just in time to keep the neighbors' houses from catching. I got there not long after."

The men looked at each other for a long moment, Jasper in the doorway, George by the porch steps. George could have sworn Jasper's eyes burrowed right to his soul, so piercing were they in the face of this weary, powerful man.

"What was her name?" Jasper asked finally, his voice quiet and even.

"Liese." Somewhere in George's heart, a dam broke free. He hadn't said her name aloud since she died. "Liese, my wife."

Then he turned into the thickening rainfall, jogging as fast as his gimp leg would allow.

When he knocked on the door of the Stones' cottage, Hanna answered. She stuck a dishrag into the pocket of a stained apron and folded her arms.

"What d'you want?" Her voice was curt, but George heard the slightest bit of waver in it.

He cleared his throat. "We're going to finish the song, Hanna. I want you and your brother to come."

Her eyes narrowed. "Last time, you walked out on us."

"Yeah, well, the time before that, you threw a fit and called me names."

Hanna's mouth dropped open. She closed it quickly and looked away. After a few seconds, she unlocked her arms and fiddled with the end of her braid.

"There've been a lot of disappointments in the last hundred fifty years." Her voice had lost its edge. "I'm not sure I can take much more of 'em."

"Fair enough." The rain was falling harder now. It coursed over George's arms, head, and shoulders, and ran in streams off the porch steps. He pulled the hood further over his forehead.

"I thought..." Hanna took a deep breath. "I thought you were goin' to fix things somehow. Like my pa used to do. He could always make everything alright. I thought maybe, when you showed up, things were changin'."

"Listen, Hanna," George said, speaking loud enough to be heard over the rain. "I don't know how I ended up involved in all this. I really don't. And I don't know for sure what's going to happen. But I do know there's a chance here, and now is the time to take it."

He wiped rain off his nose and looked her in the eye. "I want you free, Hanna. Not trapped here living without living." He shrugged. "And maybe I *can't* fix it. Maybe I can't do a thing to help you. But we have to at least try." George hunched his shoulders under the rainfall. "So what do you say? You coming?"

Hanna stared at him for a moment, a thousand emotions spilling across her face. At last, her expression evened. The unpredictable glint George had noticed when he first met her sparked to life again. It didn't bother him anymore.

She pulled the apron over her head and tossed it aside. "I'll find Harlan."

All in the cellar once again, George looked at the faces convened before him. Some looked wary, others eager, all questioning. George hoped he was doing right. This had to be it. It just had to be.

They picked up the melody where they had left off. Hanna joined in with her flute, not missing a single note. Once again George taught line by line, and the musicians mimicked him until they had it memorized.

They learned more quickly now. Everyone was focused, the onlookers silent. Anticipation built with each new measure, each phrase. They would finish it this time—and play it for real.

Finally, the last practice measure passed. Jasper, Tom, Peter, Marcus, and Hanna looked at one another, then glanced around the room at their families.

"Ready?" Jasper asked.

The others grinned. George felt a surge of excitement leap through his chest and lodge in his throat like a river dam. He looked at Hanna. Her eyes were burning with such fire, she reminded George of a queen, a young queen about to battle for her people. She fingered her flute and nodded at him.

Upstairs, someone pounded on the front door.

"Ignore it," George said. "I'll deal with it. You just play the song."

The musicians readied their instruments.

"Whatever happens," George said, "don't stop. Don't stop playing until the song is done." They murmured their assent. Jasper glanced at George and nodded, just once, but George thought he had never seen so much said in one small movement.

Jasper counted, and the song began. At the same moment, George heard the front door crash open.

40

CYRUS

CIRCA 1858

Cyrus strode the nearly empty streets. It was dusk. Most people were home by now, or close to it.

The street was dirty from the day's traffic. Dust and dried mud clung to the paving bricks. Manure permeated the lingering heat. It would stay until the street cleaners made their rounds again.

Cyrus moved the worst of it out of his way when he could be sure of not being seen. It was the fresh stuff, mostly, that he wanted to avoid. A flick of the wrist here, a finger pointed there, and horse dung scooted aside for his odorless, if not shiny, leather shoes.

"Alms," called a rickety voice from the shadows. "Alms if ye can spare them."

Stone buildings lined both sides of the street. Between their corners and stairwells were a myriad of dark spaces. Cyrus could not yet tell from which one the woman spoke.

"Alms, if ye please, sirs."

Two men in suits and silk hats were approaching from the other end of the street. Cyrus could just see the woman now, crouched by a stairwell not far from the two gentlemen. She was standing, it seemed, but with a painful-looking hunch to her back. A ragged shawl covered her hair, shoulders, and most of a dirty dress.

"Alms," she called again.

The gentlemen didn't even glance at her. They walked by as if they had never heard her at all, talking all the while about business partners and possible paydays.

As they passed Cyrus, they nodded politely and hurried on.

Cyrus continued toward the stairwell. The woman had quieted for a moment after the men passed, but she took up her plea again when she saw Cyrus.

"Alms, if ye please, sir. Alms if ye can spare them."

Cyrus could see her more clearly now. Her face, though mostly shrouded by her shawl, revealed a jutting chin and a bent protrusion of a nose. Oily grey hair poked out near the tattered fabric.

She held the shawl closed with one hand and extended the other toward Cyrus. Her knuckles were knobby and rigid. They twisted at odd angles from a dirty palm.

An outcast, Cyrus realized. A misshapen creature with little choice but to beg.

Beggars were not unusual in the city. Perhaps a bit less prevalent here, where the Gifted kept crops growing and averted some of the worst disasters. But people are people. Poverty will strike anywhere.

Cyrus wondered what this woman's life had been to bring her to this stairwell, asking for any scrap of coin from passing strangers. Had he seen her before? He had spent many years in this city. He couldn't say he had done much for the beggars, though, or even really noticed them. To his shame, he was usually more caught up in seeking other potentials for the Gifts or supervising the members under his lead.

"Alms?" The woman's voice croaked.

Would Ada become like this woman? The thought made him wince. Surely not. Not Ada. Cyrus dug in his pocket and pulled out a handful of coins.

"Oh, thank ye, sir," she said, holding out a trembling palm.

Gently, he tipped the whole pile into her gnarled, twisted hand.

She gasped. "Oh, oh, oh," she said, her cracked voice filled with awe. She clutched the coins and danced side to side in a hobbling jig. "Oh, thank the Maker. Oh wonders. Oh, Maker bless ye," she said gleefully, peering at Cyrus with small, shining eyes. Her mouth was all a wide grin. Gaps showed between half-rotten teeth. Her gums were covered with sores.

Cyrus cringed, but he smiled at the woman before moving on.

He must find Ada. It had been four days since the Cranes disappeared, and still there was no sign of her. He had begun a systematic search of the city. He would leave no stone unturned. She could not have gone far.

A nagging thought reminded him that she could have, perhaps, boarded a train. He might never find her then.

No. That could not be. He would not let it be.

It's not up to you.

Cyrus dismissed the thought and hurried on. He would find her. He must find her.

He had already searched much of the city's center. He would move toward the outskirts now. He checked the train station first, always aware of that possibility. There was still no sign of Ada.

"Have you seen an old woman traveling alone?" he asked the ticket master, the conductors, any passengers willing to give him a minute.

"No," they all said. "Try the police station or the poorhouse."

He did. Nothing.

Cyrus turned away from the city center. He passed an open barroom where lights blared and raucous laughter boomed. Men in worn-out shirts and trousers stood around fire barrels and glared at him as he passed. One spit tobacco juice at his shoes. It splattered on the dirt only inches away, but Cyrus ignored it. He did not have time for petty quarrels.

Finally, he made it to more pleasant streets. This was the northern section of the city. These were not the bustle and madness of the busiest areas, though in the daytime they still bore traffic.

They weren't rich quarters, either. Those would be mostly south and east, where his own home and the Magister's mansion stood. No, these buildings were smaller and far from ostentatious. They were, he thought, the kind of places Ada might like. She had never cared much for wealth. In fact, she had told him once that if she had her choice, she would find a little nook somewhere and run a bookshop—

Cyrus froze. A dozen yards away, a curtain moved. It was a green curtain at the window of a squat, standalone building with two stories. A nook, compared to the larger buildings around it.

But that was not what mattered.

What mattered was that he had just seen Ada's face. The shriveled Ada. Worn and withered. It was only for a second. Just a flash, as she adjusted the curtain.

Had she seen him? He suspected so. That look on her face, just for an instant before the curtain fell closed... Cyrus' heart pounded like a bass drum. It was her. He had found her. He looked around. There was no one in sight.

That was good. This might not be easy.

He crossed the street and ascended the few steps to the main door. Cyrus knocked. "Ada?"

He could have just opened the door. Forced the locks and turned the latch. But no. Not to Ada. His regard for her was too high. He had already given her plenty of trouble she did not deserve. She deserved to choose whether or not she opened the door. He would leave her that.

"Ada?"

He knocked again. Firm, but not loud. No answer.

"Ada, please."

Another knock.

"I know you're there. It's me. Cyrus." *Dumb thing to say. She knows that.* "It's only me, Ada. No one else. No one else knows you're here."

Nothing. A dog barked in the distance. Somewhere, a woman laughed. It sounded far away—a careless, passing sound, perhaps by an open window. Horse hooves clopped a distant racket. Street lamps flickered. A cat dashed over the paving stones and disappeared into the shadows.

"Ada?" Cyrus leaned his head against the door. He closed his eyes. "Ada, please. I'm sorry."

The lock slid. Cyrus' heart leaped. He jerked upright. Metal gears clicked into place. The knob turned, and the door opened.

There stood Ada, tiny and wrinkled. Instead of the dahlia purple, she wore a simple cotton dress. A purple shawl lay over her shoulders. She clutched the ends together over her sternum.

"I told you not to look for me." Her voice was raspy and small.

"I know." Cyrus stared at her eyes. Her eyes were the same. Bright, clever, wiser than he.

"But here you are."

"I know. I..." Cyrus tried to think what to say. How could he explain himself? The turmoil, the fear, anger at Isabella, the terrible sense of loss, hope, anguish.

"I couldn't not." It sounded lame, even to him. But it was all he could manage.

Ada studied him. For a long moment they stood like that, Ada in the doorway, Cyrus on the step. Her withered shoulders moved with her breaths. Up, down. Up, down. Finally, without replying, she stepped back and pulled the door wide.

Cyrus' chest unclenched. Relief flooded his veins. He stepped over the threshold, moving aside so Ada could close the door behind them.

"Well." She looked at his face. "I'll get tea."

She tottered through the entry. Cyrus followed. Ada led him through the large front room and into a smaller set of rooms at the back.

She motioned him to a chair. He sat and watched while she heated water and poured tea. She seemed so small. So fragile. But her movements were sure, even if her hands wobbled.

He felt terrible just sitting there, waiting to be served. But he didn't dare offer to help; she might kick him out for good.

Cyrus looked around the small quarters. He was in a sitting room, of sorts. There was a yellow sofa and a squat table at this end, and a kitchen at the other.

The kitchen was tiny—just a corner. It had a few cabinets and a stove. A loaf of bread and a butter dish took up most of the countertop, accompanied by a few apples that sat in a haphazard row near the stove.

"I send the neighbor boy for groceries," Ada said, eyeing his perusal of the kitchen. "I don't have much strength back yet, but I'll make do."

"Ada—"

"Don't." She cut him off. "Don't say it, Cyrus. I don't want to hear it. It doesn't change anything."

He groaned and slumped against the back of the sofa. "What *can* I say?" he asked, shoving fingers through dark, disheveled hair.

"The truth." Ada glared at him. "How about you tell me the truth."

"Ada, I've never lied to you."

"But you've never been entirely honest, either. Stop playing the Magister's game, Cyrus. Just for a second. Tell me what's really happened." She carried two tea cups to the table. They only sloshed a little as she set them down.

Cyrus watched her settle carefully into the sofa's other end. She pulled her feet up under her, leaned against the cushion, and looked at him. "Well?"

"What part of the truth do you want me to tell?" Cyrus' voice was quiet. His eyes pleaded with hers.

Ada's gaze remained cool and firm. "What *part*? There aren't parts to the truth, Cyrus. Truth is truth. It's a whole."

"Not always."

"Always." Her eyes pierced him. "Always, Cyrus."

He leaned forward, resting his elbows on his knees. "What am I supposed to tell you, Ada? You know I hold the Magister's confidence. I'm the only one who does. I did what I had to do, but..."

"But what?"

Cyrus looked at Ada. Her eyes betrayed nothing. No emotion.

"But I've also failed. I stood my ground on one side, kept my commitment to the Code and the Magister, but failed you in the process. And that truth, that I failed you..." He trailed off.

"Failed me how? You owe me nothing."

"I owe you everything." She looked away, but Cyrus moved to catch her gaze. "Everything, Ada. After all that's happened..." He lifted both hands and dropped them in his lap. "It's my fault. But I had to. You know how the Code works."

Ada laughed, jarring Cyrus. She shook her frazzled head. "I never cared about the Code. Never cared beans about it one way or the other. It's a rich man's means of control." Her eyes narrowed. "I saw through that in an instant, Cyrus. You could see it too, if you opened your eyes enough to the truth. The *whole* truth."

She pulled her shawl more tightly around her shoulders. "I only cared to stay near my sister. She was all I had left. The Code, the Gifted..." Ada shook her head. Her feathery grey hair wisped like poppies in the breeze. "They've brought nothing but pain and brokenness. Except my Luxy. He's the one good thing out of all this. The one beautiful thing. And now he's gone, too."

She turned her head away from Cyrus. He didn't know what to say. It was true. Everything good that Ada had was gone because of the Code and the Gifted. She had joined the Gifted to stay with Isabella, and lost everything.

He sat still, feeling the pain of her loss. There was no assuaging that grief.

"Ada." Cyrus took hold of her hand. It was cold. So small. So fragile. Like holding a bird with a broken neck. "There's no fixing it. I know that. And I've been a fool. You're here because of me."

"It's not all on you, Cyrus. Other people made choices." She didn't look at him. One tear rolled down the side of her cheek.

"Ada." He reached, brushed the tear away with his fingers. "Ada." Tenderness filled his every word. The words so long kept. "I love you."

For one brief second, Ada's eyes closed. Her face drew together in pain. Then she stiffened. Cooled. She pulled her hand from his, brushed the last marks of the tear, and stood.

"It's too late for that." She looked at him, her eyes as steady as stone. "Let me be, Cyrus. Go. Please. And don't come back."

41

LUX

CIRCA 1873

Lux stood, once again, in Auntie's bookshop. After the quarrel with his mother, he had stayed at Green Meadows only long enough to clean up and eat, then packed a satchel and caught the next train back to the city.

It was raining. Perhaps the drought was coming to an end.

He brought a cloak this time, and a low hat to cover his face. Despite his resolve not to fear, he was wary of Cyrus finding him again.

"What am I missing?" he asked Auntie when he finally stepped into her bookshop, dripping with rain, and locked the door behind him. "What is it I don't understand?"

Auntie peeked around a bookshelf, a feather duster in one hand. Her face lit up like a daisy bloom.

"Ah, Luxy, I've been waiting for you." She dropped the duster and hurried to him, tsking about the puddles forming around his feet. She laughed, almost girlishly, then sobered. "You mean it, Luxy? You really want to know?"

"I want to know."

Auntie tossed his cloak and hat onto the back of a scuffed chair. She took his hand. "Come," she said, her voice soft and wondering. "Let me play it for you."

She led him to the back of her little shop. Her piano was in a store room, behind crates of books. It was old and dinged, but the wood still shone like honey, and the keys still played true.

"It might change everything," Auntie said, looking steadily in his eyes. "It might remake you entirely."

Lux's heart thudded. "I don't know what you mean."

"Well..." Auntie shrugged. "There's no saying, really, what it'll do. Except that it makes you whole." She tilted her head. "Do you want to be whole, Luxy?"

Lux nodded. He did want to be whole. *Whatever it costs.*

"Then listen." She smiled. Her eyes glistened. "Listen all the way, Luxy." Auntie put her bony fingers on the ivory and began to play.

As the notes filled the little room, Lux closed his eyes and surrendered himself to the song. It poured through him, coursing life in every fiber of his being. It was terrifying, still, but not the way it had been. It could kill him. He knew it could. But it was also life. The sound that he had once rejected now felt like water to his very soul, an ocean filling a dry well. The power of it scared him beyond reckoning, but he relished it. Gave himself to it.

Every longing, every fear, every bit of anger and crushed hopes; it all swirled together, overcome by the beauty and strength of the music. It was as if his skin and bones, muscles and sinews, heart and mind were renewed piece by piece—rebuilt from the core into something more truly alive than it had been before.

Light he had never seen, hope he had never known, truth he had only held in misshapen bits, now whole and clear. All of it wove through his frame, his thoughts, his mortal humanity, washing away the dust and putting things to rights. It was piercing, and glorious, and wondrously, achingly beautiful.

The song slowed and quieted. It finished. Auntie turned from the piano stool and faced him.

"Do you understand now?" she asked softly.

Lux's eyes were still closed. Tears streaked his face. He hadn't realized he had been crying.

He knew, without really knowing how, that his Gifts were gone. He was ordinary. And yet more than that. It was as if something had taken the place of the Gifts. Something far better. He would not trade it for anything.

Joy settled into a steady hum, beating a whisper through his veins. He was free. A slow smile spread across his face. "I understand."

Lux was back on the train the next morning. Auntie would not let him stay longer.

"Your mother needs you," she had said back at the bookshop, "whether she knows it or not."

Auntie had pulled a sheaf of papers from her desk and pushed them toward Lux. "Here," she said. "I knew you'd come back." She grinned. "I wrote it down for you. The song. Learn it, Luxy. Learn it and play it for others. Play it for your mother. You can't force it on her, though, or on anyone. They have to want to hear."

"But what if they don't want to?"

"They may not, at first. It's a revulsion to someone who doesn't want it. Sounds like death to some, but it's the sound of life to the ones who see it for what it really is. Give them time. Worked for you, eh?"

Auntie had tapped his chest. "The song's always been in the blood, Luxy. It's how we're made. But it can't just be in the blood. We have to let it fill our soul, too. That's where the real life is."

"But where did it come from, Auntie? How did you find the song?"

"Well..." She pursed her lips. "I'd always thought of the Gifts as being a bit like music running through my blood. I couldn't hear it, but I could feel it. I never could quite figure it out; it was just a thought."

She paused, and winked at him. "Until I found it in the Arbor Pearls, of course."

Lux had stared at her with such shock that she had laughed until tears ran down her cheeks.

That was when Lux noticed that her face was less shriveled than it had been. In fact, it was almost smooth. She looked younger, taller, like a gracefully aged version of herself—like what she would have been if the Gifts, and her sister, had never touched her.

"Auntie, you're fixed!" It sounded silly, but that was what it looked like to him. A right version of Auntie.

She had felt her face, stretched her fingers. "Well, I'll be...I think it put some flesh back on my bones." She chuckled. "Wondrous thing."

"The song did it?"

"Must be, Luxy. Must be."

"Play it again, Auntie. What if it made you even younger?"

"And why would I want that?" She cocked her head. "I've been put to rights, Luxy. I can't ask for more than that. Besides," she had added, brushing soft, silver-brown hair away from her cheeks. "I think that's what the song does. It fixes what was broken. Mends the things that were rent. It gives life as the Maker intended."

"But the Pearls." Lux fixed his eyes on hers. "You have the Pearls?"

"Not anymore. I put them far away. They were never meant to be misused as they have been. The gift of the Pearls is the reminder of the Maker's goodness. Of who He is. That's all it ever should be."

"How did you ever get them from the Magister?"

Auntie had risen from her chair and tossed Lux his hat. "That, Luxy, is a story for another time." She kissed his cheek. "You have a train to catch."

"But the music," Lux had asked, returning her kiss and pulling his cloak around his shoulders. "How did the Pearls give you the music?"

Auntie shook her head and grinned. "I listened to them." She laughed. "In all those years, the Magister never once listened to them. He poked and prodded and tried to figure them out with his own head, but he never just put them to his ear and listened. It's all right there, Luxy. The tune of the Maker's own song."

Lux remembered strange old Gertie's story about the Maker singing the world into being. What was it she had said?

This world has a set of softer stones, made from the Maker's song. They capture a glimpse of the beauty and mightiness too big for our human understanding.

The Song of all songs was in the Pearls. That was something worth pondering.

Lux had paused at the door with one last question. "Auntie, why, do you think...well, why didn't it heal you when you heard it the first time?"

Auntie shrugged. "Why did it heal me at all?" The corners of her eyes crinkled into soft swoops. She tucked a bit of hair behind her ear. "I think that's what we miss. We think we know, we think we understand. We forget, sometimes, how small we are. And yet how loved."

Auntie patted Lux's shoulder. "Take it home with you, Luxy. See what happens."

Lux tried to tell his mother about the song. He tried to play it for her. She wouldn't hear of it. She became angry—more angry than he had ever seen her. And terrified.

"It will kill you, Lux. It's not safe."

"Mother, I've already heard it. It's the very opposite of death."

"It took your Gifts!"

"It was worth it."

"Don't, Lux. You tamper with things you know nothing about. I know power, son. I've learned things you wouldn't believe. Keep it away from me, you hear me? Get rid of it."

He told her about Auntie. Isabella would not listen. She stopped her ears and almost ran from the room.

So Lux tried the cottagers. He saw them in a new way now, those cottagers. They were simple, hardworking people, but always striving. Always afraid, in their own way.

He moved into a cottage, much to his mother's horror. It was the same cottage he had found as a teenage boy. It felt more like home to him now than his mother's mansion did.

Sometimes, sometimes, Lux could swear he heard the song whispering through the walls like the faintest breath. He actually pressed his ear against the wood once, but there was nothing. Nothing but the dull roar of his own ear cavity.

Perhaps if he got to know the cottagers, if he gained their trust, he could tell them about the song. They seemed eager, but wary. They just needed more time.

His mother always weighed on his mind. He rarely saw her. She seemed to both want and not want to see him. She was more moody than ever. Paranoid, even. Lux was determined to reach her.

He set out one night for the mansion. If she would just listen, if he could just get her to understand...

That night was the last time anyone in Green Meadows saw Lux Crane.

42

CYRUS

CIRCA 1873

Cyrus studied the little room. It looked untouched. The carving on the ceiling was in its precise place. No unknowing eye would guess that anyone had been here just hours before.

Cyrus was impressed. The boy was shrewder than he had hoped.

Cyrus had put Lux in this room on purpose, of course. Not even the Magister knew about the ceiling passage. He would never cramp himself in a sweaty, dusty tunnel through the roof; the Magister was too sophisticated for that. He had grown to like his nice clothes and fancy ways. No, Cyrus had made this tunnel for his own purposes. He, too, wanted a way to see the happenings of the mansion.

He left the room and closed the door. His friend was angry that Lux had escaped, but Cyrus could handle that.

The Magister did not suspect him. Cyrus had done his work well.

He had searched the mansion, knowing it would not do any good, and left the kitchen until last.

Good old Gertie. She covered for Lux like a master artist. Cyrus chuckled at the thought. Gertie was loyal. And she had loved Isabella, in those days, like she would her own niece. Cyrus knew that Isabella had sometimes sought refuge in the kitchen. She must have found something comforting being around the old woman, despite Gertie's uncouth habits and quirky ways.

Cyrus exited the mansion and crossed the yard to his own house. The city lights cast a glow on the low-hanging clouds. They threatened rain. He had searched the city too, of course, but he had given Lux enough time by then to get away.

The boy and his mother were safe once again.

It would not last forever. It couldn't. The Magister's suspicions toward Isabella had long been like searing coals. Now they had burst into flames, ready to devour.

And there was the problem of the missing Pearls. Cyrus did not think Isabella took them. If he did, he wouldn't have let Lux go.

No, it wasn't Isabella. She had always loved and feared the Magister more than she desired power. That was her downfall to becoming truly invincible. *But what she did to her sister...* Cyrus clenched his teeth.

But no. Isabella would not have stolen from the Magister. She *could* not.

Cyrus didn't know who could.

And the felled Arbor Tree? What of that? Was it directly connected to the disappearance of the Pearls? That seemed obvious, but not a given. *Why would someone cut down the tree? Just sending a message, or some other reason?*

Who else knew of the Pearls? Who would be searching?

Cyrus climbed the stairs to his bedroom. The stairs creaked, as always. His was an old house, though still in sound condition. Being right next door to the Magister's mansion had its conveniences. Cyrus' home was not a mansion, not even close, but it hardly mattered. He lived alone and was rarely here anyway. But he liked to have some privacy, a place of his own, somewhere to step away for awhile.

Darcy, his pet cat, padded through the door and rubbed her calico back on his pant leg. He reached down and scratched her head.

"What've you been up to, huh?"

She purred and arched her back. Her tail switched from side to side.

"You have any insight into all of this? It would be nice if someone did." Cyrus chuckled, gave her head a last pat, and crossed the doorway to his room.

He would figure it out. There were pieces to this puzzle that still evaded him, but he would figure it out.

Cyrus undressed by lamplight. He hung his suit carefully in the closet so it wouldn't wrinkle. He normally brought his laundry to Gertie, but he would like to avoid her for a bit. There was enough to figure out without Gertie lashing at him any more than necessary.

He blew out the lamp and climbed into bed.

What about Ada?

Ada. Cyrus did not let himself think about her very often. The thoughts came, but he usually pushed them away.

This time he let them stay. *Ada.* Would she know anything about the Pearls?

Cyrus straightened the blankets and lay still. The moon shone through a crack in the window curtain, casting pale light across his pillow. No, Ada wouldn't. She had found a new life, left the Gifted far in the past.

And yet…

Cyrus shifted to get the moonlight out of his eyes. It was just bright enough to be almost painful.

Ada had always been more clever than anyone else gave her credit for. She saw things. Noticed things. Maybe somehow, she knew something about the Pearls.

He hadn't checked on her in quite some time. It was too painful. He used to go once in awhile just to make sure she still got along fine. He wouldn't talk to her, wouldn't let her know he was there. Usually he just peeked in the front windows or got a glimpse of her when a customer opened the door.

She had set up a bookshop. It was a quirky little place. Fit her perfectly.

It was hard, still, to see her. Cyrus had stopped going years ago. She did not want anything to do with him; she had made that clear. It hurt to see that shriveled version of her, so unlike what she used to be. But it was still her. Still Ada, within that shrunken shell.

Cyrus sighed and closed his eyes.

If he was being honest with himself, which he tried to be, seeing her made him feel terribly guilty. He did not like to think much about that part.

Cyrus rolled over and pulled the blankets to a better position. Yes. Like it or not, he would talk to Ada. The Arbor Pearls in the hands of the wrong person could be an astronomical disaster. He doubted that she knew a thing about the missing Pearls, but it was worth checking.

Cyrus pulled the blankets higher over his shoulder and tried to relax. He had a plan. He would talk to Ada. It was a start.

With that in mind, he fell asleep.

43

INTERLUDE

LETTER #4

The Magister searched fifteen years for his wife. Not out of love. Not because he missed her. No—he wanted her within his bounds. His control. She had eluded him. She had left. And it drove him mad.

The truth is that he did little of the actual searching. He was brooding and angry, a lion hungry for its prey.

Cyrus searched. The city, the surrounding towns, anywhere that seemed likely. But there was no trace of an amber-haired woman with a fatherless boy.

The knowledge, when it came, that he had a son, had only added to the Magister's discontent. What did he want with a son? A son outside of his jurisdiction was only one more person Gifted and awry. And when he met that son as a twenty-year-old man, the son was weak. Disappointing. Nothing like a true progeny of the Magister.

But the son had proved resourceful in one regard, anyway. He had escaped the mansion and gone back into hiding.

That was the last straw that broke the Magister's patience. The sand that wore it paper-thin.

What had once been a desire for benevolence and the greater good was now nothing more than a riveted aim to find Isabella and destroy every trace of her and her offspring.

Within days of Lux's disappearance, the Magister disbanded the Order of the Gifted.

"Too dangerous," he told Cyrus. "Too much power in weak, useless people. It should be you and me with the Pearls' power. It should only have ever been you and me." He said this in a wrathful, half-crazed vehemence, stalking the floor of his apartments like a rabid wolf.

Cyrus did not disagree. Within the week, he summoned every living member of the Gifted to the mansion. Together in the immaculate parlor, he made them swear to cooperation and silence, on pain of death. They may use their Gifts for their personal household needs, but only in the utmost secrecy. They must never utter a word of the Magister, the previous Order, the Pearls, or the Gifts whatsoever—not even to each other or to children yet to be born.

The Order of the Gifted was closed.

As Cyrus finished his speech to the shocked gathering, the Magister stepped forward.

"I'll finish here," he said. "Bring Gertie. We must speak to her too."

Cyrus found Gertie in the kitchen. She demanded an explanation for being dragged to some meeting, but Cyrus didn't give her one.

He led her through the passageways toward the parlor door.

It was too quiet. Far too quiet.

Realization dawned. Cyrus sprinted the last steps and threw open the door.

Every member of the Gifted lay shriveled on the floor, a lifeless husk.

The Magister was nowhere to be seen.

Cyrus hardly saw Gertie push past him into the room, bobbing among the bodies like a woman in a war scene. He barely heard her sobbing or her cries to the Maker.

His ears rang. He was stunned. Frozen. The Magister had gone mad. His friend had become a monster. It had shifted so subtly. And Cyrus had not realized in time to stop him.

A note lay on the ornate, mahogany hutch. Cyrus stepped toward it as if in a dream. He picked it up. Read it.

It was the only way. I'm going to find Isabella.
Are you coming?

44

GEORGE

CIRCA 2023

"Keep playing!" George called.

The musicians bent in concentration. The listeners glanced at the cellar door, their faces painted with fear. George hauled himself up the steps and clung to the handle on the underside of the hatch.

"George!" Isabella's voice shouted from somewhere upstairs, barely audible over the sound of the music.

She will not stop this.

"Keep playing!" George said again.

The song swelled. He could feel the fire, the longing, the beauty, bursting through the cellar air like light in the pitchest dark.

"They're down thataway." It was Reuben's voice this time, loud, and gravelly, and right overhead.

George hung onto the handle, pulling the cellar hatch tight with every ounce of strength he could muster.

"Don't stop!" George shouted over his shoulder.

The song surged louder. George's heartbeat pounded to the rhythm of a thousand wings. A river rushed through him, wide, and full, and glorious in its power. He felt life springing in every cell, every blood vessel, plants pushing their way through a desert once void and dry.

The cellar door shuddered and cracked.

No! George said silently. *You will not. You will not stop it. Not this time.*

"George!" Isabella howled.

"Lady Crane, it ain't workin'," Reuben said. "The door's not breakin'."

"Get out of my way!"

Something crashed above George's head. A man, presumably Reuben, yelped and groaned.

George held onto the handle with all his might. The song coursed through his legs, his feet, his arms, his fingers, the very hairs on his head. Through the wooden door above him, Isabella shouted words he did not understand. The door quaked. Wood splinters rained on George's head and shoulders.

But the door held fast under his grip. Whether it was from some unknown depth of his own strength or an effect of the song, George was not sure. He was no match for the Lady. Was he? He didn't know. He didn't really care. He just held on.

The song rushed closer and closer to its end.

They were almost there. George closed his eyes. He had to. The power rushing through the small room was almost too much to bear. He gripped that little strip of metal, felt the wonder pour through him, through the walls and ceiling, swirling and pounding and blazing with beauty that burned and healed in the same breath.

He soaked it in. Welcoming every second, every phrase, every breath that blazed, and laughed, and burst with life.

They were at the last line, the last measure, then the last note.

The Lady screeched, and all was silent.

George was breathing hard. His eyes were still tightly shut, his fingers still glued to the door handle. Gradually, his senses unclenched. He slowed his breathing, felt his heart rate calm. The silence rang in his ears. He felt new. Alive.

Then George realized, with a jolt of fear, that everyone behind him might be dead.

Please, no. Please not that.

Slowly, painfully, he peeled each finger off the metal handle. Sweat glistened on his forehead and dripped down the back of his neck. George took a deep breath, and turned.

The cellar was empty.

No people, no instruments. Just the straw broom in its usual corner.

George stared. His brain lurched, trying to comprehend the reality of all he saw…and all he did not see. Buzzing filled his ears. He shook his head to clear it. What was this? Had it really…

"It worked," George whispered. Then louder, "It worked!"

He laughed aloud, whooped, and jumped off the steps to the dirt floor below. George ran from one end of the cellar to the other, scanning for any sign of his friends and finding none. He clattered up the cellar steps, threw the hatch open, and clambered out.

The Lady was nowhere to be seen. Reuben either. George ran to the back window and looked out. There was his backyard and the forest beyond. To his shock, he saw another house through the trees. And another. And another. Brick houses with shingled roofs and iron light fixtures on their corners.

He ran to the front window. The road was dirt no longer. Parked cars speckled the edges of the asphalt like glaring blotches on an otherwise peaceful painting. A boy and girl rode bikes in lazy circles on the pavement, laughing and calling to each other, and across the street, a man with jeans and a hoodie walked a squat, fluffy dog down the sidewalk.

George let the window curtain drop back into place. He took deep, intentional breaths, squeezed one hand around the other wrist and felt the press of fingers on skin. He counted slowly to ten. Forwards. Then backwards.

This was real. It had worked. The curse was broken. Time had caught up in some way or another, and the cottagers must be free.

And gone.

It made him both immeasurably happy and terribly sad.

George stepped away from the window. He had to go see for himself. He had to prove to himself that they were gone. He strode to the entryway and stooped to grab his shoes.

It was only then that George realized his left leg bent easily and did not hurt.

He dropped his shoes. He stood, crouched, stood, crouched again. His leg, his crooked, gimpy, stiff-kneed leg, was as strong, and healthy, and every bit as straight and bendable as his right one.

George slid to the floor, put his head in his hands, and cried.

45

GEORGE

CIRCA 2023

George poured his second cup of coffee for the morning and stepped onto the front porch. It was almost November. The sun shone warm and clear. The trees were at the peak of color, their beauty nothing short of magnificent.

Christopher, the neighbor boy next door, pulled his bike out of his garage and mounted it carefully. He waved at George, and George waved back.

All this activity had taken getting used to. The developer had built pleasant houses, at least, with large lots, and they had kept many of the trees, much to George's gratitude.

He often thought of Liese's question all those years ago. *Do you ever think the trees talk to each other?* He had answered flippantly at the time. Now he was not so sure. Everything seemed different now. Clearer. More alive.

There was much to ponder. For now, it was enough to be aware of all that had happened in Green Meadows and the changes outside his own door. It still surprised him to hear cars passing regularly on the paved road out front and see headlights wind through the woods behind him at night.

George had gone looking for anything resembling the days of the cottagers. The only relic was Isabella's mansion, now a historic estate that had passed through multiple hands and was currently owned by a man from Florida.

There were the letters, too. George found them in a metal box lodged in his barn wall—the same location, he assumed, where Jasper had once found the sheet music. There was a stack of letters, all from Jasper, placed in order of when they were written. George had found them a few days after the song changed everything.

Dear George, the first one began.

> *I hope you find these. I'm not sure how time works with us going back to the present, but it seems we are finally unstuck, and you aren't here. We are all forever grateful for your help, more than we can say. I like to think that when the clocks catch back up to where you are, you will still have ended up in Lux's old place and will still keep your horseless carriage in the barn, so I figured I would leave a note now and then so you know how things fared here in Green Meadows after you left. Many blessings to you, friend.*
>
> *—Jasper Rainwater*

That was enough to make George cough a few times to loosen the lump in his throat. He read all the letters in order out there in his shed, with his back against the battered car, tears coming freely.

They told of Jasper and Lillian's daughter being born just a few weeks after the song.

We named her Evelyn, Jasper wrote. *She's the most beautiful thing I have ever seen, George. Worth every second.*

They told of finding the Lady dead in George's house. They climbed out of the cellar, and there she was, dead on the floor. George wished he knew why.

He realized that the Lady had, in an ironic way, been correct. The song had brought death. To herself, apparently, but to the cottagers as well, no longer stuck in a prison of immortality. But it had brought life, too. Life out of the stale imprisonment of sameness. Life moving forward.

Jasper's letters told of Harlan and Hanna's parents returning, unaware of all that had happened. There was joy in the reunion, but also difficulty. The cottagers had much to get used to, interacting with other people after all that time.

He told, too, of Reuben becoming a hermit in the mansion. They had found Reuben in the pantry when they left George's cellar. He was in a shocked, crumpled heap where the Lady had flung him. Reuben lost all his vinegar after that and holed up on his own.

The letters told of the music that the cottagers loved, the endless music of folk songs, hymns, and dances, feasted upon like a banquet after long years of famine. Jasper swore that each time they played the song Lux had brought, life became richer, the light brighter, the joy deeper.

A letter further down the stack detailed Harlan Stone's wedding, and later, Hanna's. She married a trader and left town with him. She wrote letters once in awhile. She was well and happy, but she never returned to Green Meadows. That one did not surprise George. He smiled, thinking of Hanna finally free, out exploring the wider world.

Jasper and Lillian had a son, James.

Tom Donaldson fell in love with the new schoolteacher and finally convinced her to be his wife.

The cottagers harvested crops, endured storms, and watched the years pass. They lived life, beautiful in all its joys and sorrows.

Jasper's letters became sparser as the years went on. Evelyn grew up and married. James went to a university in the city.

One very smudged letter toward the end of the stack told of Lillian's death. *Just the best woman there ever was,* Jasper wrote, his lettering shaky. *Just the best. I miss her like a man misses the very breath in his lungs.*

The last letter was short. Jasper's handwriting was thinner than it used to be, and wavering, but still clear.

George wanted to copy this last letter into Uncle Barry's leather book. He turned to the front page and saw again where his uncle had written:

Only a fool runs from joy for sake of fear.—
My great-grandfather, Lux Crane.

George ran his finger over the lines. He had not decided yet how best to go about looking for more on what had happened to Lux Crane, how he had ended up outside the time stop in Green Meadows and not at all dead—for a lifetime, anyway. Lux Crane, his own great-great-grandfather. That was a strange thought.

George was baffled, still, on what had happened.

The song put things back to rights. That was all he could gather. The Lady had tried to rid Green Meadows of the song. George still didn't entirely know what she had meant by that. He didn't understand her power or where it came from. But she had somehow pulled part of life, life's richness and beauty, right out of Green Meadows' occupants. In doing so, she had brought time itself to a halt.

But not for Lux. Lux already had the song. He knew the song. It was in him the way it was now in George. The Lady, with all her power, could not pull it out of a person's soul.

Perhaps, George thought, she had flung Lux right out of Green Meadows with the music. Maybe her fear of the song was the very thing that brought about what she most feared—death, as she thought, to Lux, and her own death when things were put back to rights.

What an irony that would be.

George wanted to know what had happened to Lux after. He wanted to know why his own leg was healed.

He wanted to know where Lux had found the song to begin with.

He would start looking. Soon.

George picked up a pen, placed it under Lux's quote, and wrote Jasper's final words.

> *George, whatever happens, don't stop. Don't stop until the song is done. The best part, George, is that the song goes on. Forever.*

George knew it was true. He felt it in himself. He heard it in the ringing of bells, in the night wind, in the tottering strains of a child's violin practice coming through the neighbor's window.

George heard it. And he wondered. And the fire burned brighter, and his roots went deeper, and the joy and wonder of it all grew and grew.

46

EPILOGUE

CIRCA 2024

George read the directions on the back of the gravy packet one more time. It seemed simple enough. Stir the gravy mix and water together in a saucepan, bring to a boil, lower heat and simmer while stirring frequently.

He tossed the packet into the grocery cart. If he couldn't make something that easy, he was in for real trouble learning to cook.

Determined to build some basic cooking skills, George had bought a plug-in burner, a saucepan, and a toaster oven. If Hanna, a fourteen-year-old (or one hundred sixty-four, depending on perspective) could make mouth-watering meals with hunted game and a garden, surely he, at thirty, could learn to put a few things together. His canned and microwaved fare had not tasted the same since his days with the cottagers.

George added chicken seasoning to his smattering of groceries and went to checkout.

"Find everything you need?" the clerk asked in a cheerful voice.

"I hope so," George replied. He gave his cart a rueful look. "Too late now if I didn't."

"Well, not necessarily, though I suppose you wouldn't know 'til you got home, now would you?" She laughed and pushed glasses up over her nose. She was an older woman, maybe in her seventies, plump and pleasant-tempered. George often saw her when he came for groceries.

"How's the novel coming?" She swiped chicken breasts over the scanner. "You finish it yet?"

"I've started a new one, actually."

She gasped. "You have? After all that work, honey? Gracious me."

"Yep. Different story. More...true to life."

"Well I'll be. Sounds like quite a switch. You keep me posted, won't you? Let me know when it's done."

George grinned. "I'll do my best."

He glanced toward the supermarket's front doors and stopped short. His skin went cold.

"Marcia?"

"Hmm?" She keyed in the code for potatoes.

"Do you know anything about that man over there?"

Marcia looked up from the scanner. "Where, hon?"

George pointed. "The older man there, sitting on the bench just outside."

Marcia pulled her glasses down and squinted. "Can't say that I do. You know him?"

"Not particularly. I just...keep seeing him around."

"He looks mighty old," she said, turning back to the scanner. "I hope he isn't lost."

"Yeah. Hopefully."

Or hopefully he was lost. Or confused. Something. George had seen him one other time since the community college. He had gone to the library to return a few books. He leaned out of his car window to reach the book drop, and there the man had been, sitting on a bench just a few yards away, watching him. George had startled so hard that he smacked his head on the window frame.

The man had laughed. It was a dry, rasping laugh that contorted his face into one wrinkled mass.

George had tossed the books into the bin and made a beeline for the highway.

Now here the guy was, waiting outside the supermarket. It was not a large store. There was only one entrance and exit.

George paid for his groceries, wished Marcia a good day, and pushed the cart toward the door. There was no point in waiting it out. The guy had his hat off with his face tilted toward the sun. He did not look like he was going anywhere soon. George's best hope was to slip out without him noticing.

No such luck.

"George," the man said almost as soon as George crossed the threshold.

He knows my name? That was just great.

George stopped and turned toward him, trying to look nonchalant. "Yes?"

The man was eyeing George's leg. He leaned forward and stared at it, one brow raised. "Well now...well now, isn't that a wonder." He stood abruptly.

George stepped back.

The man raised both hands in the air, one holding his walking stick, and chuckled. "Ho now, don't get all jimmied up," he said. His mouth grinned, but his eyes narrowed. "I'm just surprised, is all. You are the same George, aren't you? The one that had the limp. What happened to it? You get it fixed somehow?"

"Something like that." George moved to walk on.

"Now just a minute, just a minute. Stay a bit, won't you? I have some things I want to ask you about."

"Look, Mr…"

"Smallguard. Mr. Smallguard."

"Mr. Smallguard, I don't know why you keep following me around like this."

"Just watching, George. Not a lot of following, as I see it."

"Watching, then. I don't know who you are, and no offense, but I really don't want to answer your questions."

Mr. Smallguard eyed him coolly, the grin still plastered on his face. He stepped sideways with sudden swiftness. George flinched.

"No fear, George, no fear," Mr. Smallguard said, leaning on his stick as if nothing had happened. "It's just some little things. I have some interest in that house of yours."

George's stomach tightened. "My house?"

"Yes, yes, that little one there by all those pretty brick places. It's a bit out of place, isn't it now? I'm surprised you never sold."

"I've only..." George stopped. He was about to say he had only been there six months, but thought better of it. The way the man was looking at him made him think he knew more than he let on.

"What I do with my house is my business," he finished.

"Ah, yes, yes, it sure is." Mr. Smallguard nodded. "You see though," he continued, smoothing a hand over stringy white hair. "There are some things I need to know. And I don't take well, George, to anyone who stands in my way. Your mum and dad knew that."

Mr. Smallguard placed his hat back on his head. "Maybe another time though, yes?"

He nodded toward George's leg. "Lucky stroke for you there. I thought I had maimed it for good." Again that smeared grin, those smug, narrow eyes. He tipped his hat and winked. "See you again soon, George."

With that, Mr. Smallguard turned and walked away. He had crossed the street and disappeared around the corner before George's brain caught up to his ears.

The blood surged to his face, then drained. George felt nauseous. He breathed once. Twice. His parents. His leg, crippled until the song. *Smallguard...*

A cold breeze bit through his thoughts and quieted the buzzing in his ears. It was early March. Springtime, but still chilly.

George stirred, unpeeled his grip on the grocery cart handle, and rattled the cart out to his station wagon. His cottage was waiting. He had dinner to make and a book to write. And apparently, a disturbing old man to contend with.

"There are some things you need to know, huh?" George mumbled, buckling his seatbelt. "Well, that makes two of us."

He jammed the gear into drive and headed home.

www.ingramcontent.com/pod-product-compliance
Lightning Source LLC
Chambersburg PA
CBHW030517310726
48979CB00010B/1702/J
* 9 7 8 1 9 5 6 6 1 1 0 8 3 *